A LITTLE DUST ON THE EYES

A LITTLE DUST ON THE EYES

MINOLI SALGADO

PEEPAL TREE

First published in Great Britain in 2014
Reprinted in 2015
Peepal Tree Press Ltd
17 King's Avenue
Leeds LS6 1QS
England

ISBN13: 9781845232405

Supported using public funding by
ARTS COUNCIL
ENGLAND

for Shaun

Close both eyes
to see with the other eye

Open your hands,
if you want to be held.

RUMI

Seven years before Renu Rodrigo's **A Postscript to The Years of Terror** *was published, the man upon whom much of the study was based disappeared in circumstances that gained global attention. Every available detail about the life and habits of Bradley Sirisena had been carefully catalogued in Rodrigo's study: his lineage as a descendent of ninth century mercenaries who settled on the southern tip of the island, having set to sea from the Coromandel coast, his scant education at the local village school that had been subject to increasingly lengthy closure under pain of death from the local insurgents, his linguistic tic that compelled him to suck air through tightened lips at intervals while speaking, and his enduring insistence that his arms did not exist, that they had, in fact, been stolen in his sleep along with his father who had disappeared on a full moon night in May.*

This apparent loss of his limbs first alarmed then infuriated his mother. She had been left without a husband and now had a son incapable of helping her earn an income. Her decision to leave the boy in the care of her elderly parents was seen by many as understandable and inevitable. The effect it had on her son, who now swayed and swung his dead arms on account of their weightlessness, was difficult to measure. Rodrigo found herself increasingly unable to distinguish between the facts relating to the disappearance of Sirisena senior and the ones relating to his son's disabilities. In a land that did not officially recognise the abduction of its less prominent citizens, bereavement slipped into the only home that could accommodate it: the private self. Exorcism rites abounded, with fires burning until dawn. For the boy there was no such release. His body registered the impact of the loss in the sheer uselessness of his arms. He could not hold anyone. He would lose the ability to write.

It was fitting, therefore, that the study of his life should lack resolution. His disappearance in the catastrophe that the international media called the 'South Asian Tsunami' could not be regarded as certain. Rodrigo could only record that he had disappeared on the

9

morning of 26 December while on his way to see a friend. His friend had disappeared too. Weeks later, when the road on which the young man had last been seen walking had been cleared of the detritus that remained of people's homes, lives and livelihoods, Rodrigo noted that Bradley's mother had resigned herself to the fact that she would only find her missing husband and son in the more fordable reaches of her heart.

1

BRIGHTHELM

small star

One by one, they fell into shade. She watched as Hannah's retreating form was absorbed into the darkness of stone steps. The last thing she saw: the pale face of the child, slumped over Hannah's shoulder, and the small star of her hand as she waved goodbye.

Savi drew her scarf around her and braced herself for the sea wind. The distant stalks of esplanade lights flickered into view, coming to her through the spray as a pale shower of young coconut flowers, waxy buds falling from golden wedding urns as she peeled them clean. Here they were again, glowing warm against the sea.

She was used to them now, these once disconcerting slips. They were to be expected in this land of shifted, shifting things, where hills rose and fell in smooth, leafless echoes, undulating like a frozen sea, and the sea itself materialised as solid waves of flint that matched the broken rocks on the shore. Brighthelm was spread between these repeating rolls of grey hills and waves, sometimes as a space of possibility, sometimes ephemeral as a dream. She would move through winding alleys that opened into gardens, pass lights that led to darkness, a pier that drew her over sea. As she walked above the moving water, she felt how much she'd left of herself behind. There were spinning wheels and trains that carried tourists into the clouds, and a language that turned chaotic on the lips. It was a place that shifted time and region, of rain from other shores. At its heart lay a royal dream of Asia – a curved and flowing building affectionately called *The Pavilion*; a prince's whim, a sideshow, where turquoise minarets and parasols of palm trees covered writhing dragons of red and gold.

Savi walked through the Lanes with her rucksack on her back, stepping out of the way of the crowds, the men and women who strode out of shops as glossy as airport magazines and dined al fresco in those sea-front hotels made famous in films. She would feel the contact of their holidays in the sun as they brushed past, their bronze against her brown, their smooth oiled skins against her dry arms, the contrast reminding her she was alone.

She was still jostled, for she walked too quickly and her rucksack was weighted with books. 'Sorry', she would say, when someone bumped into her. 'That's OK', she would respond on behalf of unsuspecting strangers, 'Thaht's OK. Zat's Okay', trying out variously a Scottish brogue, an American drawl, some version of Teutonic intonation. 'I was wondering if you could tell me the way to…? You don't have the time by any chance?'

But of course they never saw her, never responded. Just moved on as if she wasn't there.

The cobbled streets were too narrow for the jutting shop signs that festooned her native city, signs that reached out and bickered with one another. She would pause by windows spangled with lights as bright as the sequined silks within, enter the aisle and run her fingers through the skirts, feeling the texture of those places that rose in her mind – saris, shawls, shirts, sarongs that fluttered from the open stalls of the Pettah.

'How much?'

'Forty pounds.'

In the Pettah it might have been less than four.

She withdrew her hand, wondering how many people she might have touched, who they were, what form of contact this was.

In the evenings, her work done, she might emerge and step over shapes that stirred into sleeping vagrants and slip into the Greek café. She might hear the laughter of students in their uniform of club leather, light a cigarette and watch the pier illuminate into a skeleton of bright bulbs, as the waves slid into darkness and the sea was reduced to a hiss.

Time was measured in anticipation of the full moon. Savi would strike off the days in her diary, each day a match lighting their separation, her diary empty but for these strokes. She placed her pen by the table, heard it roll and tap the lamp, reached for the switch and turned the light off. In the dark, it came to her that her mother, too, might have willed her into oblivion, that their enforced separation had made this a necessary act.

Her mother had always had the ability to cauterise pain. At the airport departure gate – a memory that might be called false because it was a composite of different events – her mother had turned away with her familiar decisiveness, cleared a path through the crowd with a trolley weighted with buckled cases, and never looked back. *On poya days I will think of you* – her mother's words sealed in bright berries of crimson lipstick, uttered just moments before. The words were real but the events that framed them belonged to a different time.

She recalled the saline drip coming from her mother's arm, a crescent of paleness on the inside of her wrist, the lifeline split and trailing into vagueness. She had sat by her mother's side, stroking her hand, running her fingers down the length of her mother's fingers and locking them into hers.

It had been many months – years perhaps – since her mother had been strong enough to rise up and hold her. With their hands locked together she felt the need to be held, gently as her mother had held her, not with the abrupt and crushing need with which her father drew her to him during the last few months of her mother's life. Even in those rare moments of contact when her mother used to towel her hair dry, drawing Savi to her dimpled belly – her watalappan tummy as they both called it, smelling of sandalwood and talcum – and rolling her wet head in the large, soft folds, her mother had maintained the gentlest touch, her hands losing definition in the tumbling roll of towel that swaddled Savi's head, laughing at her exaggerated squeals of protest, their laughter frothing into one.

She had run her fingers along the ridges of her mother's left hand, around the rim of surgical tape, conscious of the looseness between skin and bone. A tight white sheet was drawn about her mother's form. Only the face shifted a little, drawn into its primary lines. The thin light in her mother's eyes seemed to be burning through Savi to a point beyond her on the window, the force of her gaze pared down to this bright filament. She was reminded of a cobra, eyes glazed in concentration as it shed its skin in the silver needles of a cactus, caught in the slow and delicate process of casting off an old self.

She had pressed her mother's hand with the pulse she wished to instill in her, and then pressed it again, more insistently, with a pressure that must have hurt, hating the stillness that had settled over the bed. She had learnt about loss in those slow hospital hours, learnt of it long before she came to England. Aloneness. Her mother's stillness a disease that threatened them all, when she could have swooped through the lengthening intervals between each breath.

It might have infected her too had not her mother smiled that last time and said the words that unravelled everything: *On poya days I will think of you*, the eyes fixed on her in the permanence of love, the words leaving her lips slack, open, with the promise of more.

Savi reached forward to kiss her but was pulled back by an attendant and led firmly to the window. Someone held her shoulder as if to stop her turning round. She heard a screen being drawn about the bed where her father had been sitting on the other side.

Plumes of smoke were rising from the burning buildings below. There were the orange flares of the city riots, the fires smudged into clouds of glowing fingerprints. *On poya days I will think of you*. Her mother's poya prayers repeating through her tears. Each full moon held a promise of sorts.

She could hear a woman's loud boots on the porch, almost certainly her landlady returning from work. She turned towards the window and opened the blind to reveal the night in slats. The railings gleamed wet. The lamp held up its globe of yellow light against a distant satellite dish. It would be a full week before the moon rounded, a full week before her mother might have lit three sticks of incense. She needed her mother now, needed to conjure with the final farewell of airport sliding glass doors, imagine that her mother had made the journey with her to become a part of a larger self that crossed the sky, place her mother there at the time of her own departure so that she might see her calling, calling and waving an arm of shiny bangles, as she turned and walked away in her new, heavy, serious, English shoes.

She was eleven years old when she left the island. By then the past was already a necessary lie.

~

'How can he remember something wrong? That is like mis-remembering, no? He's a real boru karaya. All snaky lies coming from his mouth,' Renu protested as she ran ahead, slipped off her sticky shoes, and scurried into the pantry. The girls were soaked from a sudden downpour after cycling home from tuition, and were eager for the Horlicks held in Josilin's dimpled arms.

Renu was like that, the one who ran after her but always ended up leading the way, so it sometimes felt to Savi as if someone rushed right through her when Renu sped by.

The girls had been picking over the bones of a notorious family murder that had been spoken of in their history class, a story lightly buried in casual gossip and recently exhumed and dusted off by a national newspaper. Sir Henry De Mel, a man with ancestral links to their own family, had been shot dead during a dispute over pay and working conditions on his vast coconut estate. The murderer had been apprehended and hanged. Uncertainty lay for the girls in De Mel's exact relationship to his assailant.

'Well he was treated like a son, so he might as well have been a son,' Savi reasoned, stirring the heat from her drink and downing a gulp. Did it really matter that the man accused, condemned and executed for the murder was in fact the first-cousin-once- removed of the victim? Did it really matter if their tutor referred to him as a son, as most people – including Josilin – did, when the papers dredged the details into view? It was a matter of degree rather than kind, surely.

'But he wasn't a son, he was a poor relation who was being treated as a hanger-on. How can Stiltskin get it so wrong? He talks as if it's all just a story, not true true people and facts. Anyway, he's meant to teach proper history, not fat stories about rich men.' Renu pulled her damp dress off and kicked it in exasperation.

Stiltskin was their name for the private tutor whose real name was tongue-twistingly long and whose body was half its original size from fifty years of leaning over children's desks. A large-nosed taskmaster who pranced about them, sniffing snuff.

'It doesn't matter. It's finished now and he got most things right. Redley worked for Sir Henry and was family. He was lucky to have the job and all.' Savi picked the dress up and gave it to Josilin who folded it into the sink. 'So killing Sir Henry was not just murder, it was,' she searched for the word, 'tretch – treacherri. It was *as if* Redley was a son. Stiltskin is just repeating what everyone else says and thinks. He is telling the story as it is NOW.' Her mouth expanded with emphasis. She looked to Josilin for support, but Josilin just smiled and chucked her under the chin.

'You think too much, baba.' Josilin sniffed as she went to the door. 'My baby girls both think too much.'

'It doesn't matter what is true or not. What matters is what people believe,' Savi said with a finality that she hoped would win the day.

But Renu, for whom spoken words were slippery fish, who could only find the exact words for her feelings in the quiet of her room with a pen in her hand, would not be silenced. 'That's just stupid. Belluddy Stewpid,' she shouted. 'You'd believe the moon is a pancake. You're becoming, you're becoming' and Savi could see the words coming and can still hear Renu say them across the years, *'a lost cause'*.

She knew what this meant. She had heard her father speak of lost causes when referring to a difficult case, a case so entangled in the machinery of political power that it was impossible to win. Now, in the basement flat, the words seemed to gather new weight.

The slatted blinds cast shades of light and dark on her night shirt and the foolscap she'd laid on the table. Her thesis was now called *The Manticore's Tale,* the original name lost in some filing cabinet at the university. It had begun as a study of parricide in myth and metamorphosed into what her supervisor, Dr Highfield, called *a cultural analysis of nationalist discourse in relation to ethnic fratricide* – terms which indicated his disapproval of her change of direction and his intention not to engage with her work at anything other than a cursory level.

She had not intended this change, but the study appeared to have evolved of its own accord, metamorphosing over the years as readily as the history it was attempting to reclaim. *The Manticore's Tale*. She liked the name. It had bite, like the manticore itself, the mythical man-eating creature from India, half-man, half-lion, with a tail studded with poisoned quills and three rows of teeth. Its quills sprang out and regenerated themselves each time it was attacked. The history of Sri Lanka was like that, she felt, a tale of generative violence protecting the lion men who called themselves the Sinhalese. But only the title felt certain now. The rest of her study was written in a new language with an accent all its own that she was struggling to master.

Theories of belonging, she wrote, *work on the premise of a fixed and stable originary culture.*

Here it was again, the question of origins, the perpetual problem of where to start. All beginnings were interruptions, lacerations, a tear in the fold of time. If her mother had not died in a hospital bed in central Colombo on a private wing reserved for the terminally ill, on a day when neighbour torched neighbour into bright beacons, burning 300, 400, 500 people, the numbers flaring and accumulating in charred heaps before being swept away along with broken timber, Tamil shop signs and booty, sliding into that historical crease that was marked for her only by her mother's thin hand on the whiter than white sheet, her father's tight grief, and the cries of the ambulance men as they called for haste in the corridors below, while her mother looked through the window at a sky spiralling with smoke and white flags of scrap paper; if her mother had not died at this time, the dawn of Black July, had not died at all, there might not have been this sudden collapse, this tumble into darkness between moments that could be remembered and those that could not.

It was a beginning of sorts, her mother's death. It marked the start of her own new life. She put down the pen, sat back and closed her eyes.

In the morning, she found a white envelope on the doormat with her name and address scrolled in black. Good, she thought, no junk mail or bills. Even better, a handwritten envelope. She looked at the stamps and ran a finger over the edge. There were four identical images of Kandyan drummers, their hands beating barrelled drums, and a large stamp too smudged by the date print to be distinguishable. The small, neat writing bearing her name was as unfamiliar as the mode of address. *Mrs* Savi Carter. No friend would call her that.

She used to love getting letters from the old country, would race down the school stairs in clattering English shoes, her feet carried by the rhythm of those drums. At first, she had difficulty opening the single sheet aerogrammes because her father sealed them with gum. A small tear at the top, or along the edge, could leave a gap in a sentence and she'd have to work out the missing words. She found her own way of opening them – a small nick in the corner of the envelope, a hairpin to slit the sheet.

The words inside brought the birdsong back.

The new blue curtains in her bedroom that made the room, he said, more restful and screened out the afternoon glare so she might read more easily when she got back. And the *fine thing* that happened when Renu fell off her bike on her way to a cricket match, twisting her ankle so that she had to be carried home *bellowing* on her brother's back while he *became wild*, shouting that she should shut up and be grateful that he was there, especially as she had made him miss his chance at playing first spinner and *cutting the buggers up*. And *another fine thing* happened when the stray dog they adopted – currently called Fatso, though the name seemed to change every week – chewed her sandals *into a pulp as fine as pol sambol* (*but not as appetising of course*) before swimming off into the lagoon. She had never seen the dog but her father's description of the mongrel with a scar above its eye left her sure she could see it wagging its tail before her. She knew she was unlikely to see it. Strays were notoriously fickle and disappeared without explanation – and those sandals would almost certainly not fit her now.

His letters were full of fine things, his suppressed laughter rippling from the page through the broken words that came to him in the years after her mother died. It was not a language others would understand, so different from the language blown with emotion, sentiment and paternal effusion she knew her friends received in communication with their parents, a language of compensation, thick with terms of endearment that might make up for their frailty of presence. He was not a sentimental man, and he knew better than to open this door. He had contained his grief at his wife's death in small parcels that he kept hidden from sight. He continued to go to work every day. First the office, then the court, on to the club in the evening, meeting friends as usual and swimming at weekends. There were more telephone calls of course, as experienced lawyers were much in demand at the time, and long lines of inquiry arriving at the back door, plaintiffs carrying identity cards and testimonials seeking his advice on matters that he kept to himself. But these changes seemed only to centre him, drawing him into a sure knot of certainty that seemed to grip Savi too.

He had fielded all the advice that assaulted him after his wife's death with tact, making his parents, aunts, uncles, cousins, brother and sister-in-law and a host of friends, colleagues and acquaintances, feel that he was taking all their views into consideration. Then he announced a decision that shocked them all. Savi was to be sent to a boarding school in England. He did not discuss his decision with her, and when she asked why she had to go, he just said it was for the best. He said this with such quiet assurance that, despite finding herself falling once more, she felt there might be a safe landing in those words.

And his letters had extended her trust, sealed with *Yrs affctly* and that delicate *x*, the words squeezed of vowels so she could almost feel his hug. She would still be clutching one when the corridor burst into noise as the girls rushed out for prep. 'Savi, come on! The bell has gone!'

She would be left, marooned in time and memory.

Now here was another letter edged by those distant drums. She stared at the alienating 'Mrs'. She hated being called this. Savi, she would say, just call me Savi. And on those occasions when a surname was required, watch the brief hesitation as her companion searched for a trace of anglo-saxon blanching in her uncompromisingly brown face.

She went to the kitchen and turned on the light, tearing open the envelope with one slice of her knife. Letters from the old country were now a rarity, limited in recent years to the occasional Christmas card. She lifted out a sleek card embossed with pink and silver flowers with *Wedding Invitation* angled across the middle, and on the back, in silver, *Mr and Mrs Eden Rodrigo request the pleasure of the company of…* Her gaze slid down to where, in a tidy hand, someone had written, *Do come, Savi. Don't forget us!*

This was not Fiona's hand – Aunt Fiona who had persisted in trying to teach her Scott Joplin tunes on the piano despite the fact that Savi clearly had ten thumbs instead of two, Fiona, whom her grandparents had insisted on referring to as *Piano* on account of not being able to pronounce *f*.

'Son, you must come for dinner with Piano next week,' her grandmother would call from the deep folds of a starched sari. 'Uma-Nanda has come down from Berlin. She will be expecting you.'

'Amma, her name is Fiona,' Uncle Eden would respond with practised courtesy from his desk. 'I don't think we can make it. The accountants are coming to discuss the tax returns. This meeting was delayed already.'

'What nonsense. Returns can wait,' her grandmother would say, blowing air between her teeth so Savi could almost see the tax returns scurry away with her breath. 'And if you can't come, at least send Piano. Uma will want to see her.'

This foreign aunt, with the unpronounceable name and a smile as soft as hibiscus petals, who had, over the years, been drawn into ancestral order and certified as another piece of family furniture, whose small form had expanded to reach her as her mother had retreated into illness, whose hands would tumble over and call into being the music that Savi's fingers resisted.

No, this was not Fiona's hand. Her aunt had large, looped writing that embraced you in its curves and animated words like *love* and *giggle*. Her sky-blue envelopes rustling with sheets of wispy paper had arrived steadily after Savi's father's death. They had petered to a halt after years of not hearing a word from Savi in return. This was not her aunt's hand. The script was controlled, tight, urgent.

Do come. Don't forget.

Savi took the card to her bed and read her scrawled words of the night, the idea that had found her scrambling for a pen under her pillow. *Sinhabahu's father can only be killed when his love for his son turns to anger. Parental love grants immortality of sorts (?)*

The idea had potential, but the words made her feel as if she might, at any moment, be exposed, found guilty by Dr Highfield and the entire English department of using academic artifice to paper over the cracks of an impoverished personal life. She drew the duvet about her and watched the note spill to the floor as she reached for a cigarette. She struck a match, lit up, and ran her fingers over the invitation, feeling the ridges that marked *to the marriage of their son*.

Her cousin Romesh. A boy with a tongue as sharp as his eyes, who had tugged her unruly hair, *You look like a Scarecrow! Scarecrow!* From then on she had insisted on drawing her hair back into a matronly bun until Rob had told her he loved the way the curls framed her face. She had cut it short since then.

And Renu, Romesh's sister, full-skirted as always, running along the beach like an overweight hen, her petticoats gathered and tucked behind her waist, making her bottom look enormous and her legs skinnier than ever.

Renu, *Renu Nangi*, the cousin she once called sister.

She wondered what they looked like now. Imagined Romesh taller and sobered by the years, dressed up as a groom posing for the camera with his family about him. Renu tamed into a sleek sari with jasmine cascading down her hair. 'Go on!' Renu's whisper nudged her from behind, 'Tell them you'll stay on.'

And in that company she could see Rob slipping in, joining the family as if he belonged there – Rob, the laid-back student who had been casual even in his pinstripe at the Register Office as he proffered the ring they'd bought from an antique shop in the Lanes the day before – the Rob who'd sizzled into an atom of irritability by the end of that last trip back, the trip that made her sure it was unwise to return and stir up the ashes of the past. She felt herself enter that world again as if there had been no interruption at all, no interruption at all.

the cases are falling

'Savi, for God's sake tell him to slow down. The cases are falling and the tripod's gone.'

'OK. Wait. *Heming*,' she cried, peering over the seat, trying to catch the driver's attention.

He continued to steer a jolting course through the traffic with one hand on the wheel, the other holding a phone to his ear, his head angled towards the cassette tapes that were sliding across the dashboard out of his reach.

'*Heming. Heming.* Lord, I don't know if that's the word. It's been so long. And he's not listening anyway.' She held onto the partition that separated them from Lakshman and turned, swaying, towards her seat while he carried on shouting into the phone. Now even ordinary conversations in the language sounded like an argument, and not just because of the volume at which they were conducted.

'This is crazy. He'll kill us all.'

'Everyone drives like this here. I'd forgotten it was so bad.'

The van lurched. Savi fell onto the front seat. 'Are you OK back there?'

Rob had positioned himself in the corner at the back and was holding onto the strap swinging by the window, an arm about his precious grey holdall containing the camera equipment. His view was obscured by a pleated curtain that refused to slide back.

'I think it's better we sit apart, don't you?' she found herself shouting, without meaning to. 'More room.'

The honeymoon in Sri Lanka had been entirely his idea.

'I want to see the place where you come from.'

'I told you. I don't come from one place but many. Weligama, Matara, Monschau, Brighthelm beach, the Jolly Sportsman pub...' – some of the places where she had been happiest.

'Yes. I know I'm marrying a woman of the world. But, given the fact that I am marrying her after all, it would be nice to pin her down a bit.'

'You try and you'll be sorry,' she teased, nudging him along the sofa where the travel brochures lay.

'Look, there are some good deals here,' he said, flicking to a section marked *Simply Paradise*. 'One week touring some cultural sites followed by one week on the beach free of charge. What do you say? Come on, it would be fun. You could visit some of those aunts and uncles you keep talking about and introduce me – your dashing English husband.'

'Mmm.'

'Savi?'

'I'm not sure.'

'Why?'

'I don't know if it's such a good idea to go back.'

'Don't you want to?'

'I do. In a way. But it will change things.'

'How?'

'I don't know. It just will, that's all. And Rob?'

'Yep?'

'You're not my dashing English husband.'

'No?'

'You're just dashing.'

'Got it in one.'

They had arrived at Sigiriya Village in the early evening, opening the van door to a chorus of nesting birds and amber sunlight that made the red soil incandescent. Rob looked straight towards the Rock, a grey slab streaked with the colours of the setting sun. He had been watching it appear and disappear from view for some time on the winding route to the hotel. It was impossible to get a sense of exactly how large the Rock was. With only trees and shrubs at its base and broken clouds above as points of contrast, it resisted ordinary scales of measurement.

An hour later, darkness *fell*. He understood the metaphor now. It fell, fast, clean, like a blade.

That night they slept together on a bed strewn with flowers left by an unseen hand.

In the dark, under a mosquito net that blurred their forms together, they could slip out of the light of those who locked them into colour, those who saw nothing more than their suitcases and sunglasses and the stark visual contrast between them, and slide into oneness in the anonymity of the dark, flowers crushed against their skin.

She peeled a petal off his back and licked it. It tasted of him.

'I wish,' she said, feeling her breath return from him to reach her, 'I wish I could meet the person who put these flowers here.'

'Why?'

'Because they are part of this.'

'Madam,' he said hoarsely in a voice that seemed natural in the dark, 'you want threesome?'

She smiled despite herself, smiled at the Sri Lankan lover he had conjured into being, then pursed her lips and blew across him to the moon that lay angled and fretted by the mosquito net somewhere near his left ear.

Together they had read the books, watched the TV stills, and successfully condensed a century of Rock history into their list of 'things to do in Sri Lanka'. Everyone who had been to Sigiriya mentioned it as the place to which they would like to return if they could – there was so much more to be discovered than they had time to see.

She had been just once before, with both her parents when she was about seven years old. They had taken advantage of the tourist expansion of the late 1970s that had set the country blasting its way towards a new economy, creating thousands of entrepreneurs and factories the size of football fields in the free trade zones. It had oiled the wheels that allowed her Uncle Eden to transfer money made from the sale of land before nationalization into the solid certainty of real estate.

'Sigiriya,' her uncle had said, when he knew her parents planned to take her there. 'Watch you don't fall'.

All she could really remember of the place were the interminable steps, one stone slab after another, each step seeming more solid at each gasp. Then the metal spiral staircase with the fretted base which you could see through if you let your gaze plunge beyond the grid, a terrifying collapse into emptiness. The climb led to the frescoes, upper torsos of women outlined in black, the slants of their eyes so fresh they might have been drawn by her felt tips, and etched in pastels the colour of the earth scuffed on her sandals. She had been jostled forward by the insistence of other visitors and had just caught a glimpse of eyes, palm, flower, bracelet, before being pulled on by her mother. Her mother holding her hand, their arms an unbroken line.

The site had now become another must-see venue on an established tourist route. Coaches were arriving and spilling their passengers into the heat – tourists in sun hats and shorts followed by groups of schoolchildren carrying water-bottles and notepads, and saffron-robed priests who screened their faces with black umbrellas. They were gathering into discrete groups in the shade of the trees. There was no queue yet.

'Come, I'll get the tickets.'

She regretted not buying the all-inclusive Cultural Triangle tickets that permitted them entry to all the historical sites in the area. It was a decision she had made against the advice of the travel agents, on the assumption that it might save money and grant them flexibility. Later she realized that her reasons were more personal. She wished to resist the tourist trail.

Rob had agreed, too preoccupied with planning his photographic tour and selecting film according to the anticipated saturation of light. It seemed to her that it was difficult for him to absorb any more of the country than his camera lens would allow, the trip fast becoming a spectator sport in which he could relinquish responsibility and leave practical details to her. The decision meant new tickets at every stop. It meant negotiation.

She reached into the bag slung over his shoulder and went towards the ticket barrier where two men in military green stood, one inside the barrier, the other in a small booth. They looked at her and sized her up. She was conscious of Rob zipping the bag behind her.

Perhaps it was some instinct of resistance to this unwanted

scrutiny or some desire to test the limits, but she found herself using the accent that came automatically when speaking to people here. 'Two tickets please. One foreign, one local.'

She had no idea that locals went free of charge.

'Passport.' The man in the booth flicked a finger towards her purse while the other looked on.

'Give me your passport, Rob.'

Rob was silent as she took it from him.

'Here', she pushed it forward. 'I forgot mine. Left it in Co-lombo.'

The man was nonchalant. She was of no interest to him. Just another woman with a white man who was avoiding paying up.

'Identity card.'

'I am sorry. I forgot that too.'

The man was getting restive. He was tired of these expatriates with their polkatu accents. Some German tourists were ap-proaching.

'You pay foreign rate,' the man said to the trees beyond her.

'I told you I left them in Colombo. I am local. I was born here.'

'Foreign rate.'

He hadn't bothered to look at her – she was a nuisance. And in that small interval of his lapsed gaze she said her first proper sentence in the language that had once been hers. It came to her instinctively.

'Mama mehe ipaduna.'

I was born here.

He looked up. Contact of sorts. His eyes reached and steadied her.

Then he spoke slowly, pausing between words, as English tourists do when speaking to those unfamiliar with their lan-guage: 'You. Pay. Foreign. Rate.'

~

'If I had the chance I'd go back.' Hannah shook her hair loose from the towel and rubbed it back and forth behind her neck. 'I've never been further than Gibraltar. All monkeys and rock. I'd love to go somewhere with guaranteed sunshine. Lie on the beach all day with waves lapping around. Get away from this rotten cold and rain.'

Savi loved Hannah's directness. It seemed to her that her friend had inherited the western capacity to pass judgement on whole areas of experience of which she was blissfully ignorant. Some of her peers at university were similarly inclined but their claims on her were different. She would find herself listening to an animated discussion and reluctantly nodding in agreement as they magnified her experience into a regrettable part of *the postcolonial condition* for which they felt they were responsible. With Hannah there was no such danger. The differences between them were clear. Communication free.

'It's not that simple. I have family there. And Sri Lanka is all monkeys and rock too. The waves don't lap.'

Savi slipped off her costume and looked over her shoulder. Natalie was changing behind her.

'You seem to remember a lot even though you've not been back in a while.' Hannah bent down to steady her daughter as the little girl pulled on her skirt and twisted it into shape.

But her memories were as faded and fragmented as the images on some of Rob's old slides. Her father's voice. Her mother's hand. Renu's red skirt. Images that came unsolicited and without order. She was at her most certain when tested on some element of detail – she had an absentee's sense of what the land was *not.* Such negations helped lead her back to a more a tangible truth than if she had direct access. For example she knew, for certain, that there the sea did not lap. And in the space created by this lack, the roar of churning water reached her ears. Her head began to ache.

'Here', Hannah handed her the hairdryer. 'Your turn.'

Swimming on Sundays with Hannah and Natalie was the social highlight of her life. Their relationship had been sealed when they had done a life-saving course together and learnt to resuscitate a body by applying fifteen pulses with their palms on the chest of a life-size model that lifted with a satisfying puff each time they pressed down. They had been told to pulse to the count of the opening lines of 'Nellie The Elephant'.

Natalie had sung with metronomic precision as Savi and her mother pumped away at the plastic dummies and tried not to laugh, steering clear of the temptation to compare their dummies to lovers of the past.

'I just know I'll be thinking of circus elephants when saving someone's life,' Hannah gasped, unfolding and relocking her palms as she continued pulsing. 'Look. We're even resuscitating a trunk. *Trunk,* get it?' she said bending forwards again.

Savi paused and rubbed the stiffness from her arms, then drew her hands to her lap, observing Hannah who continued to pulse, pulse, pulse and blow, pulse and blow as if she were engaged in an endurance test, as the torso below her appeared to judder into life.

An involuntary gasp and sudden release, and she knew at once the precise angle of the tilted head, the inflexibility of the swollen tongue. She'd had this knowledge in her hands since she was fifteen years old.

'You must remember to open the jaw properly, first,' she said quietly.

Natalie spun round to her mother.

'Mummy does this mean that Nellie the elephant can make a dead person wake up?'

Savi glanced at Natalie. The child became quite still, then smiled directly back at her in a way that made the fluorescent lights glow warm.

The seasons were absorbed in reading and writing, balancing ideas, looking for hidden meanings and forging connections between books. At intervals, when the words on the page seemed to resist scrutiny, she would slip on a denim jacket and go scouring the second-hand bookshops in the North Lanes, before dropping in for a cappuccino and toasted doughnut at the Arcade café. Later she might brace herself for a walk along Marine Drive where her pace would be quickened by the wind pushing her from behind.

She had first seen Hannah through the rush of water that came as Natalie slipped into the pool, falling straight into her steadying arms. That sudden contact presaged Natalie's unprompted claims upon her body when she least expected it. The girl would clamber on to her regardless of whether she was reading in the public library or lying on the beach.

It was an acceptance that was displaced like so much water onto her friendship with Natalie's mother. Hannah asked no questions and Savi felt free to speak in the verbal shorthand that others found frustrating; and Hannah would respond from the centre of her knowledge of a world in which all relationships were finite – with the exception of her relationship with her child.

Hannah's love for Natalie was limitless, and the girl carried this gift into the arms of others, nestling on Savi's lap and pulling at the earrings which dangled against her cheek.

'Go back,' Natalie breathed in her ear.

'Mmm?' She could remember the pain swelling as the earring was pulled, Natalie's cheek against hers, the child blowing words that came cold and timeless in her burning ear.

'You should go back.'

The second week of their honeymoon had been designated a 'free week'. It was literally free, in that they did not have to pay for it. It was also a week set aside for the purposes of relaxation. After a week engaged in a cultural tour of the island, they were now free to indulge in swimming, snacking and lying in the sun.

But the touring had carried them beyond the need for respite. Having made their way through the *Insight Guide*, zig-zagging their way across the country in a logic that collapsed the centuries, they were hot, tired and restless. They needed to touch some of the history they had driven through.

Lakshman was hurtling down a bend that brought them their first direct view of the sea when something snapped into place. *The sudden sea.* Her parents used to stop here to buy wine biscuits that were as smooth and dimpled brown as the beach.

'Monis biscuits.' She had not realized that she still knew the name and enjoyed the familiar taste of the words on her tongue. 'Is the Monis Bakery still here?'

Lakshman did not respond.

'Monis. Monis Bakery,' she repeated, aware of the slight imperiousness that had begun to pressure her voice.

Lakshman accelerated, took a hand off the wheel, adjusted the gear, swung round to the left and pulled up with a start outside it. She had to put a hand out to stop herself from falling.

Rob had prepared for the trip, his first outside Europe, with the same haphazard single-mindedness with which he approached his first job interviews, balancing a caution that enabled him to anticipate and negotiate unforeseen obstacles, with a natural delight in dealing with the unknown. He had studied the internet images of the region and taken account of the fact that the weather was becoming increasingly unpredictable – droughts and driving rains coming unseasonably early or late – so that the clear skies of tourist brochures, which indicated the harshest light of all, were thankfully less likely than before.

During the early months, when they still found pleasure in exploring the differences between them, she had seen his ability to adapt to change as a sign of an impetuous nature, admiring his openness and availability to the outside world, his capacity to drop everything to accommodate the fleeting moment. She would delight in the unpredictability of a day that could turn on a sudden spear of light through cloud as they paused to watch a pheasant lifting free from a field of broken wheat, its tail arcing golden in flight, Rob removing his arm from her waist and taking a photograph that froze the world about them. But later, when he gave her the picture, she found she only remembered what the image seemed to miss. She would recall not what he saw in that instant when the shutter closed, but the smell of that autumn afternoon, the chill of her cheek against the Arran sweater thrown across his shoulders, the damp tingling her toes.

He was cleaning the polarizer when she came in. She sat on the bed and covered the plastic casing with her palm, gripping it with her fingers.

'My uncle's home is not far from here.'

'I know.'

She moved from the bed and on to the balcony, her back to the sea. He twisted the lens cap on and slipped the camera back in the case, then stood up and lifted the suitcase onto the luggage rack beyond the bed, leaving the straps dangling. Then he sat down with a sigh and began to adjust the screws on the damaged tripod. She was now outside his field of vision.

She turned and let her eyes follow the stretch of beach to a promontory where the thin stands of the stilt fishermen stood unused. As a child, she used to watch the men with their dark, glistening bodies standing above the waves against the horizon, one leg extending the length of a wooden pole, the other crooked into a triangle so they looked like disjointed marionettes. She wondered if Rob would get to see them or whether she would have to conjure them into being for him from these empty stands.

In England she had shown him the photographs she dreaded looking at – her parents, arm in arm, outside a house that she only knew from this picture; herself at five years old, retreating from the camera as her mother held her, looking up, pointing towards the lens which was about to flash and blind her for a few seconds – her mother giving the smile she could not win from her daughter while her father leant against the bonnet of the new Chrysler, arms folded with pride; her cousins, after cricket on the beach, Romesh aiming the bat at Renu who held up her hands in mock surrender, her shriek of laughter burning the sky white.

She could only look at these pictures in company, when there was someone with her to talk them into narrative. She had not looked at them in years.

Rob had stayed quiet and listened hard to what she had to say because she was speaking without order or connection. All he could see were faded photographs taken on an old Instamatic, blemished by the Kodachrome colour of green-tinted skies. Some prints were out of focus, others angled so that the horizon and the human subject appeared to occupy the same spatial plane. All seemed to point to a wasted opportunity for catching things as they really were.

Now he had come to the island equipped with his own cameras. Not electronic or digital, but strictly manual SLR, and therefore cumbersome. Everything appeared to await him, ready for capture. It was something to do with the quality of light and the way time folded in on itself. *A regeneration*, he once said to himself as he ran a finger down Savi's back. Each morning had woken into a land that spread itself out just for him.

Earlier that week, as they left Anuradhapura, they had passed a military convoy heading north. Some forty-two trucks, Savi said. A couple of soldiers in the last vehicle had raised their rifles in greeting. Rob raised the tripod in response. *We're all out shooting.*

The irony was not lost on him.

It had been his decision to come to the country, but now that she was back, she found herself alone, drawn into the time of her childhood. The north and central highlands held no memories – she was able to stay detached there – but the south coast claimed her without asking and urged her to move on.

She could not talk to Rob about this, did not dare acknowledge the power of a need that was already pulling her away from him and she could not find a language to articulate what she felt.

'If we leave here after breakfast, we should get there in time for lunch.'

She was tracing an outline on the map, trebling the time she would normally allow for covering each mile and adding an extra hour. Rob did not need to ask where.

'Fine. Let's do it. There is a lot to see along the way.'

'Like what?'

'The old church and Dutch homes within the ramparts at Galle. Dominic Sansoni has done some great pictures of the old buildings. And there is Weligama – some ancient statue by the road.'

'Kustarajagala,' she murmured.

Once again, a name flared into being without warning. She remembered stumbling across the stone figure, leaving Renu and Romesh to scour the beach in search of her.

She folded the map, the north over the south.

'We won't have time to do it all.'

She tried to sound noncommittal, match his desire for exploration with the casual interest of an old hand. 'I would like to spend some time just walking around.'

She slipped the map into a plastic folder and clicked it shut.

Rob observed her, trying to place her in the new landscape, taking in the darkened face that made her eyes glow white and sharp.

'Why don't you call your uncle? See if he's free to meet. It's pointless going all that way and miss seeing him.'

She was looking down at her hands, concealing her irritation that her visit home was being reduced to just another item on the itinerary. She shrugged her shoulders.

'We might drop in on the off-chance. No one makes appointments here according to clock-time and diaries. We're not in England now. Appointments are for strangers.' She clipped her pen in her bag. 'Here time works in tune with family ties. We might drop in on the off-chance' – she relished the crisp lightness of words that conveyed that precise degree of control she was looking for – 'and just see if anyone is at home.'

Why, if she carried on like this she might even persuade herself that she had never been away at all.

The decision that they came to meant the compromise of taking two trips rather than one. On Thursday they would travel to Dolmen House and visit the old town in the Fort, and on Friday they would visit Galle. It kept the family visit and tourist trip separate, allowing them to concentrate on different areas of desire.

They were forced to change their plans on Thursday morning when Lakshman announced that his sister's father-in-law, who lived some five miles from their destination, had just died. He would therefore drop them at the Fort and return late that afternoon. He would stop off beforehand at Weligama so Rob could see Kustarajagala, but the Galle trip would require that they abandon the van for the day, as Lakshman needed to drive on to attend the funeral.

She felt she could not question these new arrangements, though it would compel them to spend almost a whole day at the Fort without knowing if anyone would be at home, and combine sightseeing with the family visit. The proposal was presented to her with customary directness and concluded with the force of a head waggle that indicated both question and resolution in one decisive tilt. She knew that for Lakshman the chance for them all to spend an extended period with their respective families made perfect sense. He could not have known that her remaining relatives were not even aware that she was back.

There is no clear approach to Kustarajagala, she thought, no entry point that might announce its presence to a passer-by.

She was standing on the inland road looking across to the point where Rob had disappeared to take photographs when she became conscious of the density of landscape, the largeness of the green leaves that seem to have absorbed Rob whole, leaving only his footsteps behind. The statue was hidden by boulders and shrubs that partially screened it from view. The sky, pale blue, would burn white within an hour.

She heard a clatter of hooves as a bakkiya drew up. She glanced at the driver, smiled and climbed inside.

'I'll be back in a few minutes,' she called to Lakshman, who lifted a hand in acknowledgement, then asked the driver to take her to the beach.

Bakki, or buggy carts, were a rare gift from the past. She could now watch the houses roll over the haunches of a bull and believe nothing had changed, the road sliding under her to the sound of the bull's hooves, which fell on the ground like a tumble of empty coconut shells. When she stepped down from the bakkiya she asked the driver to wait.

She walked across the sand, carrying her sandals, feeling the water wet her soles. She used to come here with her cousins and chase waves, running after the receding discs of foam, then rush back with the white ropes of water lassoing her heels. Her cousins would run off to find beachwood for wickets, leaving her dizzy in the lenses of light swirling at her feet.

She was moving on towards a small gully where the water lifted into rock, when she recognised the place where she used to sit. She drew closer and bent down. Under the rock, nestling between spray and stone, she found, just as she knew she would, a cache of shells, tiny and perfect. There were tellins, smooth and pink as children's fingernails, and petulant lips of cowrie shells washed into a shiny cluster under the stone. Renu and Romesh had flicked sand at her here, demanding that she at least *try* and field the ball. One day, she had run across the road with shells jingling in her pockets and then carried on running, delighting in the freedom of escape. It was some time before she realized she was lost, that the traffic was turbulent about her, that she needed to get back. The wind of a speeding car had pressed her into a clearing where the trees grew tall about her and she felt utterly alone. Alone standing before the stone figure that lifted a solemn palm.

Kustarajagala. The Leper King. A figure steeped in legend so that no one knew quite who he was or when the statue had been hewn. Only the stone and the story survived: the legend of a king from a foreign land who was cured of leprosy by drinking thambili. Josilin would bring this story to her with every glass she drank.

She had paused in the shade of the giant rock, running shells through her fingers, observing the tall form. She had watched it for so long it seemed to grow and fall upon her, the eyes swooping as they slanted down. She lowered her eyes to steady herself and saw a pool of flowers at the base.

This was no mere historical site of some unknown king, but a place of worship, a space for personal prayer.

She brought her palms together, touching her fingertips to her forehead, then ran back through town, running past homes and faded road signs till she came to the rest house and burst into the hallway, shrieking to her cousins in mock delight at an imaginary game of hide-and-seek that she had *Won!*

She returned to Kustarajagala in the bakkiya and approached Rob to show him the shells. She found him kneeling down, aiming a long lens up at the figure. All the time at the beach and here he was still taking photographs in exactly the same place. She ran the cowrie shells through her fingers so they made a faint clicking sound in her pocket.

'The light is perfect,' he called.

The sky was indeed pitched into fragile contrast. The shirt stretched across his back was stained with shadows and sweat.

'It took me ages to get some good shots. A bloody bird kept coming for me. A savage red-brown thing, like an eagle.'

'No eagles would attack you here,' she said to herself, rolling a shell inside her palm.

She felt subdued, as if she was the same lost, little girl who had stumbled on the place all those years ago. She turned towards the stone figure, her eyes glancing off the form and settling at the base. She would like to have prayed, a small personal prayer to mark her return, but the place felt bare, without sanctuary now.

The silver legs of the tripod glimmered from a ledge near by. Rob must have scared off all the birds as there were now none to be heard.

Then, as she walked to the left of the rock, her arm brushed something that jutted from a ledge. The clay mound was a recent construction that had been cleared of weeds. It had been hollowed to make room for an oil-stained niche and a small disk of stone. Inside lay some delicate stars of jasmine encircling a bright red hibiscus. The petals of the larger flower were still rounded and full. Someone must have been praying here shortly before they arrived.

She paused. The tripod beside her was propped on another votive rock. She was conscious of transgression, a boundary crossed.

'Let's go,' she said quietly, torn between the wish to be heard and the wish to remain still. 'Let's go, Rob,' she said more sharply.

He pursed his lips and let out a slow whistle as he pressed the shutter quickly, one-two-three-four, for a succession of shots.

'Hang on, what's the hurry? We've plenty of time. The driver said we can stay till 9.30 since we set off early.'

He didn't even bother to look at her as he spoke.

'I wish you'd stop.'

'Why? What is it?'

Rob was twisting off a lens and balancing the camera on his knee.

She could not explain. Nothing she said now would carry any more weight than the insect swell that rose and fell about him as he shifted.

'Nothing.'

'So what's the problem.'

She searched for words to draw him back.

'I found some shells. Exactly where I used to find them.' It sounded hopelessly inadequate; she might as well have said nothing.

She looked to see if the cloud cover was changing, as she knew that such changes could bring a quick end to these sessions. The sky remained milky as a pearl.

'Rob.'

'Yep. Just a moment.'

He reached up to brush away a leaf that had fallen on a fold of stone skin, reached out with an audacity that made her recoil.

She turned and walked on towards the road, aware of a growing fury that she did not know she was capable of, a fury aggravated by his ignorance of it, strode back, drawing her hands from her pockets so shells scattered with her cry,

'Goddamyou. Do you have to photograph *everything* you see?'

He turned, his face that of a wounded child, the boy he might once have been, fear and shock at once – her own anger thrown back at her, grown large and demonic under the gaze of the stone figure.

the only source of direct light

Her landlady lived on the two floors above and used her own front door. Savi could climb down the steps that led from the pavement, shut the door behind her and disappear. Even the dim light in the basement area was screened off by blinds so no one would know she was in. The only source of direct light slanted in from the back garden. She would look for the weather through geraniums.

She worked in the kitchen area and in bed, making notes while propped up on pillows, moving coffee mugs from the table when she needed to write. The table had a wobbly leg so, during colder spells, she would retire to the warmth of her bed with the computer on her knees, the pale patchwork quilt strewn with notes and loose files. She would drift to sleep with paper rustling about her, the pages rising and falling with her breath.

Books of all sizes were stacked against the walls, the few pieces of furniture in the flat and on the floor. She had to navigate paths around them or step over columns that also supported the routine remnants of her life: railcard, keys, washing powder, hair brush, lip balm, serrated scissors, a bottle of glacier mints, a radio alarm clock, computer disks, green gloves, matchboxes, her cigarettes.

She found things by remembering which pile of books it was on.

The stacks represented an order determined by time and sequence. Books that she had bought recently were near the surface, beneath which lay earlier borrowings and buys. Most of her books were only partly read, a reflection both of selective reading and an attraction to the new. She would sometimes rifle through a stack of books looking for some misplaced notes and find herself confronted by all the good intentions and past passions of previous weeks' buys – books that had once appeared essential but had been abandoned midway when another book called for her attention. Sometimes she would delay looking for something she needed rather than face the accusation of such neglect. The invitation to *Mrs Savi Carter* now lay inside a copy of Leonard Cohen's poems by the fireplace, not forgotten exactly, but on the cusp of remembrance.

Savi was at the kitchen table, going through her supervisor's notes, when she paused at a page that contained a section of her thesis encircled and marked with the word 'clarify' in red capitals. She read the lines again and again, and each time the words fell into place and rang out their meaning without any ambiguity.

> *The open rock door can only be a sign of 'treachery' in the play (p. 42) if we read the Lion's instincts in territorial terms. The writer may be endorsing a specific political rationale, imposing the logic of boundary marking on to the world of a beast whose every action has resisted such crude containment.*

Perhaps they weren't her best lines, but she had thought they were clear. She was in the process of rereading the section on *Sinhabahu* when the phone rang. Her mind was still focused on the play when she gathered that the lady talking to her on the phone was someone called Angela.

The voice sounded friendly but she could not match a person to the name. Instead, Dr Highfield's tired face came into view, his exasperation at trying to make sense of her thesis adding to her own difficulty at reading this briefest and vaguest of instructions: CLARIFY.

She was having difficulty focusing on what was being said by the woman at the other end of the line. Angela was talking about Rob, travel, some engagement or other, when suddenly two unrelated facts came to her almost simultaneously: that she was speaking to the person she had known as Rob's mother, and that her supervisor's note required her to distinguish between the narrator's and writer's point of view. She had blurred these in the analysis by failing to address the narrator's choric role. Her supervisor, who had almost certainly not read the play, had nevertheless picked up her mistake. She would need to reread it bearing this fundamental distinction in mind. It seemed she had been working with the bluntest of tools.

'I'm sorry, could you repeat that?'

'...he didn't think I should tell you, but I thought it prudent, given that we still have some mutual friends.'

'Thanks, Angela.'

It helped to say her name. Grounded things.

'How are you keeping, Savi?' Angela's voice dropped.

'Fine.'

'Still studying?'

'Yes.'

She was too busy writing a note in the margin of her paper to notice the slight condescension in Angela's voice.

'...You know Rob never forgot his first trip to Sri Lanka. I know things got difficult...,' the voice slowed, then suddenly gained speed like a bird skimming clear of a forest fire. 'Well, it's no good raking-over-the-past is it? Geoff was just saying-the-other-day that the past-is-another-country, one that he will never go back to, not that I have a problem with first marriage – mine a nightmare of course, forbidden territory and all – but still I think a first marriage does count for something, and Rob has never forgotten you, you know, even though he does not talk about it, he's still got-all-the-photos-of-you, and he came back with so many great shots, *stunning* shots, even if I say-so-myself, that he just had to return. He's been back many times now. I think he will always remember you for that.'

'That's good.'

'And the wedding there went beautifully. We all had a great time.'

'Good.'

The information was sinking in. He had been back *many times*, had married there, had even taken his family back.

'We saw the elephant orphanage, the botanical gardens, tea estates, climbed the Lion Rock.'

'Right.'

She put the pen down.

'Have you been back recently?' Angela's voice was warm. The intimacy of their past conversations was coming back and made Savi more defensive.

'No.'

She was struggling to think of a suitable excuse to put the phone down.

'You should. It's quite quiet there now that the ceasefire is in place. We were able to go right up north. But I know you wouldn't be interested in touring, what with family there…'

'Rob has got married?'

Savi posed the question without thinking. She suddenly realised she would rather not know if he was.

'No dear. Have you not heard anything I said?' Angela sounded as exasperated as Dr Highfield must be. '*I* got married. Rob tried talking me out of it but what the heck, you-only-live-once, and Geoff is a stickler for tradition. You really should go back some time. Rob says things are much better now than when you did your trip together.'

~

Her memories of the place were mediated by water. In every image water swelled into view, sometimes thrashing at the borders of a moment held still as her mother's hand, sometimes lifted and dashed against her dreams.

She remembered playing on the beach with the waves casting a silver rope about her ankles, walking along the esplanade with her parents and feeling the spray sting her face. There were the well baths in the garden where water came cascading from the coconut palms overhead, and the pulsing course through the river in a boat so low in the water that the reflection of her arms was broken with each push. Her strongest memory was of afternoons on the swing, when she would lift herself up above the water towards the sky and plunge back again, the dense green of grass and trees giving way to a horizon shattered by her arc over the boats, herself a bird looping the elements together. The house had been behind her and the water in front, but she could not be sure whether it was a river, lagoon or some quiet stretch of sea that she faced. The family house occupied a spit of land bordered by all three.

She and Rob were left tracing a path pieced together by those small water-borne images that led her home. They had walked again and again past a house with tumbling bougainvillea and looked at other houses in the vicinity in their search for Dolmen House. They walked up and down the ranks of the low, curd-coloured court buildings, following paths that intersected with her childhood game of shadow run. They had even circled the vast Bluffing Tree where some children were playing blind man's bluff, shouting and spinning their blindfolded victim and prodding him with sticks. After what seemed like hours, they had to admit that they were quite lost and would have to return to the Fort rest-house and start again. Rob was frustrated by this turn of events and was kicking stones as he walked. He had not spoken to her since she had shouted at him in Weligama.

'Did you notice those children playing blind man's bluff?' She wished for reconciliation with both Rob and herself.

'You know, I think it's quite funny,' she continued, trying to read the silence on his unevenly tanned face. 'They were playing around the Bluffing Tree. We used to call it that because it was where people facing trial would gather during breaks, making up stories that might get them out of trouble. And now there are children playing blind man's bluff there. Blind man's bluff under the Bluffing Tree. Quite funny, no?'

He did not look at her but it was clear that he'd been listening. He kicked another stone and watched it skitter to a ditch.

'That wasn't blind man's bluff.'

Rob drew a hand across his brow, wiping a trickle of sweat

from his eyes. The gesture softened him and slightly hardened her resolve.

'Yes, it was. Didn't you see, they were spinning a boy around who had a blindfold on.'

'Yes, but it wasn't that.'

He paused, and then continued in a tone that was self-consciously even, so she knew he was struggling to stay calm. 'You know it really pays to look about you more, Sav' – she disliked being called this, wasn't Savi short enough? – 'They were taking him away, pushing him with sticks. They were pretending to be soldiers. I believe that boy was playing the part of one of the disappeared.'

She did not know what to say, confronted by the human shape of politics like this. She glanced back at the boys who were shrieking under the tree, and then looked directly at Rob, challenging him to look at her.

He ignored her, their silence flickering in angry shadows upon the courthouse walls.

He was probably right, but she did not wish to acknowledge it, did not wish to acknowledge his foreigner's ability to see things that eluded her. She had followed the public events – the bombings, assassinations and secret killings, the violence of scandal and censure, blame and counterblame – but had done so in a way that kept her private memories intact, translating unmanageable facts into an armour-plated language she'd acquired at university.

She was not prepared to let this go and allow Rob's easy intrusions now – Rob, the child of a marriage marked by the argument of slammed doors, on his first visit to the island, fleshing it with his knowledge, grounding it in his terms, redefining her and her relationship to her past along the way.

'I love you,' he had said one night, his body a blur of damp heat, 'I love the exotic in you.' Something in her had snapped out of place then, sexed their relationship into imbalance.

She remained quiet as they approached the rest house.

'I think I'll take some pictures of the church.' He turned from her as he spoke so she was left facing the dark wetness of his back.

'I'll see you inside for lunch.'

The military base and prison were a long blaze of whitewash on their left. Some bayonets glinted from behind the outer wall. Rob began walking over the cricket green, away from the sandy path they had shared while crossing the courtroom grounds.

'At least come in and help me order something,' she cried after him. 'I'll call for you later when the food is ready.'

He dropped his shoulders and eased the camera off as he turned. He must be hungry. Either that or he was not serious about taking pictures of the shabby Dutch Reformed Church. She continued towards the rest house with the irritation of the skirt brushing her calves, conscious he was retracing his steps behind her.

'And,' she called, without turning around, so he might see she was in control, 'you should be careful taking photos round here. Those army guys won't like it.'

She was waiting in the dining hall with a soft drink of indeterminate colour and taste. A man in a turquoise shirt and dark trousers was observing her. She tried to ignore him but he continued to glance her way before walking up. He was already smiling by the time he reached her table.

'Hallo.'

'Hello,' Savi returned dryly.

'First visit to Fort?'

In England this might have been mistaken for a pick-up line. Under the spinning fans of the dim dining room, it came across as a way of establishing who he was.

'No.'

'You have been before?'

He was observing the clothes she had carefully selected that morning – the lace-trimmed vest that might have been picked up from a market stall and the ruched skirt that fell well below her knees. An effort at feminine attire in deference to the family visit.

'Yes.' She did not wish to have a tour guide and be drawn into obligation.

'Sri Lankan?'

He was still standing by the table, giving her space to turn away and dismiss him with a tilt of the head. Perhaps he was just passing the time as so many people seemed to do.

'My uncle and aunt live here,' she relented slightly, her voice thickening into a Sri Lankan accent despite herself. 'I used to come here for holidays.'

She was aware of the awkwardness of the mixed register as she reclaimed the English flutiness of the last word.

'Aaah.' He seemed to understand. 'Name?'

She deflected the inquiry as a sudden thought occurred to her. 'Dolmen House.'

He nodded.

'It is by water,' she said, gravelly once more but not caring this time. 'A large house with columns around it and a stone slab in front. There was a swing in the garden and a well at the back. Red bougainvillea overhanging the porch. And a temple quite close by, I think.'

It sounded like a child's map of the world, which it was.

He rested his arms over the back of a chair and looked towards the car park and the sea beyond. A fly shimmied across his face. He swept it away with his hand.

'Your husband?' he said, nodding in the general direction of the car park through which Rob had walked.

She buried a nod while reaching for her drink. For a split second she imagined Rob as a flying insect that might be brushed away.

'English?'

She looked up and smiled warmly. She did not know why – perhaps it was the predictability of the question, the way they were both falling into a pattern of interaction that was not entirely of their choosing – but it was enough. He smiled back and gained a more expansive tone.

'My name is Kumar. I live in the town, not in Fort. I work here.'

She was ready to shake his hand but he did not offer it.

'Are you the manager?'

'No, no. They call me the Fixer. If there is problem, I come along. I see to the small things. Details others forget.'

'More important than the manager, then.'

Self-deprecation like his was rare. An office peon might walk past the gardener who swept the dirt from his shoes without ever acknowledging him; a man with three stripes on his epaulettes would ignore a man with two.

He smiled and looked down, noting her empty glass. 'You have a long wait.'

'It's OK. We made a large order. It'll take a while.'

He called out for another drink, his voice carried into the spinning blades of the fan. There was no response. He went towards the bar, then suddenly turned to face her with a glow of recognition in his eyes.

'Dolmen House', he said thoughtfully. 'That's the Rodrigo place. I know Mr Rodrigo. He often comes here with his wife. Come to think, you,' he said, raising a finger and then touching his brow, 'look like him.'

She gave an accommodating nod that ended with a head shake, very like the customary head curl that meant *OK, maybe*, and *I understand* all at once. It was wonderful to be recognized, placed.

And she did indeed look like her uncle. Her face was generous in its contours, and when she smiled, as she did now, her eyes would be lifted in the same arced symmetry as her brow, in a way that matched his. Her parents had often laughed at the resemblance, saying she was more of a Rodrigo than any of them. Yet she had none of Eden's character. And no one had yet seen the two of them smile together at the same time. Her aunt, on the other hand, was always laughing with him, burying her pale head in one hand while cupping her glass with the other to prevent her drink from spilling. She could see Eden and Fiona clearly now. She half-expected to find them walking into the room.

'Well, I know I don't look like his wife,' she said wryly.

Kumar drew up a chair and sat down, placing his arm next to hers so she could feel the hair on his skin.

By the time Rob returned she had clear instructions on how to reach the house, which they would find at the end of the boundary road where the river met the lagoon at Land's End. Kumar shook Rob's hand and left them to the large silence of their lunch.

Before leaving the rest house she went in search of him, walking round the bar and along a corridor that led outside to a small garden tangled with bitter gourds and pumpkins. She found him seated at a table on the back patio, having a meal even larger than theirs. She thanked him for his help and said they would look him up when they were back. She wished to say more but could not. She knew Kumar couldn't have joined them for lunch. It would have broken protocol.

the wisp of an i

She reaches for the book in which the wedding invitation rests. She absorbs the words – *Do come Savi* – and tries to imagine the hand that brushed the card at this point, stroked the *S* into an *a*, carried the curve of the *v* to the small, sure wisp of an *i*.

She draws the card down the lines of print in the book in which it has been enclosed, so the words are revealed as she reads them:

No one will call you idle for dying with the sun.

They were the last lines of a poem she once loved.

~

Ribbons of wind streamed from her fingers as she thrust her hand from the window of the speeding van. There were too many relations for her to know them all, she explained, all stretching along the southern coast as plentiful as coconut palms. Every other residence seemed to be connected to her family in some way. Over here, beyond the railway track, the home of a second cousin's uncle's wife's brother; over there, across the paddy field, the walawwa of an elderly spinster so distantly related and wealthy that everybody claimed her as their own. She could only really remember those relatives who visited her parents regularly, and those who spoke too loudly or not at all.

There was Aunt Kusuma who fussed over her clothes and said she would really love to see Savi in a dress one day, a pink dress with glossy ribbons and shiny buttons on the sleeves; Aunt Sunita who would pause and blow her nose to mark her disapproval of Savi's tower of books; Uncle Cliff who always belched and whose laugh was as expansive as his splayed legs on the sofa; Great Uncle Bertie who would no sooner arrive and sit down than he would drop off into a sleep that he could only be drawn from if a cricket match was broadcast; Terry and Ameena who would squabble like chickens over everything from lashings of kitul treacle to what to watch on TV; and of course Renu and Romesh whose laughter and games still carried her into the heart of the Fort. She had given Renu her favourite books for safekeeping before she left: a compendium of Greek myths; the Jataka tales. These cousins were her closest relatives and Renu knew her better than anyone else. If he really wanted to know her he should get to know Renu as they shared everything when they were young.

She had tried telling him this but he'd just smiled in that superior way that said, Yes-yes-I-know, I understand, you-are-happy-to-be-home, which was not what she felt at all. She drew her hand in to steady the bottles of water rolling at her feet, dismayed at the realization of how ridiculous she had felt standing by him on the verge on the way to Weligama as he photographed beached catamarans and roadside fruit stalls – the king coconuts dutifully rearranged by the vendor – for contrast, Rob said – as a precariously balanced motorbike with a family of six sped by, waving and hooting into a stream of words neither of them could understand. Not being able to find her way to the house she had described in such detail to him was more than just embarrassing. It is pointless dreaming about home, she would say to Renu one day, if you don't know how to make your way back.

How different things would have been if they had been able to find her uncle's house in the morning as planned. Then they might have met Fiona who'd been at home supervising the fitting of new guttering. This had required the cutting back of a prickly swathe of bougainvillea that now lay heaped in an angry bundle on the drive and was being gathered into order by two men in striped sarongs. And if they had succeeded in finding their way back – she needed to think *they* were both responsible for this lapse – they would have missed Eden who had left early for work that day. He had taken Renu with him and left her at the hotel, bringing Bradley back home to mind the house that afternoon.

But it was past midday, a time to relax as the sun was almost at its height, and Fiona had gone to check out a new department store. Eden was home after his morning stint at the hotel, reading the newspapers on the back verandah. He had changed into a bush shirt and dark blue shorts that were just visible below the reach of the papers. He had asked for the guttering work to stop so that he could enjoy a rest in relative quiet, and told Bradley to stay by the gate and ensure that all the shrubbery was cleared before dusk. He paused from time to time to lower the papers and watch the waterbirds pick their way through the mangroves. The gardeners were gathering the last bundle of cut bougainvillea when Savi lifted the latch and walked on to the drive with Rob behind her. The men paused, one of them, bolder than the other, came forward to greet them.

'Hallo sir.'

All attention on her white shadow.

'Hello. Can you…'

'You want to see Fort? Boat trip? My brother have very good boat.'

The man smiled at Rob and hitched up the waistband of his sarong as if in readiness for the trip. The other man smirked, said something that she did not understand and tried to draw his companion back.

'Hello. Are Mr and Mrs Rodrigo in? Rod-rigo.' She repeated the name, enjoying the singsong lilt.

A mixture of mild dismay and uncertainty registered across the face of the first man. The second seemed to gain in confidence. He was about to answer when someone stepped forward from under the porch.

He was a small-made man with a shock of glossy hair whose khaki trousers and collared shirt fell loosely about him. He raised his shoulders as if in a gesture of inquiry or an adjustment to some muscles in his neck .

'Master is resting,' he rasped. 'Maybe sleeping now. If you come at,' he looked down, jerked his head, consulted the bougainvillea, 'five, he should be up.'

He seemed to draw breath between words as though he was short of air.

'We need to be getting back before then.'

It was true. They had promised Lakshman they'd be back before dusk

'What about Mrs Rodrigo or the others?' Rob felt the need to speak since the men were still watching him.

'Out.' The man's hands, prominent beneath loose sleeves, rose a fraction as if they had been pulled by invisible strings.

'That's a shame.' Her voice tightened in more than disappointment. 'I'm the Hamu Mahaththaya's niece,' she managed in Sinhala. 'I am visiting the country after a long time.'

The two gardeners relaxed a little and muttered something among themselves. They appeared to be commenting on her physical resemblance to her uncle.

The man in khaki trousers, who did not seem to be on familiar terms with the two others, asked them to wait a moment, before returning and indicating with a peremptory jerk of the chin that they should follow him to the living room where Master would be joining them shortly. He then disappeared into the darkness of the servants' quarters.

The original Dolmen House had been built during British times in a part of the old town once used by the Dutch for holding prisoners before trial. The house had been the official residence of the tax officer of the region who had named it after the large slab of stone that had once sealed a dolmen during the Neolithic age. The officer, a man with more than just a layman's interest in historical sites, had propped the two ton slab against his verandah, and publicised its provenance, thus gaining for himself a reputation as a man who defied death. Unlike other regions in the country, taxes in this coastal area tended to be paid on time.

At independence, Dolmen House was reclaimed by the government for public use and the stone slab, seen by many as a bad omen, was dumped in a gully. It had lain there undisturbed until it was reclaimed by the young Eden Rodrigo. Newly married, he had inherited a large tract of land between the sea and the river where he intended to build a home for his wife and future family. Although the slab itself had little to distinguish it, he was aware of its history, having grown up in the Fort. It was, he felt, a significant find that was in danger of being lost. On an auspicious day, he had the dolmen stone hoisted from the gully and installed as an uneven and overlarge first step under his front porch.

Savi was unaware of this story, having known the house only as a holiday retreat from the city. Her mother would convalesce here, watching her from the verandah, while her father remained in Colombo as there was always, he said, too much work to be done. She would play catch with her cousins, weaving in and out of coconut palms, before hiding under the rhubarb or behind the garage on the front drive. The game would extend beyond the boundaries of the house, on the understanding that they were only allowed to move in shades and shadows. A shadow run, they called it, their young bodies held in the darkness of blocked sunlight, in the shifting outlines of neighbouring walls and shrubs, drawing a dark thread of connection from the house to the courtrooms that then looped back to the safety of this front door. The dolmen stone under the porch was as much a part of the place as the terrazzo tiles that lined the floors. She had rolled marbles down the slab and polished stones on its rough surface, grazing her knee on it more than once. She stepped over it with Rob, removed her sandals, entered the long corridor of absence.

She was now sitting in the same place she'd occupied when she was last here, on the same ebony chair where she'd waited by her father, her arm against the flowers under which he lay. The light beyond was as harsh as it had been then, sea and sky merging into marbled glare. She had kept looking at her father's face, pulled tight and stitched behind the skull, as if it had been broken and put together again, the stubble that had grown after death making his cheeks and neck appear one. She had spent three days and nights willing him into wholeness, smoothing the fragments, the broken face in her hands.

Eden entered with the light and for a moment it was as if her father stood before her. The same eyes, she thought, before he turned them on her.

Savi got up, shaking her skirt, hearing her mother whisper as she did so, *You must wear a skirt when visiting,* then looked round to see Rob turn from an ancestral portrait on the wall and step forward to shake Eden's hand. Against the heavy, low settees Rob looked unnaturally tall.

She reached and tried to touch her uncle's cheek to hers. Some hesitation on his part, and she withdrew. She could smell the same green oil he always used to run through his hair.

52

He motioned that they should sit down.

'You should have said you were coming. Fiona would love to meet you.'

He managed just the right degree of formal geniality to accommodate them both.

Savi crossed her ankles, then ran her palms down her lap in a vague attempt to smooth out creases from a skirt that had been designed in wrinkles and pleats.

'We did not know. We just stopped by in case you were in.' She locked her fingers on her lap in an effort to stay calm.

'On the off-chance,' added Rob, repeating the words she had used with such insistence, and giving a smile that was meant for her.

Eden relaxed as he sat back, adjusting a small red cushion behind him on the settee and positioned himself so that he could easily address Rob. He had always found it easier to talk to men.

'You are staying long? You must stay for dinner. Fiona would want that.'

Rob raised an eyebrow of inquiry towards her. Savi hesitated, something in her resisting the possibility of stepping out of the frame of their arrangements – a need for order perhaps, or a lack of readiness to meet them all. She indicated that they'd need to leave before then, that the driver expected them at the main car park by five.

There was a pause. Eden looked beyond them to the open door, as if hoping or anticipating that someone might come in. The last time she had seen him he had avoided her gaze, held himself back like the others. She had looked everywhere for answers, searching their faces for something that might explain her loss, face after face closing, as if extinguished, as she entered the room. Her uncle cast a barrier of work about him, her cousins withdrew to hushed pockets of the house, her grandparents were shielded by a bevy of well-intentioned friends, as the shock, it was said, would kill them. Fiona's stiff embrace enfolded the silence of them all. Everyone was denying her entry to the meaning of her father's death. This, the loss she never dared confront.

Her mother's hospital death had been slow and sanitized, could be left behind with the island, but her father's was sudden and unseen, still open to her touch. She had not been told what killed him, just that his body had been found. She had gone straight back from the funeral to sit her mock GCSEs, surrendering herself to the demand of exams she understood. In the flurry of papers, his death became a blank sheet that one day she might write upon.

She looked at her watch. Rob was holding something in his hands. She returned to the afternoon of unseen birds and an uncle with green oil in his hair.

Rob had picked up a small, gilt-framed, black and white photo of a Western woman whose smile was a slash of light in the reflection of the glass. It was a picture of Fiona, taken shortly before marriage. Savi had been told how her uncle used to carry it with him when he was building Dolmen House, drawing it from his pocket to show his architect and friends who would all feel obliged to congratulate him on his good luck, while keeping their thoughts on this mixed marriage to themselves. Rob seemed oblivious to Eden's steady gaze.

'Your first time in Sri Lanka.' Eden's voice was brusque.

It was neither a statement nor a question, but an imperative that called for attention. Rob placed the picture back on the teapoy and drew his hands to his knees.

'Yes.'

She could tell he was unsure of how to connect.

'You like Sri Lanka?'

'Yes. It's very beautiful.'

'Where are you staying?'

Rob told him while drawing a hand over his head and down to the back of his neck. It was beginning to feel like an inquisition.

'There are better places,' Eden said as a statement of fact.

Rob glanced towards her as if unsure of what he'd heard, before slowly bringing his hand down to rest on the camera about his neck. She felt a twinge of sympathy for him and inclined her head to indicate her uncertainty. Her uncle might be assuming that he was a boyfriend that she'd brought home for approval. It would be interesting to see what they made of one another before she set her uncle right.

Eden shuffled his sandals and called into the darkness behind him for drinks to be served. The intervening years had given him bulk and presence. He scratched his arm thoughtfully, leaned against the scrolled armrest and considered Rob's exposed knees.

'You must go to Galle,' he said in a tone familiar in hotel lobbies. 'Take a walk on the ramparts.'

'We might go tomorrow,' Rob said carefully.

It was clear he thought Eden was intent on treating him like a tourist.

Her uncle now turned to her as if he was seeing her properly for the first time, his eyes following the contours of her cropped curls, the canvas strap and metal buckles of the small rucksack on her shoulder, before looking directly into her eyes with an expression that was both soft and proprietorial.

'Still studying, Savitri?'

He was looking at her as he might have done when she was eleven years old, when the quantity of books she kept in her room upstairs was a source of amusement in Dolmen House, not least because of her keen but fitful spraying to keep off the silverfish. She clenched her hand, felt her watch and rolled her finger round the dial. It was time to establish the significance of those books and the time that had elapsed.

'I finished this year. I got a First.'

'Aah.'

She could not see him clearly because of the glare and she would have preferred to stay watching this abstract form onto which she could read anything, waiting for him to ask the questions that would allow her to reveal her altered self, but Rob was opening his mouth to speak and she had to step in. She wanted to be the one to say it.

'Rob and I have just got married.'

There. It was out.

She had wondered how she might communicate this to the family she had grown apart from, wondered if they would be pleased or anxious or simply indifferent to the news. Her uncle's marriage had been a test of personal independence. Eden, who married an Englishwoman with an unpronounceable name, had seen the successful pursuit of his wife as a mark of his right to self-determination. Savi, on the other hand, carried her marriage all too lightly, as if Rob was just another book she could consult from time to time.

Eden remained silent, his face a globe of darkness.

'Rob and I have just got married.' She spoke up to make sure he'd heard.

Slowly, soundlessly, Eden leaned forward, his form growing as it moved towards her, his face now close enough for her to see the whites of his eyes. His questions were short and to the point – missing out all the important things.

When, he wanted to know. And where. Did they marry in Colombo?

'No, uncle, in England'.

They remained quite still, facing one another in the cool columned house, in a room peopled with family portraits, of shade and sudden light, the birdcalls spinning in so they felt the garden press upon them, searching for something to say that would take away the neglect of the missing years.

England. It was not just another country but another time. Her quick and painless marriage belonged there, not here.

'We wanted something quiet,' she managed. 'We also thought it would be good to come back. See people.'

Her throat was dry. She needed a drink.

Eden drew back slightly, looking from Savi to Rob, as if to see whether an embrace was in order. Rob shifted slightly but they all stayed seated in their chairs.

Her uncle leant forward, a heavy mass of concentration. He was giving closer consideration to the mosquito-bites below Rob's knees. He then looked back at her, a zig-zag glance that made her conscious of her sleeveless vest and bare arms, which she reached to cover with her hands.

'You know weddings matter here. Family matters.'

The needles of accusation in his voice were directed at Rob. They compelled him to respond in the only way he knew how, so that she was left to watch with growing wonder as he lifted the camera from his neck and placed its bulky form on to the teapoy next to Fiona's photo, the picture toppling and smashing on the tile floor, Rob picking it up with apologies that swept into one another, picking up and dropping explanations along the way, of how they had wished to keep things informal and low-key, how just his mother and a few mates from university had made it to the register office, how the whole thing was very cost-effective given that neither of them had fixed jobs, and that it was he – Rob – who had been most keen to see Sri Lanka and meet everyone, and it was he – Rob – who had persuaded Savi to return.

There was a pause that opened a space for the wall clock to be heard. Eden leaned forward and drew the photograph from Rob, tapping the remaining splinters from the frame onto the *Newsweek* magazine that lay on the coffee table between them.

In the silence that followed, Savi became aware that everything they'd said suggested that the two of them were no more than passing travellers on their way to somewhere else, subject to erasure under the hands of the ticking clock. She felt tired. The heat seemed to be entering her limbs and weighing them down.

Someone moved out of the darkness behind Eden, carrying a shimmer of glasses upon a silver tray. A woman in a sky-blue dress. Savi watched the moving figure as she came and held the tray before them and found herself searching for Josilin in the woman's stooped form – Josilin whose large arms had carried her into an embrace of warm stories and sweat. The figure who stood before her was a thin, dry wisp of a woman with a tight plait of hair that trailed down her back.

As she leaned back with her drink and looked across the room at the heavy, carved furniture, the portraits on the walls, the lampshade of amber glass that attracted a circle of clicking geckos that she would flick cardamom seeds at as a child, she wondered at how everything else had changed, how there was no correspondence between people any more, between this woman and the former cook, between the man who spoke to her and the uncle she once knew, between the Rob she made love with and the awkward figure in the chair. Then Eden cast a question that threw her completely off course.

'So what do we call you now?'

'I'm sorry?'

'Surname?'

He put a glass to his lips and drank, and then swilled the clinking ice while waiting for a response.

'What is your surname now?'

For a moment she felt relieved. She had half-expected to be questioned about Rob's salary, horoscope and medical history. She brushed the glass across her lips, then put it down, untasted.

'It's Carter.'

'Carter?'

'Yes.'

'Aah.'

The tone was settling into assurance. Then he snorted and began to wheeze in short bursts as he tried to contain the amusement that took hold.

'Carter,' softer now, then 'Carter', relaxing into his drink and almost choking as he spoke, 'Car-ter. So you're Savitri Car-ter now. What a way to return here. A Sri Lankan graduate with a First Class degree who calls herself Car-ter.'

Eden slapped his thigh as if they were all party to a joke and steadied himself, raising a finger to make a point.

'Listen, here names are important; they link us to our past. They tell us of our history, our roots. And what illustrious roots! Your mother's name, Savitri, is one of the oldest names on the island, goes back to the time of Vijaya's emissaries. And Rodrigo hails from the Portuguese court, though we never intermarried with them, of course, just took the name for form's sake.'

He was instructing her as if she was new to this, had not heard it countless times before.

'Savitri Samadara Jayani Rodrigo, a daughter of one of the Oldest Island Clans. Now become Car Ter. Car Ter.'

His eyes moved from Rob to her, moistening with amusement as he cut the name into half, delighting in seeing the two halves squirming like a bisected worm.

'Why, you need not have walked here like two American backpackers, you should have come here riding a bullock cart! You know bullock carts? Those carts pulled by bulls? We use them to carry dry goods. The people who drive them are carters, just like you!'

She opened her mouth to say something, to humour him perhaps with a description of her buggy ride, tell Rob too, as he'd not seen her take it, but found her throat too dry for words. Eden's insensitivity, Rob's discomfort and restraint: she understood them both, felt herself spinning between them. Any mention of the ride now risked placing her not as the child she had been but as the tourist she feared she might become.

Carter. A name that slipped easily into the gap between worlds.

She picked up her drink and watched her thumb expand through the liquid of the glass as she gulped down a silence that seemed to blot out the room.

~

She read the date on the wedding invitation. Christmas. The busiest time of all. Bookings had to be made months in advance to be sure of getting a flight.

She could hear Angela's voice, carried high on the excitement of her recent trip. She saw Rob going back, time and again with his family, taking in the land with his camera, rolling it up in that long spool of film and putting it in his pocket, moving into places she had once called home, going over that first journey, crossing the paths they had made, and making new tracks in the land.

So much had happened since her last trip back. The world had moved on and Sri Lanka was now taking in tourists like never before. The peace talks pushed the country off the edge of the political map, off the international news-broadcasts and broadsheets. This peace made a difference to what was known and remained unknown, to what was spoken and remained unspoken. *Peace and quiet. Peace and understanding. Peace be with you.* All the registers pointing to silence, a silence filled with her memories of the place, leaving tangled truths to the large debates of half-read books.

That afternoon she rang the travel agent and indicated that she wished to be put on the waiting list for a flight back. She was asked for her name.

'Carter,' she said, 'Mrs Savi Carter.'

She tried the name on her tongue in slack mid-American, in the crisp, open vowels of the Southern counties, in the choppy intonations of Sinhala, and with each new accent she found herself sliding into someone else's narrative.

II

DOLMEN HOUSE

'Where are you? Where are you?' In the dark, the words are hollowed out, all vowels and echo. Renu moves in space, anticipating solid objects with her outstretched arms, surfacing, surfing, the shrieks of children popping like bubbles at her touch.

'Here.'

'Here.'

'No, here.'

And they laugh to see her testing the air, measuring distance and territory.

Romesh crooks a finger and two boys scuttle under a table. Renu takes a step towards them and hits a corner hard into her stomach.

'Hey, that's not fair!' she hears Savi cry out, 'No hiding!' and turns towards her cousin's voice. There is a muffled interchange somewhere behind her, voices like fireflies to the blindfolded girl, and a movement of chairs and padded steps receding.

'Hey, don't go! Come back. You can't leave me here.' She is about to reach for the scarf about her face when her elbow brushes against something, someone.

'Got you!' In the cooling air, Renu holds onto the warmth of skin, an arm, a sleeve, moving her hands up to touch hair, feeling the trembling, the itch of stifled laughter as the body tries to hold still.

The hair is thick, slippery as seaweed. There are soft, spongy bits of skin, an articulation of muscle and a complication that rounds into an ear. Then the telltale diamond stud, the only item of jewellery Savi is allowed to wear.

'Savi. It's Savi!' And they laugh and pull the blindfold off together, Savi's eyes shining rather too brightly into the newly opened ones of her cousin. Savi is still tingling from the rummage of her face, which has made her aware of the vulnerability of her eyes and the way her lips can be pulled to slide down to her chin, but she is happy and she doesn't know why.

'I stayed because the others ran away.'

Renu's laugh ripples through her and makes her eyes light up.

'Good. We can get our own back. Let's run and hide. They'll come looking and won't know where we are.'

The girls rush out of the house together, their legs adjusting to the uneven front steps, sliding into the wet earth. They run down the road towards the offices and suddenly stop when they reach the clearing by the court buildings where a few mud-spattered vans have pulled up under the low branches of a large tree. There are people stepping out of the main building and policemen pulling them into order. Two men are led into a van with their arms pulled back behind them. If it weren't for their handcuffs they could have been any one. There seem only to be men there, gathered under the relative dryness of the Bluffing Tree. White sarongs or black trousers. The girls stand and watch, holding hands.

'I wonder what they've done. Those two men.'

'Who says they've done anything. They need to be found guilty first.' Renu, the younger of the two, likes to show that she is as informed about court proceedings as her cousin, whose father is a judge.

'I know that. But what are they here for?'

'Don't know. You'd better go and ask.'

Savi knows Renu is challenging her, pushing her to talk to one of the crowd. She had remained in the room out of loyalty to her cousin, had been sure her gesture would be seen for what it was, but Renu is pressing her as she so often does, calling on her to go forward and prove herself. Her first memories of resistance came from these tussles, not so much with her cousin as with herself. She has been raised to comply with others' expectations, even those of this young cousin, but the need to stay within the boundaries of childhood is even stronger.

'No, it's not our business. They'll tell us to shove off.'

They pause and look for Punchisoma, the jailbird who is the best source of information on such matters, to see if he is near his customary begging spot by the Bluffing Tree, but he is not to be seen.

'No harm in trying. Wait here.'

Renu runs up to the building towards a lone man who leans on a pillar near the front steps, writing in a notebook. He looks up as she approaches and they speak for a moment. Renu comes rushing back, her sandals slapping against her heels. She is smiling.

'Well what is it? What are they being tried for?'

'Not telling.'

'Go on, tell.'

'Not telling. You go ask if you want to know.'

Renu has started to walk back, forcing Savi to run after her. The flounce of her crimson skirt adds resolution to her walk and Savi is left trying to keep up with the girl whom she had felt sorry for just a little while earlier. When they return to the house, the boys are at the table eating love cake and licking the brown crumbs off their fingers.

'You girls had better come eat.' Kitsiri, Romesh's round-cheeked cricket mate, reaches for another piece. 'There are just one-two left.'

Renu takes one and hands the plate to Savi, opening her eyes wide in silent reproach at Kit's gluttony. He is two years older than Romesh and already knows how to get his way.

Years later, as she draws the cotton sheet about her to shield her from the spattered gunfire of the night, Renu will reflect on the old, enforced blindness, this reaching out in darkness, all concentration on the weight of her outstretched arms. She can still remember her body as an object without dimension until it made contact with another. She can remember the relief at recognition, of finding Savi in her hands, and of the diminution of that dizzy moment that marked her own vulnerability, before they pulled the blindfold off together and went running towards the prison walls.

For Savi, who opens her wardrobe to a jumble of clothes belonging to a season she has come to call *Wintum*, small incidents such as these have got lost somewhere in the overflowing years, but when Natalie reached for her face in the water, smudging her fingers over her eyes, that first time in the swimming pool, there was a blurred instant when she almost felt her face being pulled into Renu's hands.

~

She reached for the phone and tapped the pads. There were ten numbers for the discount service and a further thirteen numbers to reach the house. One wrong button and she could be phoning a complete stranger. The phone was ringing. Savi glanced towards her wardrobe. There were no skirts or dresses, nothing suitable for a wedding in the island. She had torn her one good skirt during a weekend break in the Lake District. No sari either, as her mother had died before teaching her how to wear one.

Someone picked up the phone. A woman's voice said something in Sinhala, and Savi found herself stumbling as she tried to respond. The woman evidently could not understand her and the line crackled as a male voice broke through.

Rodrigo residence.

He was also speaking Sinhala. She had to find the language again.

'Hello. I want Rodrigo Master to speak to.'

'He's not here. He'll be back in the evening.'

'Ah. So, is there anybody there?' That was ridiculous. Of course there was someone there. She was speaking to him. She had forgotten the formal language that would make it possible to ask for her aunt and cousins.

He spoke fast, and she gathered from scattered words that everyone was out and it would be better to call later.

'OK. Tell them Savi phoned. I am coming "Tuesday".' She lapsed into English. The years of absence had erased the days of the week. 'Do you understand? "Tuesday".'

'Right. Right. Toosday.'

It had not occurred to her he might know English.

'Yes. Thank you. I am coming on Tuesday. I am arriving early morning. At 2 am. Please tell them I'll make my own way down. OK?'

Silence. The line seemed to hiss in small bursts, as if someone was breathing in her ear.

'Hello?'

'Hallo. Hallo. Yes, medem.' A pause, as if he was reading aloud. 'Savi. You arrive Toosday. 2 ayem.'

'Yes. Thank you.'

'Thank you, medem.'

It occurred to her later, after she had put the phone down, that she had not asked who he was.

It is the first time Bradley has spoken on the phone. He speaks automatically, as he has heard others talk on the line, but is disorientated by the foreign inflections of Savi's distant voice, until her English words come and hold him. 'Tuesday', she says. Or is it something else? He makes a mental note of the information as Malika takes the instrument from his ear. He walks back to the kitchen door and waits for Eden to return so that he can be dismissed and go back to the hotel.

He hardly spends any time at Dolmen House these days. Most of his time is absorbed in watching and waiting between light sleep and the dark of the open car park where he works. It is seven years now since he began work at the hotel. His body has learned to count the hours, to feel them pass through him like the beam of headlights that roll by.

In quiet moments, before daybreak, when the first cyclists emerge from the coastal road, he may sometimes look back and recall his father throwing him onto the metal grid of his pillion seat and spinning round in a dizzying circle about the grassy compound by their home, his father's raucous cries throwing spokes of laughter into air, his own shrieks of alarm as the wheels wobble and zig-zag into a path like the nose of a lost dog. The memory dissipates as the sun begins to bleach the sky and he returns to his cabin to listen to tourist coaches pulling in; to the stutter of trishaws, growling motorbikes and the slur of vans; to the angry blare of lorries hooting round the bend.

In the evenings he gets up as darkness makes the landscape one dimensional. He walks towards the traffic barrier and stands in the small island that separates the two paths leading to the main entrance of Eden's Bay. Under slender cones of light, his shadow is frail and fleeting, absorbed into shapes that grow wild in the gloom. He is a small man with precise hands, all energy drained into the tips of his fingers. His arms are loose bands, dangling at his sides, but if you startle him they may rise and the hands reach to strike you, as if they belong to a different episode of his body.

So people are careful not to startle him. The drivers, porters and gatekeeper keep a safe distance and are sure to call out to announce themselves – especially at night, when they see him searching the dark for the sound of tyres. Bradley, they say, knows the identity of each vehicle by the sound of its approach, can match the rasp of a tyre's traction to a numberplate and name.

After the last cars have pulled in, he may pause against a boulder and absorb sounds that gather about him: the splash of fruitbats in the trees, the chips of glassy laughter and distant beat of music from the swimming pool. A rustle of lovers – or robbers – treading barefoot on the grass, and he slides from the shadows into metallic slabs of light. Between the resting cars of Eden's Bay, he searches the dark, testing each level of the night as it builds up about him.

~

It is a country of lost time. To enter is to encounter a new form of solitude. Neruda spent his loneliest hours in this place, *cortando el tiempo en mitades inaccesibles*, cutting time into inaccessible halves. Perhaps he had seen the copper cups that were once used to measure time here. Punctured copper cups lifted onto water, sinking gently down to mark the hours like setting suns, so that all water took on the colour of the time.

They will not call you idle for dying with the sun.

There is a word for such solitude, *thanikama*, a solitude of soul. Yet there is no easy recognition of soul here, no ego to take flight from. *Thanikama.* The word used by a poet who meandered in search of a dead father, feeling objects through the fingertips of memory. *Thanikama.* It is the language she moves into, a language she knows through touch.

The flight carries her into a new day. It would take eleven hours to reach Colombo, wiping out five and a half hours of her life as she moves forward in time. She recalls an astrophysicist's complicated explanations for this lost time, offering a diagnosis of the problem she could feel quickening inside her. But she did not need to be told about the spatial properties of hours, their thickness and vulnerability to being stretched, thinned and broken; she knows, she understands, has drawn breath through the tears.

She is watching the light change, moving through this space of no time, a space where, for a while, she has ceased to exist.

~

The landscape had not changed. As they meandered between Colombo cars, negotiating the fits and starts of blaring horns that had been roused by the lightening sky, she caught sudden glimpses of previous journeys, journeys that she had repeated in the dark of her basement flat and strayed from in her imagination, so that now it was difficult to distinguish between those places she had actually been to and those places that existed as an extension of dreams. By the time they reached Kalutara, the sky had broken into an ocean of streaked clouds. The driver pulled up and got out and she slipped him some coins to offer at the temple on her behalf. She was not sure if such offerings by proxy really counted, but she was not ready to step outside and take her place in the crowd gathering for morning prayers. The driver returned and the journey resumed.

The tiled towns gave way to tin-roofed houses that scattered into occasional thatched huts as the land began to level into the somnolence of paddy fields. They were driving on the coastal road that linked the peripheral places of the island into a seamless ribbon. The homes here marked sites of dwelling and barter, sprung up through contact with people from other shores. In the green wind of the speeding car there were half-houses everywhere – houses of raw brick and bamboo splints, houses of open floors and open steps leading from one open level to the next – as if the missing walls, windows and roof were mere supplements to cover the nakedness of hope. Occasionally, an effigy of a trousered man could be seen stuck on a pole against a half-built wall, or strung from a frameless window, to ward off envy and the evil eye, to ward off thieves who might seek to steal bricks. Such half-houses marked a dream that could stay incomplete for years, the brick steps scrambling towards air, the floors catching shadows of the clouds and being washed by winds as the vegetable darkness thickened and tendrils of the jungle vine reached in. But somehow they stayed clean, tidy, complete in their incompletion, like elaborate statements of intent.

'Where are we?'

She was given the name of a town she did not recognise.

'Have we passed Ambalangoda?'

'Ambalangoda coming soon.'

Like advertising a forthcoming film.

She relaxed in the back seat and let the images slip by till the sea broke into view with the shriek of a passing train, and she found herself scattered on the many journeys she had made on this road before.

The last thing she was prepared for was a direct return to roots – the slim columns of the porch and the long glare of a white balcony spattered with crimson flowers. Fiona was there this time, drawn into birdlike sharpness, the years concentrated into a keen point of vitality. She was standing on the verandah, flicking a yellow feather duster in a brisk wave.

'Savi, my dear,' she trilled. 'How wonderful. I'm so glad you could make it. Come, come, we weren't sure of the day but I got the room ready just in case. It's the same room you used to have – but the house is a little different now. Uncle decided to extend, but we can see all that later. Come, put that bag down and sit. Watch the steps, they are uneven. My, how you've grown!'

Fiona reached for an embrace and sniffed Savi's cheek, her hand pressing her upper arm, 'Have you had lunch? Malika, some aerated water! Or would you prefer juice or thambili? Thambili? That's good. It's very good for the kidneys. Now tell me about the flight. You were lucky to get a seat.'

Her cases were carried away; a fan overhead began whisking cool air; a drink materialised by her hand. Fiona blinked as she sat down drawing her skirt under her. She blinked again. She was English. She knew the importance of waiting for the right time.

'Yes. Christmas is busy. Everything is fully booked by late summer.' Savi released the bag from her shoulder and drew her hand over her head, tucking a stray wisp of hair under the band of her scarf. 'I was only told I got a seat last week. I rang straight away and left a message. I hope it's OK, my coming here last minute.'

She was conscious of her late, indirect response to an invitation received a month before, suddenly aware that she could have done more to ease herself into whatever space these relatives might choose to make for her.

'My dear, we very much wanted to see you,' Fiona said crisply. 'Renu will be especially pleased. It's been such a long time since you two last met and you've both grown up so much. She's been asking after you for some time. I must say you look well. It's good to see you've put on some weight.'

Savi smiled despite herself. When they were young, she and Renu would argue over who would make it to forty-four pounds first, forty-four pounds being the baggage allowance for a foreign trip and thus a measure of independence for the girls. Renu had beaten her to it by six months and twenty days when she was nine and Savi almost ten. The game had been taken up by Savi just before she left for England. She had weighed her case, heaving it on to the scales and checked the dial. 'I will be twice forty-four pounds when we next meet.' Renu had just laughed and said, 'We'll see.'

When Savi did eventually return it was to sit by her father's coffin, refusing all meals. Food could not be brought into the home as long as the body lay indoors. Despite the dim light of the candles they could see how thin she'd become.

Savi took a sip of thambili, then drank it all, savouring the translucent coconut flesh as it slid down her throat.

'I don't think thambili will make me put on any more.' She laughed to herself as she put the glass down.

Fiona drew her hands together into a small knot, clicking her fingers as she did so. She was lean and sinewy, her body contracted into taut lines. Her rheumatism was getting worse despite her work-outs on the exercise bike. She was looking at Savi as if she might be able to read the missing years in her face.

Savi had taken several routes in her imagined journeys home and all of them involved accidental encounters. She might wander through the Fort and lose her way, ask for directions and find herself talking to Romesh, who happened to be returning home;

she might be lifting a book from a library shelf at the British Council and see Eden in the space between books, his face spliced into segments; she might be in the Pettah at a clothes stall and brush her arm against the pale skin of a foreigner, turn and find herself facing Fiona; or she might be giving a presentation and there, at the back of the audience, would be Renu, restlessly shuffling her feet and twisting her hair around her wrist.

In all these scenes mutual recognition was hesitant, uncertain. She liked to believe that she might not be known. There was an element of spectatorship involved, too, in which she was sometimes the voyeur, sometimes the object of another's gaze.

It was close and direct contact, when things came to meet her without warning that she had difficulty coping with: the sharp sunlight now reflected from the water beyond; the fan of awkward angles cutting the air; the face of the woman she had known, trying to pin her down to a specific memory. She was reaching for a cigarette, with the remnants of a smile still pulling her lips, when her uncle walked in and forced her to look up again.

'Hello Savitri. So you've arrived.'

He was in his hotel clothes – black trousers, white shirt, pinned tie, polished shoes.

'We didn't know if it was to be Tuesday or Thursday.' Then registering the sudden withdrawal on her face, he added, 'Tuesday is better. You'll have more time to settle in. The wedding has taken over, I'm afraid. Normally it's the bride's family who have the headache but Romesh has found himself a Vietnamese lass who likes Sri Lanka, so it's all fallen on us.'

She sensed it was his way of welcoming her, making her feel she had walked into an ongoing conversation, but she would have preferred coolness to this forced familiarity.

'Come, I hear lunch is ready. It is late; you must be famished. Josilin is on leave for a couple of days but Malika's cooking is just as good. This way,' he said, leading her between settees that seemed to have multiplied in number in her absence, 'We've got a new dining room now that overlooks the garden.'

She was led to the new room, her uncle fussing and shifting a teapoy and majolica vase to make way for her case, rucksack and trainers, taking her from the dark house she knew into the brightness of the extension. The sudden light made her happy, as if she had come up for air.

The original house reflected Eden's taste for traditional high ceilings and deep wings, opening into an encircling verandah that, at the back and the side, lapsed down stone steps into the garden, so there was a gradual eclipse from the chalky whiteness of the house into the dark gloss of large-leaved vegetation. The new extension came off the kitchen wing, breaking the darkest part of the house into a riot of red hibiscus and dappled sunlight. Sliding windows spread down the length of the room. It meant the loss of part of the shrubbery and verandah but gave a sudden explosion of light.

As she drew up a chair she noticed Eden motion to his wife to remove the dirt-creased trainers she had placed by the dining room door. Fiona padded over, knelt down with clicking joints, and took the shoes outside. Savi drew her bare feet under the rung of her chair and squeezed the carved indentations between her toes. She felt like an unwanted gift that Eden was having to find room for in a display cabinet already full of prized possessions. She wondered about her uncle, the history behind his quiet control.

Eden had been born three years after Independence, a day after Henry Edward Dannister Rodrigo made a staggering win of 97,000 rupees on the Governor's Cup stakes. *Willow Green*, he sang in honour of the thoroughbred, *I love Willow Green!* Champagne was flowing and his father still in high spirits when a fluted glass of arishta, a health tonic laced with suitably generous amounts of alcohol, was taken on a silver salver by a soft-soled nursemaid to his pillow-propped mother. Henry followed in a flush of congratulations, his steps quickened by the cheers of his parents who were whooping with delight while dictating telegrams that were full of dashes and dots of excitement conveying the safe and blessed delivery of a grandson and heir. Eden was assuredly the product of honeymoon years. His parents had fallen fashionably and whimsically in love after a brief and heady courtship (which involved a mutual obsession with Henry's black felt hat), and speedily produced a son during a time when the country was being held up as an exemplar of peaceful transition to self-government. The economy was strong. The people at peace. Ceylon was internationally proclaimed a model postcolonial nation – 'an oasis of stability and order'. Henry and Lavinia entered this new world fortified by the cries of first one, then two strapping sons.

Something of the romance of these times had rubbed off on the older boy and could still be detected in his flair for presiding over social functions that were guaranteed hand-thumping dinner table gossip for many years to come. With his parents, he travelled around Europe as if it were a continent created for his delectation, sampling the ski slopes of Verbier and foie gras in Cannes with the same delight that he took in a leisured round of golf in the central hills. A sun-drained Eden, paler and fuller-bodied, returned home with dreams of building a holiday retreat that would be in dialogue with the southern sea.

This dream was fleshed with domesticity one memorable English summer, when strawberries at Ascot came to be intimately connected with an interest in exposed creamy calves and cleavages that looked tantalizingly naked under wide, feathered hats, and he met Fiona at the home of a mutual friend. She had smooth, athletic limbs, pink cheeks and blonde hair and a smile that lit up the room. She also had parents who wished to see her complete her secretarial course at Cambridge and settle down with that nice Ted Winthrop, a childhood friend who had lank hair and nostrils that flared like a horse when he laughed and, even more problematically, a semi-detached house with three bedrooms that lay just three tree-lined streets away from her parents' home.

Eden and Fiona were married when he was twenty-two and she was twenty-six in a beach pavilion at Mirissa that was hot with her absent parents' disapproval. Eden's bond with his younger brother Dominic, who had been born within a year of his own birth, was strengthened by the friendship between their wives who exchanged recipes and health tips from their respective lands. On the regular occasions when Eden had business in the capital, the couples would go for evening walks along the promenade by the Green, the wives linking arms and calling their children to stay close, as the brothers walked behind, drawn on by the connection between the women whose bodies blended under the shade of a shared parasol.

But unlike Eden, Dominic had chosen to love the wife his parents had found for him from a family closely connected to their own. Dominic, whose natural grace and self-assurance won him the support of his large extended family, was able to extend this charm and confidence to others from backgrounds and communities very different from his own. His legal secretary would be invited to a working lunch with a village grama sevaka, his silk-saried mother would be rustled down from her toilette to shake hands with a man who ran a roadside stall. He was the younger brother. He was free. He had all the time in the world to grow into his responsibilities and ideals. In contrast, Eden, who accepted his privileged status as a product of natural order and karmic law, could never shake off the snub he received from his wife's parents, whose experience of Indian coolies in Malaya relegated him to *that wog from Ceylon*. He still remembered the altercation before Fiona quickly closed the door.

The change in their older son made Henry and Lavinia wonder. Eden, they reflected after dinner at their rambling Panadura home, had become *more* controlled in the connections he made, an effect perhaps of *settling down with that English girl*. More strangely, he seemed to have become quite anxious to learn the unwritten rules that snaked the land, had become edgy in the presence of his younger brother who was outshining him by making a name for himself at the courts. The couple chose not to discuss the fact that their boys were drifting apart, putting this change down to the early loss of the charming wife they had found for Dominic.

'And you know,' Lavinia shook her head once again as she remembered the difficulties of arranging the funeral outside curfew hours, squeezing through the crowds scrambling for information outside the hospital morgue where the bodies of Tamil riot victims lay, and Dominic's sudden withdrawal from them all, 'there was nothing in that poor girl's horoscope to indicate that she would die so young, not even a hint of bad health. It's a damn sin.'

Something had gone wrong. The time dislocated. Even astrologers didn't seem to be able to work things out any more.

~

Savi and Renu had grown up in a time of silence, of events with blind, buried witnesses, when it was not what was said, but what was left unspoken that carried the burden of truth. Their lives were enmeshed in a hidden war that failed to make the international news, a war masked by shrieking headlines on the larger war between the government and the LTTE, so that the killings, disappearances and abductions in the south that claimed many thousands of lives came to gather dust in the files of human rights observers. This war lacked the comfortable logic of race and ethnicity, the logic of religious, cultural difference, the easy distinctions favoured by those who liked to keep things simple and clean. This was a class war among the Sinhalese – young insurgents against a paternalist state, cousin against cousin, brother against brother, a settling of scores where long-standing fears, ancient rivalries, secrets, betrayals, mistrust, grudges, inequities and resentments determined the call to arms. It was a family war, an internal matter of blood, marking a violence that could not be reasoned away. And like all dirty secrets, it grew in the silence it imposed.

Savi had travelled through this time on the wings of her father's letters, having been transported abroad just two years after her mother died in Black July. But for Renu there was no respite. She lived in and through this time, could feel the small shards of history embedded in her skin. When she heard her father raise his voice to Uncle Dom, she scurried to the door and listened. She never told anyone what she heard that day.

'Dom, it's time you stopped encouraging these cases,' her father spluttered, trying hard to keep his voice steady. 'People are talking. They even threatened me directly.'

'You're living in the heart of it here at Fort,' her uncle replied. 'Turn a blind eye to what's happening about you, brother, and you can be sure you might be next.'

'Carry on like this and I will be! You're putting far too much faith in the law.'

'We have to have faith in something. The law is all we have left.'

'You need to fight fire with fire, damn it.' Her father slammed the desk. 'It's the only way to get the brutes in line. Why if they'd carried on – and *you* of all people know what these men are capable of – I would've had to shut up shop. Then where'd we be. Out on the street with nothing but your fancy ideals for breakfast. Can't you see that your activities are putting us all at risk. Your faith in this bloody law will get us killed!'

'I know, but I have no choice,' her uncle sighed. 'When the state turns against its own people we are all at risk anyway.'

'Dom, it's easy for you. You can dress up in your ideals and parade around like a hero because your daughter is out of danger and you can join her at a moment's notice. I have family here, children. Where are we to go, mmm? Where are we to go when the bloodhounds come sniffing at my door? My god, take a good look at those people who come to you, take a good look at their eyes, red from weeping, red from searching for sons, brothers, fathers they have lost, take a good look at them, Dom, and know that could be you too, that none of us is safe. You've got to end this bloody crusade before it is too late, or else – or else go! Go, get the hell out and don't come back.' A chair scrapped on the floor as her father stood up.

Renu drew back from the seam of sunlight that broke from the open door and went quickly to her room in the silence of bare feet. She knew how to walk in shadow, shadow run, to move in panels of shade so she would not be seen. When she closed the door of her room behind her she was still holding this last fragment of conversation. She began sifting through its cadences, extracting the vital elements that might connect it to all the other essential facts.

Chequered sunlight came through the bars of the window and caught her in its net, turning her cheek light then dark as she reached below her mattress to draw out a blue file. She opened it on her knees and began to lay the delicate clippings on the bed. The papers made a patchwork of print on the white cotton sheet. Each evening she would examine the clippings, one at a time, framing it in the symmetry of her palms.

A year later, she noted: *We are all tainted by what is happening around us. It's in the air we breathe. There is no longer a place of innocence from which to testify.*

solving case 8591

If anyone had asked him why he spent the night listening for the rolling tread of tyres and checking faces, shouts and the distinguishing features of men's exposed arms, Bradley would have told them he was involved in solving case 8591. This was the identity granted his father upon his disappearance. He was not sure if it had been given to him by the police or by one of the officials from the many NGOs that had come into being in the wake of the disappearances, but for some time now, after the word for father had been torn out of him when he saw him pulled into the van, he'd found comfort in a language that registered the emptiness he felt. Case 8591 was the husk that was left, the official line of inquiry that kept his father alive. His involvement in the case had led him to take up the offer of the nightwatchman's job Renu had found him at Eden's Bay. It was a line of employment that allowed for a different sense of time. He worked the night shift until dawn and then went to sleep as the sun burned away the clouds. By early afternoon, when the staff and guests retired from the heat to sleep, he would wake to the mirrored glare of light magnified on sea waves.

He got up from the wooden pallet with the sun expanding inside his head, and reached to wipe his eyes. He felt the familiar shift in his shoulders and looked at the useless weight of hands, the crescents of dirt that gave definition to the nails. He had got used to this disconnection between will and action, the burden of having a body that resisted his control. But the memory of wholeness was still there and he would sometimes imagine his arms doing his bidding, feel them shift and test the air.

He turned from the sea and rose to walk towards the outdoor tap that permanently gushed water, its nozzle gagged by a browned cloth that someone had tied as a filter. He moved onto the grass and carefully slipped off his sandals, scratching one foot against the other, the cool rush of water darkening his feet. He heard

Jazeel's incoming three-wheeler sputter to a halt and turned to see Miss Renu stepping inside. She took a canvas bag from her shoulder and placed it on the seat beside her so her palm was resting on the top.

He knew where she was going, where she always went after work at the hotel. The place, after all, was where he had seen her first, when he and his mother had been drawn into a queue marking a broken line of inquiry that had ended with the official recognition that his father was indeed *missing*. After months and years of calling at this police station, this check point and that army camp, being told again and again by officers that his father was not there and had never been seen, a man from the city had come into the heart of his village and reclaimed this one truth that his father had indeed disappeared. Renu and her canvas bag of questions had followed in that man's wake. Bradley stepped from the tap, shaking the water from his feet, and slipped his sandals on. As the car turned past him, he nodded towards Miss Renu and was sure he felt his left hand lift to wave her by.

The drive took her inland, down a rutted road past luminous green paddy fields, and then thinned into a dirt track before suddenly widening as they passed a densely screened dagoba, invisible but for its white tip. A black and white board beyond announced in broken shells of Sinhala script that she was at the *Rehabilitation Centre for Families of the Disappeared*. The door of the mobile centre was open. Navin was talking on his cellphone inside.

Renu nodded in response to his raised hand, stepped in, put down her bag and drew from it brown plastic bottles. Each bottle had a label scripted in blue ink. She was conscious that they rattled as she placed them on the desk.

Navin switched off the phone and turned towards her.

'Hi. I didn't know if you'd make it.'

'I wasn't sure myself,' Renu was keeping a mental tally of the number of bottles as she took them from her bag, 'but the dispensary was open and I nipped in. Here. I've labelled them all. Make sure that the Dissanayakas know that the lotion is toxic – for external use only.' She checked her bag to make sure she'd not missed anything and lifted a brown envelope that had got caught under a seam. 'Tablets for the Seneviratne boy. The instructions are on the front.'

Navin was leaning against the desk with his arms folded so he looked slightly smaller than he was. 'Has your cousin arrived?'

It was rare for him to pick up on her personal life, but today he seemed to want to talk. His sleeves were rolled up above the elbow and his hair was tousled making him look vulnerable and young. Looking at him now she regretted giving him this personal information.

'I don't know. I need to head back in case.'

'I've just had some great news.' His exhaustion was wiped out by a smile so generous that it reached right into her. 'We've managed to get hold of a counsellor.' He said the last word with suitable gravitas, then brightened with excitement. 'A minor miracle!' He clapped his hands. 'He should arrive in a couple of weeks.'

It took Renu a moment to register what he'd said. She was looking at the fine hairs on his hand, at the way the laughter flickered through him and made him come alive. In that instant it would have been easy to miss his meaning. But she was attuned to listening. She knew how to pick up bright bones of words from a blaze.

'A man? The counsellor is a man?'

Navin's eyes contracted. 'You know the score. It's all they've got.'

He reached for a canister and took out a pen, cutting her off with a deft flick of the wrist, then said hoarsely under his breath, 'It could be a good thing. Some of these women might like to talk to a man for a change.'

She was conscious of the reproach and regretted her bluntness. Navin knew just as well she did that a female counsellor was necessary. There was a long understanding about the things that could not be said. But with less than thirty trained psychiatrists on the island, a male counsellor at Kurundupola would surely be better than none at all.

'Well done.'

But it was too late. He had already dismissed her and was talking to one of the field workers who'd come in.

She made way for the man and brushed Navin's arm in passing. She was still conscious of the contact – his skin against hers – as she returned to the Fort, as they drove past the cricket green by the Dutch Reformed Church. 'You know the score', he had said, the words falling hard. She was sure he would not have said that when he first started working there.

She reached for the metal bar as the three-wheeler drew under the Bluffing Tree, and felt the shadows of leaves flash upon her exposed arm. The security men by the court house glanced towards her as she passed. Instinctively, she reached for her bag and leashed the strap about her wrist. The vehicle drew noisily along the road, leaving behind the order of the court house complex as it entered the clutter of rambling homes with high walls and open gates. Children shrieked in bordered gardens that were interrupted by the river, their chatter spraying the brightest family gossip onto their neighbours' lawns.

Renu peered across Jazeel's shoulder as the vehicle stalled. A squawk of the horn shifted an idle dog from the drive. Savi should have arrived by now. There was so much she wanted to ask her. So many questions and no clear point of entry from which to begin.

Travel well, travel well, Savi's father would say, *for every journey is incomplete.* He would talk in parables and clipped aphoristic gestures when saying goodbye. His parting from her, from her mother, was constrained – limited to a pat on the back and a wave to them both, with a glance so brief and intense that Savi left clutching his words, felt them filling her arms as they drew away from the city of falling houses. She would wrap the words about her in the long, expanding intervals when only letters marked his presence.

Suba gamanak – travel well – her palm sliding on the banisters. Travel well, for every journey is incomplete. He rarely joined them on the trip to Dolmen House. His tall form stretched into a frail line of loneliness as the car pulled away.

The last time she had been here, she had left without going up these stairs, following Rob's lengthening shadow as they hurried down the road, her voice magnified in his denial of her call. Each time she cried out she had become more sure that they would never come back here together again. She hadn't shown Rob the house, never completed that journey, never taken him through the only home she cared about.

Where is home? Rob would ask, trying to provoke her into connection. But she could never be drawn, could still remember the easy rationalizations that made home *a mobile space of belonging*, gestures that made sense only in closed seminar rooms. Released to open air, the moment she touched these banisters, this wall, this glass shade in this house where objects were released into memory and claimed, the words grew weightless and hollow.

Travel well. She opened the door, was in her room once more.

The room faced west and remained cool till the evening when it flared tangerine in the light of the dying sun. It was not her room exactly, just another guest room in a house that expanded for visiting relatives. Yet she had been permitted to personalize the space and string up the shadow puppets her parents had given her after their last trip abroad. They hung about her bed, circling the blue fountain of a mosquito net, dangling their distended arms, caught in the orange glow like figures flailing in fire. What it needed, Renu once said, looking up from the bed as she sucked a boiled sweet that leached colour across her lips, was music.

So she had placed a tape-recorder on the desk and watched the puppets sway to the liquid rhythms of a voice that rang *Goodbye to love,* singing along with this voice so that the two became one. The figures moved through shadows of guava leaves, of *all I know of love is how to live without it,* and the cries of parakeets that gathered on the tree outside the window at dusk. Two pictures were on the wall: her uncle's pastel portrait of his pale young wife, whose cloud-coloured eyes would follow her wherever she lay, and her own childhood painting of a peacock's energy. The riot of angry feathers made her wonder why it had been selected for display. Her parents did not allow her to stick things on the walls of their city house, and this picture, she knew, was certainly not her best.

Her belongings were kept in an ebony almirah that had been gifted to her grandmother upon marriage – her clothes, books and toys squeezed into one small shelf between faded files, albums, tissue-wrapped saris, and drawers full of glinting silverware and

Venetian crystal. She loved to unfold into this space and thrust her hands into the cluttered darkness above, lifting small heirlooms into light, to feel a shift in the order of things as she replaced them in the dark.

The almirah had been moved to a wall by the door and been replaced by a teak wardrobe that stood open to reveal a few metal hangers and a packet of naphthalene balls. The ceiling was clear but for the exposed hook of the missing mosquito net and two sun-bleached puppets that dangled helpless on extended strings. There was a wicker chair, weatherworn from the verandah, a half-empty book case with a glass screen, a desk by the window and a bedside table with a white watermark where someone had placed a glass. There were landscape photos on the walls as well as her blue peacock and her uncle's painting and, of course, the bed, a cane bed with a crescent moon headrest and embroidered white sheets. It looked as smooth and cool as she remembered it to be. She leaned back, drawing the bag off her shoulder, and touched the almirah, her fingers in the dark grooves of wood, as if reaching for what lay behind.

At Dolmen House family life expanded and the days ran together in uneven eddies. It was easy to slip into the arms of this time, to be drawn into belonging by those who lived here, as if her city life were a mere interruption to these days moved by water, between still and moving water, between river and lagoon and the echo of the sea. She would kick off her canvas shoes and plunge into the calls of cousins, climb trees with her toes, spray-cycle through puddles, chase chickens and stray dogs into days that gleamed bright as the brass she polished with her aunt. Here the hours would unfold in her drift past a kachcheri full of court-case conversations where she gathered small stories of adultery and theft, later drawing them from her pockets to examine with Renu in the privacy of her room. This, after the somnolence of a ride in a skiff. This, after an illicit swim among blue lilies.

Even her mother, who in the last years had veered between restlessness and sleep, gave in to the wholeness of this unbroken time. She would sit in her rocking chair, alone among the restive water birds, communication between them intact.

Savi had relaxed too. Too, too much, as Renu would say. She relaxed so much that it seemed to her she became someone she did not recognize any more. Her body gained in power as she ran from room to room, from garden to garage, to the beach and back before breakfast, scrambling into Renu's bed with *Nakitinna LazyBones!* before being turfed out by ayah who said her dirty feet would muss it all up, and clattering downstairs to gather the still warm eggs, without sense of boundary or time. Here she gained a fortified sense of self, an energy that filled her before wearing her out, returning at night to the sanctuary of her moonstruck bed to slide into dreams under the watchful gaze of shadow puppets and her aunt's pastel eyes. Years later she would read of *the devastating totality of childhood* and know exactly what the words meant.

She had slipped free from her mother in the expanding silence between them, as her mother lay in the still warm centre, blurred between tablets and sleep. But one time her mother had roused herself to speech. One time she had wanted to talk.

'Savi, please bring that book and read to me.'

It was a quiet command, all the more powerful for the tone in which it was said. Savi looked about for shelter but no excuses could be found. Renu was inside, busy with a violin lesson that was stopping and starting in time with Fiona's fingers on the piano. Romesh was out with a friend. She reached over the table for the book and ran her fingertips over the ridges of the embossed title.

'Which story would you like?' She tried to hide her reluctance to read, aware that this was the first time her mother had asked anything of her for some time.

'Any one. It doesn't matter. You don't mind do you?'

'No of course not,' she said too quickly.

She opened the book and flicked through the pages to the point where a ribboned bookmark lay. She held the book open and turned the bookmark sideways so it supported a clean line of print.

'The Visitor', she began, sitting back against the light and drawing one leg under her. 'His hands were weary' – this might mean something like 'wary' or 'wiry' so she slurred her reading to allow for both possibilities – 'though all night they had lain over the sheets of his bed and he moved them only to his mouth and his wild heart.'

She paused and reread this in silence as the meaning gradually came to her and the words touched the woman behind. Her mother's face was blocked by the page, her hair just a small wing above the cover. Trust her to have picked a story about a sick man! She sat up, refolded her legs and continued.

'The veins ran, unhealthily blue streams, into the white sea.'

This was not what she wanted. She wished to go. Renu must be finishing her lesson now. She looked towards the dining hall and saw the table lamps had been lit, then turned back to her mother who seemed to be somewhere else.

'Sounds too strong, no? Do you want me to carry on?'

Her mother drew her gaze from the water and looked straight at her. Savi tried to deflect its directness by looking as blank as possible.

'Putha.' Her mother never called her *daughter*, only *son*. Savi knew she was going to say something she might not wish to hear. 'Listen. This thing inside,' she was always vague when referring to her illness, 'it will not go away.'

So here it was. The Talk her parents were always muttering about. The Talk that would help her Adjust. Her mother had avoided it for too long, Savi heard her father say one night through the beaded curtain of her bedroom in the city. She looked away but her mother's silence forced her to look back.

'We must accept.' Her mother was all-too-present now. 'You must accept as I have done. If you accept you will find there is nothing to be scared of. This thing…'

Savi hated Thing. She wished it had another name, something personal that could be confronted. Her mother's eyes, brilliant in their darkness, would not let her go. Thing had changed her. She looked different, her face pulled into the contradictions of the last few months. Her skin was too pale against the shining eyes, her hair too black against the wasted neck, the lips too full against the angle of her cheek – and she was far, far too young to be saying the words she was now saying as she reached out her arms and began to smile in a way both puzzling and strange, releasing her into a softness that made Savi feel she was about to tumble in space.

'It's a rubbish story. I hate it!'

She dropped the book and ran into the house, scrambling up the stairs so Renu paused and put her violin down and saw the earthy smudges that followed her as she went running straight up to her room where she flung the window open and thrust her face into guava leaves, into the pungency of fruit, breathing green air in, out, in, out, till ants crept into her ears and she shook her head free.

She did not remember the bars above the windows. Just the sweet, sickly smell of guavas and salt and mud and sun on mouldering lilies. It was the muddled smell of everything at once and it was still there now, shuttered in the room. She lifted the catch and released the grille, felt a momentary loss of gravity as she thrust her face into the light, the glare of the afternoon tightening her eyes.

No leaves. The tree had gone, in its place a thin papaya tree with disproportionately tiny fruit, struggling through shrubs. Her eyes followed the spread of lawn extending to the thickening reeds on the river bank, and the dark shade of the mango trees at the water's edge screening the lilies on the lagoon. The lotuses had gone, plucked into oblivion by temple sellers, but the lily pads remained. She pushed a twist of hair under the fold of her scarf. Somewhere behind her she heard a motorbike drawing a low guttural stream of sound along the river road. She kept looking ahead as the sound of the bike gave way to birdsong and the rolling hush of the sea, adjusting her gaze to the marbled expanse of sky and the interruption of distant leaves. She became conscious, for the first time, of the lack of human interplay before her, that her window faced away from the town, that all the buildings were behind her – the neighbourhood kitchens of gossip; the kachcheri stacked with restless clerks and rusty filing cabinets; the courts bustling with the self-importance of armed police; the small white temple, drowsy with pirith prayers; the echoing arches of the church with its single sonorous bell; the clinking glasses of the rest house where businessmen and western backpackers shared an evening beer. It was as if in all the time spent in this room she had been looking in the wrong direction, had been facing the wrong way, and if she were to turn around and walk steadily towards town she might come face to face with a different story of her past.

As she watched the white light of the afternoon annihilate the lawn, stripping it naked before her, she began to wonder what might have been unravelling behind her as she had rushed to rouse these green gardens into colour.

Tuesdays were laundry days or dhobi days as Fiona now called them. First, a clothes wash at 8 am, and then sheets and towels before lunch. Fiona would set the washing machine on at the appropriate time and then organize the preparation of the two main meals, measuring out the rice, onions, garlic, cinnamon, cloves, cardamom and curry leaves that were required. She was as fastidious about such things as she was about the cleaning of chatti pots, the washing of all the vegetables in a solution of vinegar before use. Malika, who in recent months increasingly covered for Josilin since the old cook had hurt her leg when she was struck by a car, did the ironing in the annex in the afternoon.

Eden had never understood why his wife didn't permit him to take the dirty washing to the hotel where it could all be sorted, ironed and pressed for her, but Fiona had always insisted on doing everything herself. She had taken to managing the house as if she had been to the manner born, but had reserved the smaller, personal, more refined tasks, such as polishing the family silver and cleaning the glass screens of the old photographs, for herself. Sitting behind the screened light of the back verandah on the old hansiputuwa, she would polish serving bowls scrolled with her father-in-laws's initials and become quiet with the knowledge that she was the custodian of an old inheritance.

The regularity she imposed on her days was sustained not only by her natural sense of order but also by her ability to draw on hotel staff whenever her own domestics let her down. It was this sense of temporal certainty, her steady claim upon past, present and future, that made her feel increasingly sure that Dolmen House might truly be hers. Years ago, she mused, writing to Savi had once been scheduled for Saturdays, some-where between settling the bills and seeing to workmen, but now her focus was on staving off the advancing years. For a brisk ten minutes shortly before lunch, she would go upstairs to her dressing room, change into her white tennis shorts and aertex vest, and pedal feverishly on the exercise bike Eden had bought her for her fiftieth birthday, focusing all the while on an oil painting that took her into an English landscape that was serenely misty and flat. 'Aiyo,' Lavinia had despaired at the predictability imposed upon her own days when she came to visit her son in Dolmen House, 'that wife of yours is too strict. Everything tick-tock by the clock like England!'

Fiona was hanging the wet sheets on the line when Renu peered round from behind a pillar. The green nylon line was strung between metal poles behind the garage in the one part of the garden that was left to grow wild. It was possible to talk here without being seen or heard.

'Hi Ma. Is she here?'

Fiona turned around and nodded. She had a peg in her mouth, and her arms were held out across a line of towel. She removed the peg and called Renu over with a whisper.

'Yes, but she looks tired – not surprising with an eleven hour flight. She's now resting. Went straight to her room like she couldn't wait. But she's really quiet. Eden asked her why the Galle Face to try and get her to smile, but she just looked blank. She's put on weight which is good, but she looks much older, too old.' She compressed her lips in concentration. 'It must be the winters and bad food – and, you know, dear, she smokes! Lit up after lunch so we had to turn the fan to the max. She's really let herself go, been away far too long in that blighted land. Dom should never have sent her, arranging all those guardians and trust funds so she had no choice but to stay.'

She picked up a towel and turned back to the line, concealing the nagging possibility that perhaps they should have insisted Savi come home after Dominic's death. 'It's good we called her back. A holiday here will do her the world of good.'

Renu smiled at her mother's change of heart, as they both remembered the heated family debate after dinner when they had discussed whether it was wise to invite Savi to the wedding after she had dropped contact of her own accord. Her parents had gone through the manifold possibilities that lay behind this silence; Romesh had said that it was just an invitation, and after all *he* was the one getting married and putting himself on the line; it was high time his cousin came back and saw them all. Her mother had been torn between her genuine concern for Savi and her desire to keep the peace at home, when Renu had said, 'OK, if you don't invite her, you can count me out,' and had slammed the door, sealing a deal that meant she would now be held responsible for all twenty-six children that would need to be kept quiet during the reception. She hoped Savi knew how to handle children as she was sure she would be hopeless.

'A good thing you left England,' Renu said, picking up a sheet and folding it into a manageable square. 'You would have become positively decrepit if you had stayed there.'

Renu pegged the sheet on the line and turned to go back in. Her mother stooped to pick up another towel.

'Ma,' she looked back, waiting for her to straighten up, 'did she say anything about what happened?'

Savi's failed marriage had been a subject of speculation ever since they had received her postcard giving them the news. Her father said that it was probably just as well as camera Carter would probably have not come to much anyway, and as he was the only one to have met Rob, they usually let him have the final word.

'No,' her mother whispered hoarsely, shaking her head. 'Best not to mention it.'

~

Savi had withdrawn from the window and begun to unpack her belongings, stacking items on the bed, bookcase and table in a way that marked the bedroom as her territory once more. At first she didn't recognize the small, shiny hardback that lay on top of her clothes. It was the size of a pocket notebook and had a pencil portrait of a boy etched on the front. *Jona Oberski*. The name was certainly not on her reading list, the title unfamiliar. She then recalled being about to close her case and seeing the book on a stack near the fireplace. She had just moved a box of Kleenex from the top of this pile and that had left the book exposed; it was one she had bought in Edward's Antiquarian Bookstore just a few days before. According to the blurb, it was a small memoir on the Holocaust written with chilling clarity from a child's point of view. She thought of some of the books she had packed – the thoroughly thumbed and underlined copy of *Sinhabahu* that almost fell apart in her hands, a couple of theoretical tomes full of coloured stickers directing their small tongues towards the most useful points, a transparent file containing her most recent notes and, of course, her lunar diary, all lying at the bottom of her case, under her clothes, forming a hard protective shell – and had suddenly felt the need for something new to take along. This small, plain book was perfect. It was something she might actually read during her month away.

She placed the book on the desk by the window, glad now that she had brought it, and leant down to fix the travel adaptor in the socket underneath. She was on her hands and knees when someone knocked and came inside.

'Hi Akki,' Renu called, 'I see you're a seasoned traveller, but those adaptors don't take account of power cuts. Come evening and you will find the trip switch going off.'

Savi stood up, reached out and really hugged Renu for that, for ignoring the lapsed years, for restoring her to the family with that one word, *Akki,* that gave her the sister she never had. She embraced all the lost time in her cousin, held it fast in her arms, and then drew back and began searching for something inside her case.

'Here, a small something for you.' She pressed a round item wrapped in gold tissue into her cousin's hand. Renu smiled and touched her cousin's wrist before she could withdraw.

'You came.'

'Because you asked. It was you who invited me, isn't it?' Savi pulled away and opened the wardrobe door.

Renu placed her gift on the desk, glanced uncertainly at Savi who was sliding a blouse onto a hanger, and picked up a small hardback book. She opened it, her hair falling loose about her shoulders and framing her face into a pale heart-shape, so that Savi saw long lashes and the bridge of a small aquiline nose.

'You know, Akki,' Renu was skimming a page as she spoke, 'a lot has happened while you have been away.'

'I know.'

'You need to stay here for some proper time. Otherwise everything slips like earth sliding from under you and you have nothing to come back to.'

Savi observed the quick flame of Renu's face, how quickly it arranged and rearranged itself, as if absorbing events to obliterate them, a change in her cousin that marked more than elapsed years.

'Not everything has changed,' she said, reaching for her rucksack and pulling out a CD of their favourite '70's musical. 'Here, we must listen to this sometime.'

Renu remained silent, contemplating the book.

'What is this?'

'Nothing. A memoir.'

'That's strange.' Renu looked up, her eyes flashing cinnamon and amber in an impish smile. 'When I heard you were doing a Ph.D. I thought you would come back with big, fat academic books. You know, full of all those long, impenetrable oxymorons that make English sound like another language.'

Savi's laugh was uncertain, measuring the distance between them. 'No, no I don't want to be reading those. This is a holiday – or at least a break.'

'Good.' Renu nodded her approval, 'That's good. You were always here on holiday before. But this time we have a wedding!'

Savi fell silent, unsure how to proceed. Before she left for England she'd heard that Renu's horoscope was being recast. It was no family secret that her cousin had been born with Mars in the seventh house: 'a bad bet in the marriage stakes' as Eden had put it. Renu had come to her own conclusions and told her with a theatrical sigh, 'Anyone I love is Doomed to Die.' Now her brother was slipping into marriage as easily as Renu had kept clear of it. Intimate histories lay hidden but there was something else Savi needed to know.

'You left school?' She needed to know what the differences were.

Renu sank down on the bed beside her, smiling an old, old smile. She touched Savi's cheek as if she was still a child. 'No,' she said, slowly shaking her head, her eyes settling into steadiness as her smile faded, 'school left me.' She stiffened, drawing a tired hand over her head so her hair was pulled over one shoulder, and continued talking in a calm, neutral vein, speaking of Romesh and his future wife who was studying ancient Buddhist art, of her mother being so so happy, but worn out by the long distance wedding, of her work at the hotel and her father's sky-high development plans. She spoke on and on as Savi leant back upon a pillow that released a sweet familiar smell.

At some point Renu was saying, 'But that's all blood under the bridge.' Savi had wanted to say 'water' but her eyelids were trembling with sleep. All blood under the bridge, the things that happened when school was closed, when students waited for years to sit exams and only florists and coffin-makers thrived, when soldiers read out the TV news so that all events came charged with the threat of war, when rivers were so contaminated no one ate fish any more and things streamed by as quick and fast as fresh clouds so that it was impossible to keep up, facts shifting like the moon as soon as they were written down, how to write, how to make sense of what was happening...

Savi felt her eyes becoming heavier as her cousin's voice flowed on. The room seemed to be glowing orange, the shadows casting mangled shapes upon the wall. There were figures with loose limbs, faces from ancestral photographs sliding on the wall, slowly congealing into blocks of darkness. Just before she dropped off she thought she saw Renu stand dark above her, the book glancing fire from her outstretched hand. 'I will read and return this, read and return,' someone called from the closing door.

almost twelve cries from his home

Eight month's before his disappearance, Bradley's father purchased a plot of land. It was a small agricultural plot, across the bay from a neighbouring hamlet, almost twelve cries from his home. The boy had begged his father to take him to see this land, but some reluctance in Sirisena made him resist. He wanted his boy to grow up and work in town, to turn to his studies rather than submit to the vagaries of the weather.

'It is twelve cries away, son, a long time away. Get ready for school now. One day I will take you.' He would ruffle Bradley's hair and leave with his bike rattling with tools.

Bradley would listen till the sound was absorbed by the cries of woken birds, and wonder how far twelve cries might be, the distance from which a call, a hoowa, could be heard, a distance, the boy reasoned, that must vary with terrain, the density of trees, the sound of waves, of wind. He would call to his friends to measure the distance of a shout, calling at ever increasing intervals on his way home from school.

'See you machang! See you! Hoo-wee,' again and again through cupped hands.

At first they would call back. 'Till tomorrow!' – the thread of sound getting thinner as they walked apart, but in time his friends grew tired of the game.

'Why all this screaming your guts out when you're only going home?'

'I want to see how far I get before I stop hearing yo-ou.'

'You think we are village oafs to go hoo-hoo for you. You might as well carry a pingo on your back and go to market.'

The boy would throw his satchel in the air and catch it and continue to walk home by himself, drawing cries behind him with each step. After his father's abduction he would hear calls leaping on the road like stones on water and know the precise distance between them.

Renu observed the subtle changes that took place in the run-up to the first general election to be held in twelve years – the shift in the tide of conversations when she entered her parents' room, and a new language in the house. Cooks, cleaners and gardeners now spoke of concern for their families rather than hers. They would discuss relatives who lost their jobs and new dangers on the buses and in town. Her parents would listen closely and join the servants in speaking of politicians as if they were as much a part of their domestic arrangements as members of their family or close friends.

These were the first signs of the hidden war, the violence stealing in under cover of darkness. She would go to bed and wake each morning to new surroundings. The view from her window was different. There was a new order to the day.

She could not remember when she first noticed the posters by her school, or the ring of the doorbell that marked nothing other than the leaving of leaflets on the drive demanding the closure of shops. She could not remember when her school first closed for the day, without warning it seemed, and she was left to look for Romesh who could not be found anywhere, preferring as he did the company of older friends such as Kit. Her brother seemed aware of a larger pattern to events, conscious that an order lay behind the lack of discipline of those years. Renu felt she was increasingly being left behind, tied to one place and one gradually unfolding time.

'Josilin's husband is missing,' her brother said one day, reminding her that their garrulous cook had a life outside the kitchen of Dolmen House.

'Where has he gone?'

'Don't know. He might have joined the JVP or he might have been taken by them. It's hard to say.'

She had read of the activities of this communist movement, the reports and elusive talk granting it iconic status, but all the information in the papers was dissipated in detail, as if the larger narrative was missing or unknown. Her parents would lower their voices and hiss the word 'communist', in the same way they would whisper of shameful, secret things, and any mention of the JVP or the Indian Peace Keeping Force always raised the temperature of their talk. Now the JVP appeared to be directly responsible for cook's strained face.

'Can't Thatha go to the police?'

'He already might have, but you know how he doesn't trust the police. And it could make things worse for Josilin if her husband is involved.'

The more she asked, the more muddled things became.

'Wouldn't Josilin know if her husband was a member or not?'

'He had friends. She does not know who they were. People sometimes keep things to themselves to protect their families.' Romesh picked up a stone and started digging into the ground, working the soil loose with his nails.

This was a time when to be young was a danger; this movement of disaffected youth was too far from natural death to fear its other forms. The military crackdown on the JVP became even more brutal than the intimidation and violence of the young insurgents. When the insurgents began to target and kill members of the families of the security forces, the latter announced that for every one of their family members killed they would take the lives of twelve from the families of the JVP.

Death squads sprang up from jungle ranks. The Black Cats, Green Tigers, Scorpions, Eagles of the Central Hills, all slick killers who struck under cover of military sanction. They were abducting and killing village men and boys regardless of their political past or affiliation. Personal grudges could be resolved by these means. A lottery win, a failed promotion, a new house, an elopement, a cross word, any of these might result in a disappearance, a death. The insurgents' trademark warning to potential police informers required the victim to be shot and left hanging from a lamp post. This was being countered by death squad reprisals that resulted in the burning of young men strapped to petrol-filled tyres. Their charred remains were left on display by public roads, remnants of flesh and limbs melded with the melted rubber. More bodies were dumped in the river. More bodies were thrown in the sea. Trees bloomed with the brightest of posters: 12 for 1. An Eye for An Eye.

One day Renu heard that some boys had been reported missing from her school. Several police officers arrived in a brown truck and summoned the teachers from their rooms. The teachers had left, one by one, to be interviewed in the school office, and the pupils left to chat and read. The children discussed among themselves who the missing boys might be, until Romesh had suggested the names of five classmates whom she knew only by sight. She tried to call them into view, the details of their faces already blurring. A door had then opened and everything went quiet. She saw a man pulled between the officers, a man drawn into smallness by the handcuffs on his wrists, and it had taken her a moment to recognize Mr Devananda in this diminished form, the teacher responsible for making the past electric to her touch. She never saw him again. She failed history that year. Remembers this as if his disappearance was made real only by her disgrace.

It was at about this time that she began taking newspapers to her room and reading them while her mother slept in the afternoon. She would use Fiona's sharp sewing scissors to cut small windows of news from the papers, placing the cuttings in a blue folder that she kept under her bed. They were stories of random killings from the larger war, 'Suspected LTTE militants kill 47 villagers as they sleep', '100 shot police officers found in a mass grave', interspersed with global news of the end of the Iran-Iraq war, the massacre in Tiananmen Square, the fall of the Berlin Wall. The bloodletting in the south coast had become so routine it no longer made front-page news, and she was left looking for small squares of events between the prominent photographs of smiling ministers shaking hands. In one month alone she counted 112 political killings. A further 212 murders were officially classified as the work of the JVP. These killings, it was reasoned, required an immediate response. They resulted in over 30,000 disappearances in the course of three years. In later years, the numbers were revised up to forty, fifty, sixty, then seventy thousand deaths.

There seemed to be a surfeit of information coming in, but no context for her to connect to. Even the very the land on which she lived – between the river, sea and the gathered silt of generations – was now being broken up and demarcated into safe and forbidden zones. She was not permitted to walk to school, near the prison or too close to the court houses. She was told that the heat she had always lived with now required the comfort of her father's car. She would be driven from the town along unfamiliar routes, with events held at a distance, the tree-line disturbed by slow smoke from bodies left burning on the roads. A small, acrid smell would lie suspended in air and still be discernible on her journey home.

She learnt to walk quietly within the shadow of high walls, to measure the weight of silence between words. She would gather all the stray scraps from her father's office conversations, her mother's phonecalls, kitchen gossip and the hot fire of courtroom talk, and try to link these to the fragments of news she held in her hands. She needed to find connections, the hidden logic to events, because more than anything she believed in the knowability of her world, believed this more fiercely the more it came to be denied.

One day she sliced the tip of her finger while snipping out a small item of news. It described how someone had been taken in for questioning by 'officers in uniforms as well as in civils'. She had placed the bloodstained cutting in her folder as an event to follow up. The next day she scoured the paper and found an amendment that could barely be seen. It recorded that the man had in fact been taken away by 'unidentified gunmen'. She cut this out too, aware that she had evidence here that the instability of the times was connected with the instability of truth. And between articles on cultural history and world news, between information to be found on *The Ayurvedic Properties of Spices* and *Medically Important Snakes of Sri Lanka,* she heard of the murder of a Tamil professor, a human rights activist, who'd been shot by a man as she cycled home from work. 'It is better not to be sure about who killed her,' the woman's distraught parents had said. Doubt had now become an instrument of will.

By the time Savi had begun her study of Sri Lankan myth at university, Renu had already completed years of self-directed education at home, events filed away in a folder with her rust-red fingerprint.

One late afternoon following Savi's arrival, the cousins were resting in the green shade of trees, under the calls of roosting birds. Savi sat on the swing, gently pushing with her toes, the branch above her creaking slightly as she swayed.

'Do you remember swimming in the lagoon?'

Renu looked up from her notes, squinting in the light. Savi seemed to have fed herself the question to take her back in time.

Renu did remember. She reflected how their parents had never found out about these illicit swims, recollecting, too, how they would hurry to the well to wash the silt from their face, hair and feet, before creeping back to their rooms to shower off the rest. She would find thin creases of dried earth behind her ears, between her toes, weeks after such a swim.

'I'm sure they knew,' Savi said, kicking herself into motion. 'Parents always know. We must have smelt horribly of mud and muck.'

Savi's mock disgust brought the childhood image back.

'And all those little snails in your hair!' Renu cried. She could see the watersnails stuck in Savi's unruly curls, Romesh teasing them out with a lollipop stick, Savi squealing while he roared with laughter, saying she would make a great slug lollilop, what with snails-and-weeds-and-all.

Savi continued to swing towards the leaves. The reeds shook as some curlews lifted from the grasses and steadied themselves in the air. Renu returned to the book, drawn into Oberski's calm, steady journey into the concentration camps.

The writing was compelling, luminous. She felt drawn from the garden shadows, led by a child's hand into an experience so cold, so crystalline and sharp that events were being stripped clean to their bright human bones. There was utter conviction here, utter certainty, a clarity of boyhood vision, the ability to recount the past with the recovered innocence of the child. *With one hand I clutched my mother's hand, and with the other I covered my mouth to make sure I wouldn't ask my mother something by mistake.* How many times had Oberski rehearsed this experience before it became communicable, linear, logical? She would never have believed in the possibility of such a return, such a steady walk back into terror if she had not found it here, in these pages, in this book in her hands. Her hands were trembling as an image from the lagoon, the one she did not need to remember, slowly came back.

'Do you think,' Renu said quietly to herself, 'there is ever an experience so intolerable that there is no language to contain it?' She was testing the words out, to see if they made sense. She drew an unsteady pencil across the open pages of her notebook as if she might write something down. 'Do you think some things are lost because they can no longer be borne or carried on?'

Savi was swinging with more force, moving her feet forward and back, looking as if she might suddenly catch flight. The sun dipped below the trees, spreading shadows that reached across the rest of the lawn, pulling them into the shade. Renu remained in the wide circles of her questions, feeling them rippling about them both.

She was conscious of Savi saying something between the push and pull of her sway, saying something about memory, about different kinds of memory, the different names for describing the experience – field memory, observer memory, collective memory, cultural memory, autobiographical memory, textual memory, trauma, telepathy, nostalgia, 'anamnesis', memory moving forward and 'ontologising' itself so new origins were born, the list went on. She was saying it was all relative and dependent on your view of the world and the past, using a language so clouded that it spun out of meaning and released Renu from the swaying moment.

This cousin of hers had left the country with lollipop hair and returned laden with these bags of woolly words – her 'high-flown language', as her mother would call it – now being carried into the leaves.

She thought of Savi's travel in other lands and her own still, untravelled life.

'Are you happy in England?'

She asked this without thinking, but she needed to know.

Savi was suspended in the air, the white of her clothes lifting light into the darkness of high leaves. She said that it was a different world out there, that she was still working it out.

Renu looked at the arms stretched along the line of rope, the legs reaching and folding back as if Savi was being sucked forwards and then blown back by the sea, every push a loosening of the years, trying to focus on this to hold back the image that rose from the water and stayed clammy in her hands. For years she had never gone to the lagoon, the place a deep hole in the past through which she could fall at any time. She snapped the book shut and concentrated her attention on her cousin's bare legs and arms.

'Poor girl,' her mother had said after Savi had returned to England after her father's funeral, 'poor girl, she has no one now.'

Her mother wrote regularly after that, large generous letters that carried the censorship of care, empty of events that might deepen Savi's pain.

'It is best she's outside,' her father had replied. 'The way she looked at us over Dom's dead body made me feel as if I had killed him myself.'

That was the last time Renu had seen her, before her mother's ardent words, before the darkness of the lagoon, when Savi had been no more than a girl in a white skirt who sat still as a candle, day after day, by her father's still form. Renu had remained in her room and Romesh stayed outdoors, both in retreat, both unable to absorb any more tears.

Savi loved the sense of flight, this stretching out in air and sudden plunge into gravity, as if she lost her body and then reclaimed it in the fall. She could lose herself in air and enter the old world as if she had never left it behind, finding herself in this possibility of weightlessness, in the addition and subtraction of her movement through leaves of broken light. In the brush against birdsong she could remember how her father could distinguish between the cries, picking at the weave of sound to find the thread that marked the ruffled chat of magpies or the clear silk of the black bulbul – a community of different birds, each with their own language, each insistent on being heard. If she elected to hear just one she became aware of the argument between them, the territoriality of their lives.

Those were early years, before her mother became ill, before sirens seared the city and the sky broke open to the scorpion tails of black helicopters. A different time, when they'd visit Dolmen House together, relaxing in the idleness of green. You need silence to hear birdsong well, her father would say. Savi was now aware that just one bird was calling, a coucal whose call sounded like a clatter.

She kicked harder and was carried over water once more, felt the lack of completion in the swing that might carry her over and under, over and under, remembered tumbling on the swingboat at Brighthelm pier, clutching Rob's arm as she turned upside down when they had been tipped over the sea together, here in this moment when Renu was asking her about memory, here in this time when she was reliving it all.

She began to run through terms and definitions as if she were flicking through the pages of a book. There were so many kinds of memory. If she reeled them off this quickly she might slough them off like dead skin.

'It's a different world,' she glanced at Renu, steadied by her swing back, 'I'm still working on it.'

Renu was sitting on the steps with a black notebook and the borrowed hardback on her lap. She was sucking the tip of a pencil and looking at Savi as if seeing her for the first time. Savi noted with a tinge of pleasure that her gift, the bangle of red and gold, was glistening on her cousin's right arm. She was conscious of her bare legs sweeping the air. She kicked harder to move on but felt she was growing older and heavier under the gravity of her cousin's gaze.

'What are you working on?' she asked, carrying the words forward towards the sunlit leaves. When she swung back she saw Renu was standing up.

'You always liked that swing,' Renu said with a smile as she brushed her skirt. 'That's good. No one uses it now.'

Renu turned and walked back to the house, striding through the grass, into all the other times when Savi had seen her walking ahead, walking on alone, leaving her wondering if she should follow in her wake.

Savi was left to find her own path through the day. She would wake up in the early hours, before the sun came up, and drop off to sleep again as everyone else began to rouse, so her mornings began shortly before lunch was served. She had spent one afternoon walking through the Fort, taking in physical changes to the land. There were more houses now, fewer trees, and the homes themselves had gained new identities with extensions and new rooms. She paused by some familiar homes, neighbours whose gardens she had run through as a child, hoping that someone might recognize her and invite her in. The houses stayed quiet, folded into themselves, and she was left by the gate to the sound of children's play. With fewer trees and larger homes, the landscape seemed sandier and dustier than before. She went past the court houses and on to the rest house, noticed a fountain by the drive and wondered if it had always been there. She approached the reception and asked after Kumar. No one at the rest house seemed to know who Kumar was.

The next day she got up earlier than usual and found herself walking past the boundary walls, along the esplanade and beyond the clock tower and market noise that came up behind her, carried on the wind. She kept walking on till the houses gave way to the coastal road and beach, and the beach itself petered into a scramble of rocky coves. She picked up some loose mussels and rolled them in her palms feeling the crystalline deposits rub off on her fingertips. She was heading back, climbing down from the rocks and onto the beach when someone tapped her on the shoulder. An urchin with sandy knees opened up a blackened palm. There was a steeliness in his eyes, eight years of wariness hardened by need. She reached for her purse and pulled out a hundred rupee note. It was the smallest change she had. The boy snatched it, beamed at his luck and ran off before she had time to change her mind.

'Miss Rodrigo?'

At last, she was being recognized. A bespectacled man with wisps of white hair appeared by her.

'It's Freddie Vaas.'

'Hello.'

'You don't know who I am?' He seemed mildly amused.

'No. I've been away a long time.'

'I know. I know,' he nodded and kept looking at her as if trying to flesh a memory from the contours of her face. 'I worked with your father. I came to the funeral. I saw you but we didn't speak.'

People had come and stood behind her, looking at her father over her shoulder. She had kept her back turned, to block them from view.

'Your father used to carry you into the office when he worked in the Fort. You were just a baby then.'

'You recognized me from a baby?'

He laughed, showing his teeth in a way that made him look like a friendly camel.

'The Fort is a small place. We heard you were back and you have been seen,' he said. 'By the way, you should be careful about money, not to give too much. Other beggars will come.'

'I wasn't aware I was being watched.'

'We are all being watched. As I said, the Fort is a small place.'

They were walking towards the wooden bridge that led to a

small island and stretched into connection with an uninterrupted sea. Freddie held on to the handrail and paused as he looked towards the arched entrance to the Fort. He was speaking of her father, how much he had been missed when he left.

'But he said it was best to stay in Colombo as your mother was so ill. All the good hospitals are in the city. And of course,' he added with a dry smile, 'he was able to do much more for his clients from there.'

He asked her about her life in England and she found herself speaking of the food and the weather and other bland, neutral things, all the while thinking of her father's life at the Fort, of these friends who had known him in a way she never would.

'My father's letters used to give me news of the Fort even though he wasn't here. It was as if he missed it too.'

The truth of this came to her only as she spoke. She was thinking of him for the first time perhaps, as a man rather than her father, as a widower, a respected lawyer, a parent without a child, his separation from his family, his friends, from her and the long, tidal years that had kept them apart, finding in his isolation an isolation that might match her own; thinking of him on those evenings after her mother had left the city house for the last time; following his shadow before it withdrew behind the metal cabinets that flanked the office door. And the time she discovered his early morning ritual of watering the blowsy extravagance of her mother's favourite red orchids, still flowering on the unswept balcony, months after she was gone, watching with wonder as the bright blooms, leafy tongues and tentacled roots began to curl and fade into mould.

'They don't really need watering when it's this humid,' she said softly, uncertain whether her advice was wanted or not. Then noticing his quietened hand, 'If you stop watering and give them time, they might grow back.'

He had turned towards her and smiled.

'Savitri Samadara.' He recited her name in a way that invoked her mother too.

'Time is the gift of kings and the prize of paupers, and I,' he paused for emphasis, raising a finger of his free hand in the air, 'am poor in time.'

He had laughed, his eyes moistening with a mix of amusement at his own theatricality and a sense of strangeness at their altered circumstances, and then did something that brought everything into focus at once. He pulled his shirt out, stretching it down to reveal the gap where a missing button showed the dark hairs on his chest, exposing – in an instant – her mother's absence, her own neglect, the dark space of his beating heart.

'I'll call you.' Freddie touched her arm as they parted by the boundary wall, 'after Poya when you've had time to settle down. My wife would love to see you. She remembers you when you were a baby, too.'

She returned to Dolmen just in time for a shower and late lunch, trying to shake off the knowledge that she had been claimed by a stranger, that her ownership of her past was incomplete. She opened the door to voices. Fiona was in the kitchen talking to – could it be? Yes, it was! – Josilin, who had come specially to see her and who, she had been told, had agreed to work for them daily for the rest of her stay. The cook was complaining of the delay she had experienced on the bus to the Fort, her voice swooping up and down like a bird. Savi rushed into the kitchen and the smell of freshly picked curry leaves, and found herself laughing. Yes, she was laughing and she didn't know why.

Josilin's face creased into the warmth of an embrace she could not, as a servant, give, creased all the more warmly to make up for the absence of this touch.

'Aney, Podi Hamu,' Josilin cried, gently couching Savi's cheeks in her hands, 'you have your father's face and you have your mother's smile.'

Savi squeezed her arm, felt herself expand into the time when she would lean on the cook's shoulder, when the smell of fried onions mingled with the stories she told.

Josilin was the same, older of course, with silver threads scrambling through the dark grey hair, and plumper, with a slice of slack flesh bulging between her jacket and cloth, but she still beamed the same generous smile that creased her eyes up into a deep twinkle. Savi sensed that Josilin was looking at her as if she had a knowledge of her that she herself had lost – an easy, deep acceptance of everything she was, stripping off the unnecessary years so that her core self was exposed. This was a time for simple words, the only kind of words she had left in the language.

'I am happy, very happy to see you, Josilin.' Savi squeezed the small shoulders and felt how much frailer they had become.

Josilin chuckled and shook her head into an even broader smile. Savi needed nothing more. There was nothing more to say. She laughed again and ran up the stairs to her room, delighted she had found the words to bring her home.

The first two weeks after her arrival were the happiest, most hopeful and wretched days of Savi's adult life. For most of the day she shared the house with Fiona while Josilin kept busy in the kitchen. Romesh was in Yala with his future wife and in-laws, carrying out Eden's meticulous instructions for a wedding that was sure to beat all other weddings in the south. Her uncle and Renu left for work at the hotel at a time when she was still rousing from sleep. She would hear the car doors close, the gravel crushed as it pulled out of the drive and find herself stretching into the expanse of a clear day, not even aware that she had started to sing. Later, she would come downstairs to the dull thud of a pounding wooden pestle and hear Fiona's disembodied voice as she spoke to someone outside.

So this was it. The real world of flapping slippers and domestic chatter, the life lost during years at boarding school where every minute of her time was accounted for, even the length of time of her weekly hot bath. In those seven years she came to associate specific days with specific duties and rights: on Wednesday afternoons she was permitted to wear denim jeans, on Sunday at 10 she had to shine her shoes for church. At university things had changed, her time stretched, though regulated by writing deadlines and the length and depth of books that gave structure and purpose to her day. The new, loose time at Dolmen brought a freedom that was almost frightening in its lack of anchorage. She did not know what to do with all the empty hours that fell into her hands.

It began to make her restless, these days punctuated by bird calls, the roll and rasp of a grinding stone, the hooting of passing cars full of people focused on a life of which she was not a part. Even Josilin had found her old place in a kitchen that demanded her full attention as she cleaned, washed, chopped, scraped, ground, sliced, boiled and fried with help from the dry, thin Malika. Savi knew she could not join and help her, to do so would be to admit that she had changed, but life here had moved on and she had slipped out of its grasp. One morning she snapped at her aunt, instantly shamed by the petulance in her voice.

'The De Sarams have moved on. Some houses are a shambles. The court houses are cordoned off. And the place at Prison Lane has been extended so it is not recognizable any more. The only person I've met who knew me was someone I did not recognize. Houses and neighbours, all changed!'

Fiona smiled and shook the duster, adjusting a framed photograph that had been hanging at an angle on the wall. Savi noticed that her aunt seemed to be especially fond of these ancestral portraits, peopled with relations that Savi never knew.

'Yes, there have been many changes. Lots of people left during the troubles. Just locked up and left. It was a difficult time, but we stayed on. So not everything has changed. And many people you know will be coming to the wedding in Yala in a few days. Cliff and Sunita said they might drop in to see us even before then.'

She sat down opposite Savi and handed her an empty sugar bowl and a bottle of Silvo. Savi picked up the cloth and tipped the polish onto it, feeling the white milk moisten her fingertips. She had no real desire to see Aunt Sunita and Uncle Cliff, or to be polishing dishes.

'You did not wish to go when everybody left?'

Fiona examined a serving tray and slowly began to polish it into grey strokes, gradually wiping it clear to reveal the desired shine.

'Eden said it was safer to stay. The army camp was busy so security was tight. And of course his work is here. Anyway, where would we go, people like us?' Fiona was looking at her reflection in the tray.

Savi recognized the emptiness that lay behind the words. She wondered at the past this English aunt had left behind. She had not returned to England since her marriage to Eden, a separation made permanent by her parents' disapproval. She wondered if her aunt's loss made her sympathetic to her own. Fiona seemed to be accepting her without history, without regret.

Would she ever wish to go back to England?

'No never,' Fiona said. 'Why would I want to return?'

'To see family, friends, the place where you grew up.'

Fiona smiled and leant towards her, putting the tray down.

'I belong here now,' she said, 'and, my dear,' she whispered, placing a firm hand upon hers, 'so do you.'

They looked at one another in a silence that gave depth to the words. Her aunt then leant back, releasing the stiffness from her joints.

'You know, when we're young we make decisions that – how can I put it – belong to the present. You think you're planning ahead, moving into some great future, but you're not. What you're really doing is following some instinct that tells you that everything is up to you, that power lies in your hands, that you can change things – even people – to suit you. It's only as you get older that you realize you're just a small speck in a larger pattern of events. That all the time you think you're changing things, what you're really doing is adapting to them. I have no regrets, no regrets at all. Dolmen House is my home. It's pointless looking back except to remember how different life was then. Whoever said the past is a foreign country was absolutely right. But it's not just a foreign country, it's a country without a map. The best way to move through it is simply to follow your nose.'

She laughed and poured herself a glass of water. Savi smiled at the unspoken understanding that fed the words, the acknowledgement that they'd both married foreigners who had led them away from home, the fact that they both were stranded in the present without maps to the past.

She continued polishing a dish and listened, her hands moving in smooth circles, while Fiona's voice quickened as she began to tell her of the time when she had first met Eden at a friend's twenty-fifth birthday party at Blatchington Mill, and my, how Eden had taken her the length and breadth of the country and got her to place bets at every race, how – and she was embarrassed to say this – she spent *all* the money he gave her at Ascot and lost far more than she made, but he had wanted her to share this forbidden passion – racing was banned here then, you see, as the government said gambling was sacrilegious – but the Ceylonese carried on betting on all the English races, and some of them, who did not even know any English, used to memorize the shape of words that spelled the name of their favourite horse – they would not be stopped from taking a wager – working out the odds while hidden away at the back of a barber's saloon. They might not drink on Poya days, but Buddhists love a flutter. Had she not noticed how people here bet on everything, even on which crow might fly from a wall first?

Savi waited till Fiona had finished and got up quietly from her chair, leaving her aunt sitting in a room brightened by the silver moons of family dishes. She felt her way up the stairs and sat by her desk, glancing at the yellowed books she had drawn from the bookshelf earlier in the day. They were the English books she had been given as a child, *The Wind in the Willows, The World of Peter Rabbit and Friends, Winnie-the-Pooh,* all of them revealing what she later felt was a curious obsession with anthropomorphosis. She had never shared these books with Rob, never discussed this muddled introduction to his native land, and wondered if her denial, the desire to keep this world secret and untouched, had been ultimately responsible for the break between them. The English must adore animals, she had thought before she left the island. Later, she learned that they really did eat lambs.

There was just one book that she had carried inside her, a lavishly illustrated compendium of Greek and Roman myths along with tales from the Odyssey. It fell open on the stories she had read again and again: Persephone, Aeneas in the Underworld, Orpheus and Eurydice, the images of anguished figures twisted against their loved ones glowing crimson, blue and gold through the gnarled rocks and blossoming vines. The colours were as rich as they had always been. They dazzled in the drab room.

She put the book down and shifted the papers on the desk, the diary with red strokes that marked the coming full moon, the list of wedding invitees that Renu had left so she would know whom she might be meeting soon. There were three hundred and fifty names she vaguely recognized; they must belong to relatives, family, friends for generations. At some time their lives must have been a part of hers.

She flipped her laptop open and began writing a letter of return, like the ones she used to write from school, on Sunday evenings before Lights Out, writing as if she was trying to find a way back. *Things are better than expected. Everybody is friendly and keen to see me settled. Aunt F. is kind, sympathique you might say. She gives me room to explore but is there if I need anything.* This, she realized, was for her father who made the French term real. *And it's great to have string hoppers and moju again. Lusciously hot and squelchy!* This for her mother who used to blend the food in her fingers before sliding it into Savi's mouth when she had grown too tired to feed herself. She would close her mouth around her mother's fingers and try not to smile as her mother said, *Stop that nonsense! Now, open. I said, open, otherwise I will make you use a fork and spoon next time!*

And as she continued, she found that they were all together again, her mother, her father, herself, together in the island of time she had made for them to share. She kept on tapping, calling them to her, calling so that she might complete her return.

When Renu came back from work she found the laptop open and her cousin asleep on the bed with the guest list in her hand, her face speckled by evening light under the spinning wings of the fan.

~

The window is moonless for the room faces west. If she is to see the waxing moon Savi knows she needs to stay awake longer and turn her face towards the sea. Every night of her return she wakes at three am to an olive black moon.

~

She kept looking at the white dial until it was spliced into even halves: 6 o'clock. It was time. Savi drew back the curtains as the screech of parakeets entered her room. She was pleased with herself. For the first time since her return she had got up at the same time as everyone else.

'Can I join you today at Tel?' she called out to Renu from the top of the stairs. 'I won't get in the way.'

Renu looked up, sighed and shrugged her shoulders in a gesture of dismissal.

'It's just reception work. Book keeping, guest lists, that's all. You'll be bored senseless.'

Savi wanted to say that she was in danger of this already, but kept quiet.

'I should have asked you before but I dropped off early. Still getting over jet lag. I'll keep out of the way. Go for a swim or explore. I've packed a bag.'

Eden came out from the office below the stairs and smiled up at her as he straightened his cuffs.

'I see we've been neglecting you what with the wedding and all. I'm sure Renu would be glad to take you along.'

Her uncle continued to make an effort to put her at ease during the drive to the hotel, pointing out Renu's old school, the rebuilt post-office that had been gutted by fire, the new mosque with its gold crescent moon, the old superstore with a storage unit requisitioned as a check point, observing that there were hardly any troops to be seen.

So this was the journey that her uncle and Renu made to work every morning while she slept. For a brief moment it seemed as if the broken hours were being made whole.

'You've come to Sri Lanka at the right time,' Eden observed, as they turned into the hotel drive. 'This ceasefire has allowed us to get back to normal life.'

Renu remained quiet, stroking the bangle Savi had given her. She had been looking out of the window so that Savi could only see the hair flowing over her shoulder and the red canvas bag slung across her arm. As Renu got out of the back seat she turned around and leant towards Savi as if to kiss her. Savi smiled, felt the long hair brush her cheek and was about to respond when Renu hissed in her ear, 'I thought you might have done some research while you were here. You've been sleeping the whole week!'

The reprimand was not new; she had been chiding herself for abandoning her work since she arrived. It was not what Renu said but the bitterness with which she said it that made Savi stiffen with surprise.

Renu's coolness, her reluctance to take her with them, and her uncle's efforts to put her at her ease, to ground her in the present, these things suddenly fell into place as she climbed the steps behind them. She was not wanted, not welcome here at Eden's Bay. They were moving away from her as if she was a dangerous thing to touch, withdrawing from her with glances that flickered about her form. She felt her temperature rise, aware in that instant of what she was doing, climbing up towards the marble columns and opening the door of a history that had been kept firmly closed till now.

People turned to watch her as she walked through the foyer, as she moved on and beyond, her steps quickening and taking her beyond the bar and bright blue swimming pools. The sea breeze was prickling her face as she began to run, run across the dry lawn fringed with palm trees and on to the open beach, her forehead moist, her feet suddenly faltering, sinking into sand, as she breathed in the sea, breathed in the sea where her father disappeared.

This was where they had last seen him, walking into water with his arms reaching for a wave, the thrash and roll of it embracing him so close they had turned their heads away from the intimacy of it all. Turned and walked straight into a narrative of blame and counterblame, each of them asking who had seen him last, who had spoken, heard, touched him, as if this last witness might hold the key to his return, the water leaping into light and a sudden collapse in density, her breath quickening into hollowness, becoming weightless in the wind.

Her father had died in her fourth year in England after she had become accustomed to his absence, after she had learned the art of self-deception, of imagining him there. He had died at a time when the island was in the international news and the violence seemed endemic, with wars being fought on several fronts. Earlier her friends at school had kept asking questions that placed him at the centre of events, as if in this bomb blast, that assassination, she might have direct access to him in the same way that they could only know the country in terms of headlines that had no connection to their lives. Yet her father never wrote of such things. His letters remained steady, personal in their reach. He was safe, he'd assured her. There was no cause for concern.

It became easy for her to protect him with her will, to keep him to herself, separate from events that had become too public, hurtful, as they brought the shame of brutality to the land she loved. It was necessary, perhaps, for her to set him apart, to mark him as a bystander, on the margins, to set him beside her in this. He belonged to the one profession that had gained public trust, as lawyers fought hard to keep in common memory the importance of human rights. Under Emergency Regulations it became lawful to bury a body without official inquiry and the last defence against killing was habeas corpus, the demand for physical evidence of a victim, a human being, of a life being lived. Lawyers who filed these were themselves abducted or killed. When the news of her father's disappearance came she tried to displace her fear, drawing him into the time they might have shared.

The news of his death had begun with a phone call at school.

'Savitri?'

The accent was from home. Something was wrong. Savi had leant against the cubicle door and closed her eyes. The darkness brought with it too many possibilities. She opened her eyes and saw the girls outside, heading out for breakfast.

'Yes?' The word was folded in echo and her 'yes' was repeated back to her.

'It's Uncle Eden here. You haven't heard from your father have you?'

She knew then it was serious. An unbidden plea began to pound in her head, magnified by the silence down the line. She could see Jane putting on lip gloss in front of the mirror in the hall.

'Not to worry, I'm sure he's fine,' he said hoarsely. 'But look here, your father went swimming yesterday and has not been seen since. He might have taken himself off somewhere. He didn't leave a message so we can't contact him. Listen,' she could see Eden searching the walls for words 'If you hear anything will you contact us direct?'

Suddenly the possibility of her father was everywhere. On the beach. In the hotel. In the car driving back to Colombo. In the club. In the law courts at the Fort. In hospital. The absurd thought that he might have caught a plane to visit her in England made her feel momentarily giddy.

'Have you called the hospital?' Again the repetition of her words down the line that began as she spoke, so she had to speak against the sound of her own words.

'Yes.' There was silence. 'But this is not England.'

It had taken a further twelve hours to find his body. A fisherman found it in an inlet near a prawn farm. How it had drifted so far up the coast was anybody's guess. The distance of time and place heightened speculation, but there were too, too many bodies surfacing at the time, and there was no doubt at all that he'd chosen to go swimming. The postmortem would later show that he'd drowned. His lungs were engorged. Blood had leaked into his mouth. There was no external injury apart from a small bruise at the front of his neck that was almost certainly the result of pressure from the mortician's knife. Set against the disappearances of anonymised village youth and high profile political assassinations, she had the luxury of containing the news as a private matter, a private death.

She had still been searching for a way of accepting the news when her father's last letter arrived. It had been date-stamped a week before he disappeared. *Darling daughter, another day of thundering rain and I am confined to the office...* She could see him writing it, the blue paper pressed against the leather pad by his wrist as the rain drummed against the window and smeared it into a blur of blended colour. She had felt the pressure of wet glass and become conscious of moving through the cold towards him, tracing his steps from the hotel as he walked towards the beach into a sea of thrashing water. She remembered how he'd lift her high above the anger of the waves, his body swaying as he strained to keep her in his arms, the turbulence of the surge about them, the thrill of tested safety.

Just once she had slipped from his grasp, caught the blind confusion of the loss, and been scraped ashore, her knees and arms stinging from the tumble in sand. He had emerged with a burst of spray towards her, laughing at her concern. He had always had a habit of doing that, generating anxiety and keeping her suspended in its logic, coming back and restoring order.

Then a thud had alerted her to someone closing the front door. The winter wind picked up and beat into the front porch. She folded the letter into her schoolbag, placed the bag over her shoulder, and walked steadily towards playing fields that lay smooth and frosted like parchment in the light.

III

THE LEPER KING

Navin put down the phone and watched Renu step into the three-wheeler, her long hair blending into the darkness inside the vehicle. He sat down and heard the three-wheeler recede, making a note of the counsellor's request for an amanuensis. He was not sure if Renu would undertake this work, was not sure if he wished to ask her and risk being turned down. She was not being paid, was free to come and go at will, so everything she did here had become a matter of trust.

He picked up a file marked 'inactive' and read the case notes of a woman who had accepted compensation for a husband who had been disappeared. The case was closed so there was no reason to read it, but he often went through old files as they set a benchmark for financial claims. Reading it, he noted how much of the woman's story had been left out of the official record. He remembered how he heard that in their years together the disappeared man, prone to drink while out of work, had abused his wife, beating her and pressing her with implements of fire so that her arms were etched with past domestic conflicts. She was a daily in the Fort, in service to Renu's father, so Navin would sometimes see her leave as he arrived. He would pass her without acknowledgement, his eyes drawn to the pale enamel of small scars, and feel some warmth spread up his own arms, pricking his skin.

He had been warned to stay focused on the facts that could be filed, verifying each incident as part of a process that would produce a result. There were compensation claims, employment needs, medical requirements and the vague, distant possibility of a legal inquiry, all details that would need marshalling till a case was complete. Complete, closed, never resolved. If he learned to stay close to the solid wall of formal procedures he might just be safe.

He was also told that he should never be alone when he spoke to the families. This was to ensure the legality of the proceedings and to avoid personal risk. For the first few months a student had accompanied him during interviews, but a lack of funds, and an inability to anticipate when and where people might wish to speak, had led him to learn to work on his own. He wrote down all the necessary details, taping the entire interview on a recorder, and returned to his room to hear everything again, this time taking in everything that could not be written down.

In the sulphur glow of an exposed bulb he would strip off his formal clothes and cast them into a pool on the floor. He would sit naked but for the sarong tight across his waist, turn on the tape and draw his forehead into his hand. His eyes might be closing when they would suddenly open wide as he stumbled on the moment of abduction and he was not a listener any more. He'd be drawn into the voice, find himself sliding into the event. The tape would keep turning as he slumped at the table, aware of an arm about his neck, his body assailed by unseen blows. He could feel a struggle quicken, even though he had barely moved, generating an indiscriminate energy that made him feel he had lashed out. In a giddy instant he was free, no longer victim but assailant, enjoying the release of fighting back. The recorded voice would carry on but he no longer heard the words, as he suddenly realized the physical damage he wished to do. This haphazard violence that he had taken into himself would leave him empty and exhausted at the end of the day.

He knew he needed to focus on ordinary things. This blue pen upon the table. His feet level against the floor. He breathed deeply and became conscious of sweat trickling from his scalp down the side of his nose. He looked out through a window grimy with dust, and became aware of the patterns on the glass. His office was stuffy, far removed from the open verandahs and paneless windows of the houses outside. He had got used to the sensation of drawing deep, uneven breaths from a space sucked dry of air. He put his tongue to his lip and licked off the sweat, then put down the file and glanced at his watch, noting the deep crease on the worn leather strap. His brother had given him this watch before he went overseas.

He had been a field worker at the centre for eight years now. His brother, two years older and broad-boned with ambition, had left for the States on a sports scholarship. Navin stayed behind, unable to break free from the NGO he had started working for during university closures. He could not remember when his reasons for work became personal, but he knew that his continued residence in the country was part of an untold pact with parents who had waved their first son off into a future studded with foreign success. His brother was their lode star, he the young sibling his parents held close in the wake of their loss.

At first he had been confined to deskwork at the office in Colombo where he was responsible for the collation and evaluation of resources. It was his first job, his first step beyond his family. He accepted the role as if it was the beginning of a new life. His briefcase, another of his brother's gifts, felt satisfyingly heavy. There was even a secretary who would bring him tea. She occupied a neighbouring desk and would place a fresh cup on the shelf by the window, just out of reach, so he would have to get up and walk towards her to pick it up. He would be conscious of her lateral glance as he went past, would sometimes pause at the window to hear her breathe. Zuleika was a Muslim girl from a Tamil suburb whose smile on his first day at work had kept drawing him back. Her background meant that there was no future here that he could carry to his parents; her daily presence by his side meant that he could think of little else. From his desk by the fan he would observe the arc of her neck and the stray wisps of hair blowing behind her ears. When she reached for the phone the bangles on her arm would ripple into a spectrum of colour. He would carry this rainbow with him at the end of the day.

Three years later, many years it seemed to him, he was instructed to travel, first to southern villages he was familiar with, and then to the north. He would decamp in schools and temple courtyards and spend time explaining the nature of his work. At first the villagers would be cautious, asking him the kind of questions that might draw him into their ambit of experience. Was he from the government or was he working for a foreign organization? Why did he work in both the north and the south? Why did he visit this village, that family? Was he related to the Ranatungas who owned the distillery in Mirissa? Did he work with the Mothers' Front who'd organized the protest marches? They had to be sure to whom they were speaking. It was possible that revealing a truth might do them further harm.

He was aware that many stayed away in silence, perhaps because they lacked language, perhaps because of fear. 'I have not the words…', 'I cannot speak about such things…' and he would be left at the brink of a dangerous memory. At such moments he would be divided between the need to respect their silence and the desire to ensure that their memories were not lost. Some of the women still lived amongst the killers. The very policemen who now protected them when they came forward with their stories were responsible for abductions. In government commissions of in-quiry, the culpability of senior military perpetrators was marked by enforced army leave, creating a climate of impunity that contaminated the air they breathed. He began to realize that his complicity in their silence would protect both victims and killers.

He kept coming back to them, relying on an instinct for preservation, because reason was not reliable any more. He would draw up a chair or sit on the floor and ask about the present rather than the past. This was a space they could enter without fear. They would begin to speak of troubles with employment, problems with relatives, and of their children who were the future they lived for. Some would lift the past onto a distant shelf, 'Why speak of these things? Nothing will bring him back.' 'It is better not to have an opinion on such matters', and find comfort in the smoothness of a child's glossy head. Then suddenly, without warning, the ground would give way and he would drop into another time, flung into it as if into an open river. There were fragments – a shout, a blow, a torch – and then an abrupt return to the facts of material loss. The talk of income and support allowed him to clamber into dry language. This language of security was one they all understood.

With the men gone, the women now had sole responsibility. Neither wives nor widows, what was most certain in their status was that they were alone. The women would see the sudden change in Navin as they shifted between times, and try to find words that would keep him within reach. It was safer to discuss death certificates, compensation, than to talk of other things. But it was often too late. He had already grasped a different truth, had found in the expression of their hands an emptiness that gave way to a surge of blood memories. The last connection. The last witness. That last touch. He took the tape-recorder back to his room, the collective loss expanding in all the unclaimed space inside him. There was no book to close here, no office door to lock. It was as if he had been brought in for the express purpose of absorbing their pain.

In quieter moments he would think back and wonder how different his life might have been if he had taken Zuleika for himself and not remained alone. Perhaps such a connection, such a break with convention, might have better equipped him to listen to the women. For he was now, indisputably, in the business of healing. The stated objective was rehabilitation, a return to order, as if order and disorder were distinct territories with boundaries that could be mapped. He could see that distinctions were unclear, that order was an illusion, the fabrication of those who spoke ardently of the need for 'normalcy' while breaking jaws and spinal histories. Silence had as many colours as the bruises on boys' backs. It was for this reason that he had come to engage a volunteer to transcribe the recordings. It was for this reason that he kept the typescripts in stiff folders, three for each centre, each fastened with thick rubber bands and locked in the briefcase his brother had brought back from Singapore. He would place the briefcase under his bed and stretch out in the darkness, listening to the myriad possibilities of the night.

Seven cries inland was a village where moonstones could be found. The gems lay buried in earth at about the depth of four men. Windswept lean-tos and tumbling pyramids of soil indicated that this was a place that had shifted identity as it grew. The villagers were farmers who cultivated rice and grew seasonal fruit. For generations they had felt the milky gems between their toes, in fields of still water and irrigation ducts as they dug the soil clear to drain the nurseries. The stones were a secret the farmers kept for themselves, before speculators entered and tore the earth raw.

Workmen came from the coast, trousered traders in Pajeros, and finally tourists with cameras and many tongues. More and more moonstones were found, spilling riches to the very edge of village homes. The villagers spoke to each other, the speculators spoke to the village headman and the villagers gradually moved, first from one house, then another, till their original homes stood empty of all but memories. They now lived in whitewashed houses on the boundary of their land, close to the groves where cinnamon peelers stacked their crops.

There were other changes too. For as long as they could remember, these tenant farmers stayed constant in their connections. Not still, but constant, as a river is constant in its reach towards the sea. The mine brought shifts in time and geography, a realignment of relationships and neighbourhood logic. Some villagers, such as Sirisena, felt invigorated by the change and began to reach for new horizons, saving up and buying land that they could cultivate as they wished. Others felt threatened by the strangers in their midst. When the troubles began a few months later, the villagers of Kurundupola were still adjusting to change. They agreed to build a barrier between themselves and the mine. They made a rattan fence and planted thrusting yellow spears of bamboo. They would rather walk to the coastal road and sell their fruit than be forced to barter with these mining strangers, these men who emerged from the earth, their bodies white with mud.

Navin had first come across Kurundupola when searching for a suitable site for the mobile unit of the rehabilitation centre. He had been given the freedom to choose where his office should be. This was years after the troubles had been quashed by state violence, years after some villages in the area had been cleared of young men. Little did he know that the centre's mobile unit would remain here, alongside the survivors, marking a permanent feature in the landscape of change.

He had checked in at a rest house, and gone to bed early, as the light in his room was too dim to read by. He made a note in his diary to bring a 100 watt bulb with him next time. He had stripped and stretched out under a white sheet, surrendering himself to mosquito stings. Minutes later his body exploded to the sound of his pounding heart. The boom was loud and borderless, as large as the dark about him. He got up and reached for the window, looking out towards the grove. The beating drums came from the direction of the mine, the darkness pulsing with the distant flare of fire. He had heard of such rituals of drums and demons, of fire, strange tongues and cut limes. He knew that for those who had lost their men, these rituals offered hope for a kind of peace. It meant rousing all the evil in the world and calling it to account. He stood and watched, feeling the small glow of flame grow and pulse inside his chest, booming all the time. He knew better than to turn the light on, knew better than to open the door. Knew all too well that this was the hour when the world was being set to rights.

The next day he set off on the road towards the mine. His initial hesitations about which of these villages to choose as a site had begun to resolve. There were several villages in the area that had been broken by the violence, but this village by the mine was battling demons on its own. He drove down the rutted road till he came to a clearing where a gleaming white dagoba raised a spire towards the sky. At its base was a small ledge of fresh red flowers. He drove on, wondering at this mark of silent worship so close to where the boom of spells had torched the previous night. He stopped when the barricaded posts that marked the entrance to the mine stood ahead of him. There was no sign of a village anywhere. Then, almost out of his line of vision, he saw a track that might just be navigable. He eased the car down the path and found himself in a compound of about a dozen homes.

He turned off the engine and got out. It was still, quiet, the sky clear of birdsong, as if the drums of the previous night had beaten out any sound. The houses were shuttered, the only movement a tracery of smoke by a patch of scorched earth. Behind this stood a construction of palm leaves in which the patient must have sat while the exorcist worked. Navin turned, sensing he was being watched, and saw a figure by a washroom wall. The boy was perhaps sixteen, leaning with his knee raised against the wall. He might have been there for some time, but something about the angle of his body made Navin feel he'd just emerged. He wore a pair of loose brown shorts, his face framed by an untidy shock of hair that exaggerated the whiteness of his eyes. Navin felt his skin prickle under the boy's scrutiny. Bradley was the one child in the village who did not shrink from strangers, who alone did not mind seeing and being seen.

'Hello,' Navin called with cupped hands, 'Come. I'm here to help. There is no need to fear.'

He understood the need to keep his reach communal, of not selecting a single person, a single home; these were people who had been singled out for breaking. Navin would wait till the villagers came to him.

'I am an officer for the rehabilitation centre. Your headman might have mentioned us. We are local, not foreigners. We have come to help you with your troubles.'

The houses about him looked clean with a fresh coat of paint. A heap of crushed coral used for undercoating walls lay under the shade of mango trees.

Two women appeared at a door on his left, then Navin spotted an old man in a small cluster of figures. As he began to speak to them, he almost forgot the boy who had been watching him. When he turned back to the washroom the boy had gone.

Three days later his assistant had arrived and Navin was ready to start work. He walked towards his office feeling that the future lay open before him, feeling that anything was possible in this new village in the south. It came easily to him, this shouldering through the crowd, opening the door and sorting his items on the desk as someone called people to order outside. There was a complete lack of ceremony to mark his new life that made it seem all the more natural.

On his way into the office he noted some of the people he'd spoken to before. Ellen and Ranjan L. were there with several others, and a neighbour whom he recognized from his first visit to the village. Ellen had asked him, again and again, which department he worked for while her husband stood by in silence. The fact that the rehabilitation centre had no history in the region made him an outsider and suspect in their eyes. Now, the old couple's female neighbour was urging her to speak.

'It is so many years ago,' Ellen observed; 'what can be done for us today?'

'So long ago,' muttered her husband, 'so why's he asking questions now?'

Navin acknowledged them with a nod. The old couple held back but the neighbour smiled and came forward.

'You start now?' The woman spoke with an authority marked by the urgency of hope.

'Yes.'

'I told them to come. I told them not to worry. That you would help us. I've been round to other houses. We have suffered long. We thought we were forgotten.'

She was a small, plump woman with bright eyes and large hands. He noted the black burns above her fingers, the pale smudges on her arms.

'Your name?'

'Josilin T.' He was making a mental note of the name, opening his briefcase, when he heard the woman tell his assistant, 'Put them first. They must go first. Anoma and child, you too. Anoma, you can speak English. He is from Colombo'.

Then an altercation started as Ellen shook off her husband's protests and Josilin pushed forward the woman who had been with them and all sprang before him as he stood up to quiet them down. Josilin's friend was pressed forward and urged again to speak. She hesitated, rubbing her arm, and looked towards her son who stood a little apart from them. It was the boy from the washroom who'd not responded when he called. The boy was watching without moving, looking directly at Navin, with an intensity that made him feel exposed. Navin took in the restlessness of the mother's hands, the uncertainty of the fractured foreign words, then was drawn back into the long clear road of the boy's scrutiny. He called for order, his voice rising as he struggled to break the intensity of that gaze.

Bradley had disappeared without warning when Navin had first seen him. The boy knew this was not the man, not the vehicle, he was searching for. He still carried the memory of his father's abduction, had called every detail of it aloud for weeks after the event. His mother would shush and tell him to stop; it was not safe to call out like this, but his voice would get louder in a bid to draw her in.

He had been playing with a wooden toy on the night of his father's disappearance, counting black seeds and placing them inside a small cart. The seeds were glossy black moons he had found on the beach, and the cart had been made for him by his father when he was a very small boy.

'Here son, it's for you. I'll put a string on it soon so you can pull it along.' His father had run the cart on the floor to show him the smooth movement of the wheels. The toy had never been strung, but Bradley still played with it after school, after he'd finished copying all the English letters into his exercise book.

That evening the village fell quiet as some people had gone away to visit relatives, or so it was thought. Some women had gone to the temple and were making their way home. Those who remained were preparing the last meal. A clatter of clay cooking pots and a splash of running water could be heard. His mother was expected back soon.

Bradley's father had got up from his chair. He was going to the table where he kept his transistor radio when he registered the noise of a motor engine and turned towards the door. A large vehicle had drawn up outside their home.

The boy heard the door of the vehicle slide open and shut, the tread of footsteps coming right up to their house. He stopped playing in response to his father's call to be still. Then the door burst open and three young men came in, shouting. They *came with their eyes empty of everything* and forced his father's outstretched arms, his father struggling between them and crying out *God, no!* One youth had a rifle slung over his right arm. He gave an order and together the other men held his father stumbling and unpredictable between them. They lashed his father's hands together behind him with twine.

It might have ended there. They might have taken him then. But his father cried and lunged forward, bringing two of the young men to the ground. He was a strong man who was accustomed to using his strength. They came down beside the

126

table where his father stored his tools. A large noose of rope was by them on the floor, the rope his father used for securing goods. The youths pulled at his father, picking the rope up as they rose.

'Let's teach him a lesson!' They laughed, then bound the rope to his arms and slung it across an exposed beam, holding themselves steady as his father thrashed and lashed out. Their home had no ceiling, just the beams up above.

His father's body twisted in the air as they pulled him up by his flipped-back arms. Then something snapped that made his father scream in pain. The men called out to one another, enjoying the game.

'He's hurt,' cried one. 'Let's go,' another, and his father fell to the floor with a shoulder that had shifted loose. It lifted at an angle away from his body. One youth leant forward and cast the rope to one side. His father cried out and cursed them for generations to come.

'Best cover him.' Together two of the men began to pull up his father's white vest. Pulling it up over his chest, tearing it over the limp arms, over the sliding smear of his father's shocked face. The other held his father's body steady as he cried out in pain.

Bradley remained as still as his father told him to, his father's instruction pinioning his arms to his sides. They hooded his father with the vest, held down the pale cloth ball of his head between them, but his father struck out and one of the young men shouted with pain. The youth with the rifle stabbed his father's head with the butt. His father cried out, *Please don't, don't,* his chest heaving into a ridge of ribs. Bradley saw the cloth bag reddening with blood. His father struggled on, his legs kicking out from below so the men were forced into a strange dance. Then the youth with the rifle struck again and his father slumped down, his body reduced to a loud cry.

This is what they had seen done at the military camp. This is what they'd been told it took to keep the brutes in line. Sirisena cycled the coastal road from one rebel village to the next, buying land and giving money to the JVP. Sirisena was a trade union activist. Sirisena believed his son should be educated above the rest. It was upstarts like these who were threatening them all. His name had been first on the list provided by a fellow villager.

Then the youth with rough skin stamped on his father's outstretched legs, as if to ensure he could not strike out. His father's body no longer lifted with the blow. The one who was thinner than the others was barking cries and calling his father *Dog, faggot, tree-fucker*, his yellow teeth showing beneath a spray of hair on his upper lip. The man's glossy boots then began to kick too, kicking deep into his father's belly as if it was a car that wouldn't start. His father was broken now.

Then it finally came, a disembodied cry without origin, his father's scream his own scream, his voice rising into an angry lash of words, *Don't! You bastards! Leave him alone!* Too late, of course, this sudden release. The third man turned and told him to *Shut up!* They all now looked at Bradley and were still. They wore black trousers and green T-shirts, each man's face defined and distinguished by the boy's violent fear. Bradley stopped crying then, stunned by this moment when he came to exist for the young men, stunned by the sudden clarity in which they too could be seen. Each of them drawn into precision in the light of a naked bulb.

Then the rough-skinned youth coughed a laugh, muttered *Let's go*, and they hauled his father up to take him from the room, his father so small now without a face, so large now in the scream that came from him as they dragged him outside. As they stepped past Bradley a polished boot came down on the wooden toy, crushing it so the wheels went spinning across the room. They were dragging his father backwards by his arms, pulling him with his unhinged shoulder into the open doors of a white van. The engine spat into action, the men got inside, and the van doors pulled closed with a grating sound. No number plate, just a bent exhaust, the bumper rattling loose as the van drew away, taking his father into an endless night.

In the long oblong of light that came from the open door, he could see two lines of darkness where his father's legs had trailed upon the ground. He remained on the mat for hours it seemed, till neighbours dared to come forward and tried to quiet him down. He was numb and senseless. He could not feel anything any more. They drew his shaking body to them, the trembling of the boy now running through them all. The father's crushed resistance running through them all.

~

Bradley has told Renu all that he remembers. She has written it down and finds herself reaching for more. She has moved on from noting details of the abduction to finding out what she can about Bradley himself. He is young, but in the seven years since she met him she feels she barely knows him at all. She's observed him through the grille of the hotel gate when she arrives at daybreak, has seen him withdraw into his cabin to go to sleep, as if the times they occupy barely touch. She feels she's been writing him through some blind memory, through Anoma's hopes, through the limitation of his limbs, a desperate act that interpreters of silence might understand. For though Bradley has spoken she knows she cannot reach him, reach the boy who'd seen his father through the young man who speaks now. There is some distrust of words in him, a hidden resistance to speech. Renu feels as if something has altered in the order of things. She had once imagined that established events could not be changed, that the historical past was as solid and secure as her grandparent's home, but everything is breaking open as she steps into unknown events, into the uncertainty of the people she speaks to and needs to move within – the space between memory and the present moment shaped by censorship, by fear.

She gleans what she can from the young man and the other villagers, disciplining the information as if there is a hidden order there. There are victims and aggressors, different forms of loss. There are names, dates and times that she can write with some assurance, and then the clashing claims, mixed memories that have her cross-referencing facts and inventing codes. She's no more passive in her listening than a swimmer carried into the arms of an indifferent wave.

From her earliest years, Renu has been rooted in the present and the certain past, been impatient with larger tales that drew her into distant times. When she was a child she would hear the cook tell island stories by the coolness of the porch and would wait for them to end so she could talk of real events. She would sit with Savi on the wicker chairs of the front verandah while Josilin stretched her legs out on the dolmen stone, holding an enamel mug of milky tea, swirling the last grains of sugar as if swirling wet rice in the nambiliya. Josilin would have spent the morning preparing rice, separating the grain from the husk, winnowing the chaff outdoors and washing out the small stones from a grooved silver bowl. Then language would flow through her as she began her tale, her voice changing, entering the times when her own mother too had told stories, sifting bright stones of narrative from the rough seeds. Her voice would lose its husk, lift clear into her mother, as if their bodies had been drawn into a single grain. The island stirred in the swirl of these stories, bringing estrangement and enchantment to the place where they lived. There were folk tales and myths, there were stories from the river and legends that had been inscribed in art on temple walls. There was the story of the Leper King, a man who might have been a god, who lived, it was said, not far from the Fort.

Once in a certain country lived a good and kindly king who was afflicted by an illness for which there was no known cure. His subjects travelled the length and breadth of the land in search of healers, and even sent emissaries by ship to foreign realms. Many physicians tried their luck, bringing potions of bright colours and oils tinselled with rare gems. Still the king remained afflicted and a cure unfound. Then one day a humble herdsman came to court and offered the king a drink from a freshly cut coconut. The common fruit shone as bright as a sun lifted from the sea. The king's court was shocked, believing their monarch was being mocked, but he commanded them to silence and ignored their pleas not to drink. He put the coconut to his lips and duly drained it dry as his chief minister called out sharply that This might be a plot to poison their king! But as he drank the liquid his body slowly changed. His skin became smooth, his legs grew firm and strong, even his hair appeared thicker than it had ever been before. When he finished, all his subjects stepped back in wonder, some tumbling down the court steps as they did so, for none could believe the transformation that met their eyes. The king's body glowed like that of a coming god and his limbs were as shapely as if he was reborn. The herdsman…

Renu's ears would be warm against her palms but she remained curled in her chair waiting patiently for Josilin to finish, certain of the titbits of town gossip that would follow the tale. The old cook would move from the timelessness of the tales that Savi loved to the present of real events as if they were part of a single narrative thread. She would wait for the cook's voice to drop, thicken, become grainy with new knowledge and listen fingering the stones that lay in the metal bowl – these hard, dark tales of infidelity and drunkenness, of rumour and truth – as Savi would drift to sleep in the brightness of a *sun lifted from the sea*.

~

Savi has got used to the sound of sea and wind in the house, has carved herself a shelter in the fall of a dying wave. The last time she had breathed in time to this rhythm she had been fifteen years old. She had lain on her bed and breathed in the water, taking it deep into her body so that her chest felt full, just as her father's must have been. She had felt the pressure carrying to her ears and the extremities of her skull, the world sealing over, carrying her into the darkness with him. She now curls into the swell, allowing it to carry her into the space he left behind.

Her eyes are resting upon a black dragonfly on her bedside table. It has translucent wings with a black spot on each tip so its body makes the shape of **o | o**. She is breathing the sea, reduced to the calligraphy of the creature's form, when the door opens and Renu comes in.

'Are you ready?'

Savi hears the words as if they came from a distant place.

'You don't have to come if you don't want to.'

'Mmm?'

'I told you there was someone I wanted you to meet.'

Savi stretches and feels the afternoon break into light. The ocean recedes. She is released into the clarity of a dragonfly on wood.

~

She had once associated the road to Kurundupola with the quality cinnamon reserved for love cake and watalappan. Now as they travelled on in the three-wheeler, they were on a path she did not know. Renu told her about the moonstone mine and the village where a rehabilitation centre was supporting the families of the disappeared.

'You know the woman who gave you a massage today is one of the people who is being helped by the centre. Her husband was a victim. Her son was traumatised. So was she in a different way.'

Savi wanted to say something, but her body was still suspended in a moment without time. Earlier that day she had gone to Eden's Bay with Renu and succumbed to an ayurvedic massage from a woman she was told was the senior masseuse. She had stripped naked and lain on the mattress as the woman's hands ran like a river through her. She was conscious of having grown darker after each morning swim, her body divided between her English and native selves by the telltale yellow shading of her swimming costume. She had relinquished herself as she was pummelled, plucked and rolled into wholeness, becoming part of the rhythm of Anoma's hands, feeling no distinction between them and her body as she was released into a syrup of muscle and fluent tissue. When Renu came in and suggested that she might like to meet a friend of hers, Savi was still aware only of the soothing circles of hands on her heels and the small pulses triggered by the plucking of each toe. She could remember the woman only through touch as she wondered about the son and the history that they shared.

'Is he the person you want me to meet?'

Renu was about to answer when the three-wheeler hit a stone and threw the words from her. Her response was to a question that Savi had not asked.

'He needs physiotherapy but the centre cannot provide it.'

'Why not?' She was willing to be carried in whichever direction Renu might wish go.

'Because he's not a victim of torture. We don't have the funds to cope with the effects of trauma.'

Savi remembered the pressure of Anoma's hands upon her body, the sense of release that led to loss of boundary.

'His mother is a wonderful masseuse. Can't she help?' She caught a glimpse of a dagoba through the trees before being swerved into a dust road.

'She's tried. His needs are different. She does not see him much now.'

Savi stepped down from the three-wheeler into a sandy clearing where whitewashed houses were grouped on the edge of a grove. There were fruit trees interspersed with tall coconut palms. Opposite her the office of the rehabilitation centre, a grey cabin jacked up on rusty wheels. Cables extending from the side of the mobile unit connected to a generator, so the office had a source of electricity independent of the homes. She followed Renu inside, her step sounding hollow on the board, and instantly felt the temperature rise. Someone was standing up from a desk in front of them.

Renu introduced her to a slim, unshaven man in blue jeans. This was Navin Ranatunga, Renu's unofficial boss. Her cousin was smiling as she said this, but he looked sharply away, embarrassed almost, his quick, intense glance a matter of crisp formality that instantly rendered her an intruder. He sat down and picked up a sheaf of notes, perhaps signing off some papers. Savi looked at the dark hair of his arm, the cream dial of the wristwatch with the worn leather strap, and wondered what kind of work could be picked up so casually and undertaken with a stranger looking on. It took her a moment to realise that Renu had left the office and she had been left alone with him.

She looked outside, uncertain if she should follow her cousin or whether she was expected to talk to this man who had just asked her if it was good to be back, while continuing to write.

'Renu tells me you're doing a PhD on Sinhala nationalism.'

It sounded grand, weighty, far too large for this cramped space.

'Amongst other things.' Her words were airy, dismissive. She was conscious she might have made things worse. She remained silent, watching his moving hand.

'Well that must keep you busy. There is a lot happening here that relates to your work.'

She felt the irony of the words coming from a man whose work stopped him from even looking at her. No, she was not busy, there was nothing to do. Even the war seemed to have stopped and cut her loose. Those sharp eyes must have taken all this in, her utter irrelevance to events. She could not remain in the office within the tight compass of such knowledge.

133

Through the window she saw Renu talking to someone, writing in a black book that she held close to her chest. Her cousin had knotted her hair so it hung in a loose bun down her neck. With her head lowered, she looked like a student taking notes and for a moment she saw in her cousin's form the person she might have been if she had not left.

Savi stepped out to join Renu, into a compound burnt colourless by heat, though there was some relief in a small breeze. She could now see the figures that were a blur from the office window – an old man sitting on the ground, a child drawing in the sand, a woman in a red dress, gathering leaves into a heap with an ekel broom. She turned to go up the path that led back to the road when Renu's shadow engulfed her from behind as she touched her arm.

'Would you like to join us?'

'Sure. What are you doing?'

'Just keeping up with things.' Renu was withdrawing from her once more.

For over an hour Savi sat on the cement floor with Renu and the villagers, listening as they talked in the shade of the stoop. Several people had gathered – women of all ages, a few old men with rheumy eyes. Most of the children were attending the last day of school. Savi listened to them speak, picking up words that once were hers. *Kammali, amaruy, varadi, kalabala, karadara.* She tried to make connections between the words she knew, filling the gaps between them, but she knew she was guessing, that any meaning was probably the product of her imagination, and the gaps grew large as potholes as she stumbled over a profusion of rocky, adult words. *Prayojana. Balaporoththu. Prashnaya.* She did not interrupt to ask what they might mean.

A woman of about forty was sitting before them, speaking as if continuing an ongoing conversation. Others had gathered round, listening as though absorbing a communal tale. They sat in silence with their hands about their knees, nodding or clicking their tongues, prompting with *That's so* to carry the narrative forward. They talked so fast sometimes that Renu stopped taking notes. When her cousin did speak Savi was aware of the silence that followed, the sudden hesitation in the woman who had been speaking before. Renu would repeat the last words spoken or the last words she had noted down. The women would look at one another, as if uncertain of what to say next.

That evening they were together in the ochre light of Savi's room. Savi sat with her legs crossed on the bed and Renu was on the floor, leaning back against the almirah. She had collected some of Savi's books about her: *Antigone*, a volume of lyric poems and a glossy tome full of impressive terms that quietened her as they did indeed make English sound like a foreign language – *ontological scandal, metropolitan hybridities, disjunctive temporalities, simultaneous uncontemporaneities...* Savi saw the smile that stretched her cousin's lips as she put the book down.

'Did you enjoy the visit to the centre?'

Savi felt she was being invited to share in something.

'Mmm...' She did not wish to show how little she understood of the language. 'What exactly are you doing there?'

Renu drew a tired hand over her face and sighed. 'I ask myself the same question sometimes. I suppose you could say I am helping Navin out.'

Savi wondered if her cousin was evading her again. She thought about the man in the office – his seeming indifference to her as he kept his head down, the moist hair glistening on his exposed arm – and a sudden possibility presented itself.

'Do your parents know you go to the village?' She tried to keep her voice neutral.

'No. But I wanted you to.'

Renu's gaze was direct. Savi was sure her cousin was involved in an affair with the man who had stripped her down to nothing, but Renu was shaking her head with a smile.

'It's not what you think. He doesn't even know I'm there.'

Savi was smiling too, but didn't quite believe it. Renu's denial was coy, too soft, but she let it go.

'That makes two of us. He didn't notice me either!' And they both laughed as if they'd avoided a connection neither of them was yet ready for.

It was a relief to slip into allotted roles, Renu asking about her work in England, what it was like to still be studying after all these years, Savi entering familiar territory, explaining the long years at university in a way that might help her cousin understand that academic work played only a supplementary role in her life. She felt the need to explain these things after Renu's rebuke.

'It hasn't all been study. I did some temping for a while but decided to get back to it after Rob and I split. It felt natural to go back to university. It gave continuity. I had a sense of unfinished business, so I just returned.'

This was the first time she had mentioned Rob, but Renu steered clear, a silent swerve to avoid a maimed bird.

'What are you writing on? I thought you were working on something political. Literature from a political angle, wasn't that what you said?'

'When did I say that?'

'Just the other day after lunch.'

'Well yes, I guess that's it. Though I must say,' Savi drew her legs up and wrapped her arms around them, 'politics seems to mean so much more here where you live and breathe it every day. There was this South African writer who said that in South Africa, politics is fate. Perhaps that's what it is here too. Fate, destiny, a sentence carried in the blood. It's impossible for me to say, living so far away. The only thing I can be sure of, the one thing I keep coming back to,' she paused, conscious of her struggle to explain the jumble of ideas that were coming to her, the muddle of books on the floor, the frustration of not understanding the village women, 'is that the stories we tell matter. I believe they are the only thing to hold on to when everything else is gone.'

And as she said it she knew that stories helped fill the space where her home had once been.

'The only thing to hold on to,' Renu repeated solemnly in a tone that suggested she might be mimicking her. Savi could tell from the raised eyebrows that her cousin was not convinced.

'Yes.' Savi smiled to see her earnestness thrown back at her.

'I thought it was hope.'

'You mean like Pandora's box? No, hope means nothing without a story to hold on to. You need a narrative to give meaning to hope.'

'So what's your hopeful thesis called?'

Renu wasn't teasing any more. She was smiling, patient, calm.

'The Manticore's Tale'. It sounded absurd. As if she was

writing a folk tale of the sort Josilin told them when they were young.

The Manticore's Tale, Savi repeated with a gravity that caused Renu to draw herself up, was only the title. It was all that was left to link her to her original intention of studying myth in island literature – the ancient chronicles of the lion people that gave continuity and legitimacy to the island's main race. How once upon a time – and she could almost hear the old cook join her as she continued in a voice that was deliberately self-deprecating – in a certain country, a wilful princess had fallen in love with a lion and given birth to a history of pure race memory. The fantasy had congealed into scabs of pure blood.

Renu was nodding quickly, acknowledging her familiarity with the story. 'Yes, yes, I know. Our people refuse to recognise that we are all mixed-up migrants, descended from a good-for-nothing outlaw. But tell me, why the manticore? There must be other creatures that are part lion and human.'

Savi had hoped to move on from the embarrassment of the title, to explain how her research had led her to study the emotional labyrinth of personal betrayal and public duty, patricide and parental love, but Renu was observing her with an interest that compelled her to carry on.

'There are,' she measured the gaps between words, 'the Sphinx for one, but…'

'What is it?'

'You'll laugh.'

'Go on. Tell.'

She looked directly at the amber eyes and curled her lip in concentration. 'OK. But please remember that this is just a piece of writing. The manticore,' Savi paused to check that Renu's interest was genuine, 'comes from India. The word means 'man-eater'. And there's a play in my title on the word 'tale'.'

'Tale?' Renu's echo drew a band of literal meaning around the word and Savi was aware once again of how ridiculous it sounded.

'Yes, as in "ending". The manticore's tail is tipped with spikes that spring out when it's attacked and then new ones grow back. I was referring to the idea of generative violence, of stories that when repeated cause violence again and again.'

137

Savi rushed through the formula. She wanted to draw the topic to a close but her cousin was leaning on the almirah, her face pinched into a frown of concentration, her hair flowing into the grooves of a carved acanthus leaf.

'You think myths and legends matter so much? Cause violence, are destructive? My, you have changed, Akki. I would never have thought you would come to see stories that way. You used to love those old tales, wrap them about you like a cool sheet. I was the one who could not sleep when I heard them, remember?'

The years fell away as they were drawn into the time when they listened to island stories on the darkening porch, stories marked by destiny so that an individual's achievement could only be measured by the degree to which he embraced his prescribed role. Savi could almost hear Josilin now, hear the stories of the night, as she began to speak, to herself, to Renu, to her few faraway friends, of the comfort, the certainty of these tales and the difference between them and the English novels she'd read in which individuals claimed ownership of their fate. She'd once been soothed by the safety of the island tales, their assurance of continuity, but long years of study had led her to see that differences between forms led to different modes of being in the world, different approaches to the future and the past that could have different results. Perhaps the history of the island would have been different if it had been written and told in another way.

'Politicians use stories all the time to sell the idea of our glorious heritage. People have gone to war in defence of this myth.'

'And what of stories that are not myths?' Renu asked. 'The ones that do not get repeated again and again. The ones that get lost or forgotten.'

'They need to be brought back. Perhaps then new myths will be born, and perhaps we'll get to see old myths in a different light.'

They fell silent as the sun intensified, streaking Renu's hair into a river of flowing wood, her skin translucent, her face thrown into relief, as if she might dissolve and disappear. Savi stretched, reaching out, filling her skin. There was no need to say anything more. She relaxed, her eyes slowly contracting to the pale flame of Renu's face. She had seen that look before, sitting with Renu in a circle of women whose voices rose and fell, Renu listening as they spoke, their words running through her hands, like so much water, like so much dust.

~

Anoma has put the bottles back on the shelf and collected the soiled towels, folding them into thick squares that hide seaweed-coloured streaks of oil. She places them in a laundry basket, walks back to the truckle beds and wipes each plastic mat with a sponge of disinfectant, stroking the mats into dark stripes of wetness. They stay damp despite the heat. She washes her hands with soap, rolling her palms up to the elbows, folding her hands one over the other and splashes her face into coolness. It has been a full day with five new clients. The pocket at her waist is weighted with generous tips. She wipes water from her cheek and sees her face darken with moisture. Something about this gesture brings back a memory of a woman's striped body from earlier in the day. *Foreign-returned,* the woman's body said, even before she shed all her clothes on the floor. Anoma remembers the sweat on the face of the Sri Lankan tourist's face, the clothes falling off like unnecessary skin, the two-tone body scissored black and white, the movement from dry, burnt shanks into buttery caramel. She then wets her hair and runs her fingers through its greyness as if testing its texture for the first time.

She is used to knowing things through touch, enjoying the impress of her fingers on a body, the alchemy on pale creatures that redden at her touch, drawn into colour as she moves across their forms. She remembers how after Savi left, a newly arrived East European walked in, heaving himself up to receive her small palms. She rolled him over and began cupping the flesh of his back so that blossoms of blood appeared just below the surface of the skin. She then erased these with thick red strokes as she swept her hands up the length of his back towards the tension of the right upper arm and the lifted shoulder that stayed stubbornly pale. She found the hollow she was looking for under a scar on his right shoulder joint where some bone had been lost, and knew then, for sure, he was a painter of walls. The muscles and joints tell of the long hours of the body, the prevailing climate and conditions of a life being lived – the congealed tension in the neck and lower vertebrae of the sedentary office worker; the blue ridged rivers flowing down the hamstrings to the dry petals of cracked heels of a hairdresser with beautifully conditioned hair. She feels no need to practice her English when they lie before her like this; there is no language to equal the intimacy of touch. Only her son eludes the knowledge of her hands. Only her son's silent arms have come to resist speech.

She feels for the notes in her pocket with still damp hands and then draws her arm through a bag that contains little more than a faded identity card. One client had made a sexual advance, clumsy, without signature. She had dismissed this as she had learned to dismiss other irrelevant things. She climbs down the steps to the side entrance, moving past the red stars of ixora blossom and the tall lampposts, passing Bradley's whitewashed cabin on the way. She crosses the car park, keeping her face towards the drive, remembering once more the advice she had been given when she lived at Kurundupola.

'He is gone', she was told. 'Stop looking and move on,' but she had continued to insist that her husband might be alive.

She had been praying at the temple when he was taken away. It was her custom to observe *sil* every full moon. It was *Wesak*, so the temple was crowded, and it had taken her longer than usual to make her way home. The road was decked with Buddhist flags the colour of flame and sky. In the darkness they appeared to be striped into various shades of grey. She was walking on the grass verge, away from the other worshippers with their woven baskets and bags, when she saw Josilin hurrying up the road towards her with her hands raised to her mouth. She was calling, calling out sharply, so that the words grew and engulfed them both as they drew near. 'Sister, come quickly. They've taken him. He's gone. Come quickly. The boy's crying. He saw it all.'

Day after day the boy talked of what he'd seen, forcing the moment of violence on her as if she could enter that time and intervene. His memory was dangerous, she knew, far too detailed and strong, as if fear and rage had sharpened his senses. She told him to be quiet, but he wouldn't stop, her hands carrying her forward and trying to get him to obey. She was pinching and slapping him, gently at first, then with surprising, brute force, aware then of gaining release from something she could not name. One day she sprained his wrist by accident as she tried to teach him to hold a knife. Felt the thin tissue of the child's muscle stretch and yield under her palm. The blade then turned towards her, cutting a deep, fish-shaped gash on her own arm so they both cried out at once. Her shock. His fear. The flare of distrust that would never go away. There was nothing left to keep her in the village now.

Years later she came back to register the abduction and in return received a case number and advice on finding work. The rehabilitation centre drew her into a quasi-official space she understood. She believed in such things, in ritual, the large, unwritten laws of the night, the need to mediate between them. Believed in the bright hope of the young woman who worked there and got her formally trained in ayurvedic healing so that she was able to get the job at Eden's Bay. She could now use the skills she had acquired in the city, the knowledge of perfume, the supple body, the language of touch.

The young woman had then asked if she might meet her at her former village home and arranged for Bradley to be there so that she could talk to them both. It took her a moment, as it always did, to recognize the long-legged youth with wild hair, to see in the loose arms the child that she had left behind, the son she had spent her meagre earnings on to keep in clothes and books, the son she had cast off like a broken chair. It was just as well, she thought, as she contemplated the spent energy of his limbs, that she had beaten the boy, beaten him back into the childhood that was keeping him safe. No one could ever wish to harm him if he stayed like this. No one would ever touch her baby or take him away.

He had looked quickly at them both, coughed up a ball of phlegm and spat it with perfect accuracy onto a black beetle that was scuttling past her feet, so a shiny ball of spittle ran across into the grass. He then withdrew to a corner where he kept his father's mammoty and the broken cart, as the women sat down in the shuttered light of a green room.

The young woman drew a black notebook from her bag and

began to talk of Sirisena, carefully reading and enunciating his five given names, the long list strange and unfamiliar to them both. For a moment, her husband faded into an abstraction, one in a long list of men who'd been caught in the freeze-frame of a disappearance, the husband who still seemed present in the house.

The walls were a different colour from the last time she had been there, but she could still see all the old objects in the altered light of the room. Behind the young woman was the same thick grained table, the old blackened stove and the hurricane lamp he had brought home on the one night she had seen him drunk. And there, beside them, the old chair he used to sit on when he was sharpening knives. The rhythmic slicing movement up and down the granite stone had always set her on edge. She could still hear the scrape of it in the gloom.

She listened as the young woman read out her official state- ment to the police, the details of time and place of the last sighting, the clothes he had worn, the loose change in the wallet she had given him that had disappeared with him, the white van with the bobbing exhaust that the boy had seen, the bootmarks spattered across the cement floor. She turned away and looked down, her arms drawn about her to stop the tremors in her chest.

She was stroking the pain from her arms as her husband might have done. She was aware that this lady with large, inquiring eyes had asked her something and that she had begun to respond from another place, as the memories came back with many voices, hers and her husband's, as it had been at different times. Something about the way this young woman listened, her lips drawn into a firm line, her utter stillness, made the older woman relax so she was able to let him talk on.

'Here move round, he said, and it eased when he pressed there. He had strong hands so the pain lifted fast,' Anoma began, speaking for them both. She was flexing her back against the pressure of her husband's hands.

'He would do this when he got back, after he saw to the land; things were different then, we kept different hours. He would come back at midday and leave before dawn so that he could till the new field and return to work at Kurundupola before curfew. Each day was like that. Broken into two halves.'

The lady's eyes, like liquid amber, watched her in a way that made Anoma sure that she could see her husband too, as he broke the tension in her shoulders and squeezed the aching muscles of her upper arms.

'He said the new field wouldn't yield much for it was too close to the coastal road. The tides were changing and sea water was coming in. It would take many days to block it up. But he was hopeful, always hopeful. We had been through this before.'

Suddenly she felt cold, as if her skin had turned to ice. She was being asked about the time when he had returned bruised by the threats of men he would not name. The insistence with which she was being asked this left no doubt of the specificity required.

'Can you pay them?' she said, and saw the young woman biting her lip, 'Can you pay them? But I knew it was not necessary to ask. It was a huge sum, what they asked for, more than we earned in a year. I can talk of these things now because it's known, you understand. People thought we had money because of the new land.'

Renu let out a long, slow breath that drew her head down towards the book. Anoma heard her ask about creditors and the bank loan, watched as she wrote something down.

But something stopped Anoma from speaking or responding as she wished. Her husband's tough arms were comforting and silencing her at once, as he pulled her back towards him, his lips moving soft and insistent on her neck, her mouth. He was touching her breasts, whispering in her ear.

'*Not yet. Come.* He was like that you know,' she continued chuckling quietly to herself, when the young woman sat up and drew a piece of paper from her book. Dates were put in front of her. The arrest of a lawyer on 7 January, the student demonstration of 7 June, both in 1989, before moving on to the one date that exploded at her touch – their last night together before he disappeared. She remembered this too well, found herself repeating things rehearsed over the years, as if in repeating them she might call the moment back. Their last night together. Their last night of connection. The lamp she still carried to her bed.

'The market was closed today, I don't know why but it was so. *You smell beautiful. Like citronella and sea salt.* But he smelt of it too

143

with my arms about his. The road was dark. Did you hear me calling for you?' Anoma was crooning gently while rocking on her heels. '*No one can love you as I do*. He has a soft voice, so beautiful to hear at night, but I told him the market was closed and all the river fish are bad so I haven't cooked a proper meal. My last night with him and no proper meal. Our last night together, I didn't even give him a proper meal.'

A thin high wire of sound escaped and she felt a light touch on her shoulder as her voice grew hoarse, 'Touch me there.'

The woman pulled away as if she'd touched fire.

'But it's dangerous to keep the light on,' Anoma resumed, then tumbled into a cascade of events that came too quickly for words, that had her companion getting up quietly and reaching for the door. 'Josilin always said so. Don't keep the light on, we were told all the time. Here, there, everyone muttering the same thing. Don't keep the light on after six otherwise you will be next. Inna barriyo! How to live in darkness when you work two days in one? The light was on when I got back. Someone had informed on him already he said. There are informers everywhere. *Be careful who you speak to. There is no such thing as a safe witness, no such thing!*' she hissed. 'But husband it is dangerous to keep the light on. Citronella, he said. Don't leave me. I am here, here and here.' His words hers, hot on her tongue.

Anoma carries on walking on the coastal road that will take her to the outskirts of the Fort, touching the pocket at her waist as if it is a talisman. Sirisena, she reflects, would be pleased to see her earn so much. Sirisena, she calls out quietly, and hears him laughing in reply.

~

Renu has withdrawn from Savi and sits in the arc of her wicker chair with a book on her lap, holding a newly sharpened pencil in her hand. She reads:

A mild seizure.
The facts I gave carried her into an intimate space. No new evidence

here. If she carries on like this they'll call her pissu, mad, and make her vulnerable again. Unlike others, she seems to finds no comfort in her child. To know more, I will need to know him, but he just sat in the shadows with one leg crossed, like a figure 4.

'There is no such thing as a safe witness', she said, so what does that make me?

I will ask Thatha about a job for her tomorrow, without fail.

This book is where she is most free, where the words come from her like a river, where she can write without fear.

… it had become lawful to bury a body without a public inquiry.

She reads, inhales it and feels herself expand – absorbing this shiny chip of truth that burns her from inside. She knows that she holds the fragments of a story that could grow large in her hands. She flips forward to her notes of the day, taken in the shade of the stoop, with her cousin sitting by her side.

Sumanawathie W., Lalitha W, Premawathie W.

Three women of the same family who had once given her a bitter herbal brew when a migraine had drawn her head into her lap. Insisted she drink, despite her protests, so she had swallowed three large gulps and rose into the surprise of finding her mind clear. Their faces had opened before her, the blades of pain parting to reveal eyes large with concern, with care, with an old and exhausted grief.

A husband. A brother. A son. Their individual, scattered loss gathered and grained into definition through the repetition of their shared words. *Kalabala… karadara karanava… gonubilla,* they had said.

She underlines these words, marking them out as key events, and is suddenly struck by their extraordinariness. *Kalabala, karadara karanava.* She has heard them so often she has not seen the magic they contain. They need to be stilled, written down and prised open like this for her to see the wonder of them rising now bright before her like butterflies.

What safe, comfortable words for such dangerous things! How could this be – at precisely what point in time had a 'frenzy' exploded into a state of 'civil war'? When had 'making trouble and being a nuisance' flipped like a chakra wheel into 'torture and abuse'? And exactly what had it taken to transform a *gonubilla*, the hooded monster of childhood, summoned from outside the window by parents whenever they needed to chide and goad their children to bed – Hush now, to bed, or else the billa will come and get you! – into a *political informer* who determined who was spared and who was shot?

Is this what made a war domestic, internal, bringing violence to the home? Or perhaps it was just another form of camouflage that made violence seem safe? And in the kind of parallel thinking that comes easily to her at such times, she recalls how just the other week she had drawn Romesh's attention to a similar distortion in the morning paper. Listen to this, the Americans are calling an accidental killing in Afghanistan, friendly fire. How about that!

Her brother had called back over his shoulder, 'They just reserve that for their own. The others – that's you and me – we're collateral damage!'

She had laughed then, happy to share this with him, the brother who brushed by her as if she was an invisible mat under his feet.

She continues looking at the words inked in black. Underlines them again, so the lead snaps from her hand like a spark.

clear of contact

Four nights later it begins to rain. Soft, unseasonal rain that taps the leaves awake. It grows more insistent and encloses them all. Savi is asleep upstairs in a room so dark that it seems to have lost spatial dimension.

In the bedroom below and on the other side of house, Renu lies awake, listening to the rain, her eyes open. She is remembering a time when the darkness seemed interminable, when the days drew in early and the nights were long. Clear of contact and companionship. Josilin would take the early bus home, leaving them with the understanding that she might not be able to come to work the next day. Her mother would draw the curtains, sealing them in to the dim, dancing light of six candles and the faint beam of a silver torch. Her father would secure the four brass bolts that crossed the external doors and French windows. They moved through the house like strangers testing unfamiliar ground. There was no need to declare curfew. After six o'clock the abductions would start.

History entered their homes in a wild fire of rumour. They learned to run their lives in this sudden, unpredictable light. The abrupt school closures, the staff absences at Tel, the talk of friends and relations who knew of someone who'd disappeared or been killed, the phone conversations from her father's office that had him slamming down the receiver, her mother's tight-lipped withdrawal as the order of her daily schedule was interrupted by the blind violence of the times. Renu observed how her mother had started to extol the virtues of 'tolerance', as if there was merit in patience, reward in putting up with things.

'Tolerance is not in itself a virtue. It depends on what is being tolerated,' Renu had countered, as she wiped the dust off a cabinet with impatient strokes.

'It is easy to say that when you're young,' her mother replied. 'When you're older you'll see that there are some things that can't be changed.'

The nights were fractured by sharp noises that had no clear origin or source. Renu would hear a cry, wake to shots in the dark. She'd be told not to worry, to ignore the sound of fruit bats and festive crackers. Her sheet would be drawn across her and she'd be told to go to sleep. It was impossible, of course, as the shrieks and blasts would continue. She'd lie awake and imagine what was taking place outside. The night rain would have her lifting her head from her pillow, listening closely for what might be hidden by the patter of its fall. The Fort prison was just half a mile from her home. *Curfew,* she had looked it up in the dictionary: *to cover a fire.*

She gets up from bed and walks through the house, turning on the lights so they mark her way. She draws the latch open and steps onto the verandah with its cluster of curved wicker chairs drawn into pale shrouds. She moves silently to sit upon a step, stretching her legs so she feels the dampness of raindrops splattering her skin. Everything blends in the darkness beyond. Her eyes rest on the darkness of invisible trees as she tries to form an image of what they look like in the day. The extinguished landscape allows her to imagine them there. It is her memory of the garden that provides a sense of place. Without this knowledge she feels she could be anywhere.

She finds herself reaching out in time, searching for the date of an event that might order the time that is coming back to her now. The abductions had begun when she was in secondary school, some years after Savi had gone abroad. She had always liked the wholesome certainty of written dates, their clean, sharp neutrality, but for some reason she has difficulty pinning down her own past in this way.

A date drifts to her with the falling rain. Has she written it down somewhere? A day in late March 1989, the month her uncle Dominic had gone swimming and drowned. Her cousin had come and gone, come and gone like a quick shadow, and barely spoken to them in Dolmen House. Her mother, her father trying to salvage the old order, her brother away at Kit's home in a town five miles away. Her sudden illness two weeks later had been absorbed into the disruption of the time. It was best she stayed at home anyway, her parents said, as she was growing up too fast. Their desire had been quickened by the discovery that some of her brother's friends had expressed an adult interest in her.

Renu continues listening, hearing the wind lift through the sweep of rain. There is water beyond the trees, there are reeds and water lilies that she can smell as if she were at the water's edge. The lagoon is defined by accumulating silt, the slow mixed deposits from salt marsh and river bed gathered over years. The sandbar rises, falls, changes shape with the tides. The lilies have stems that reach six metres deep. Slate grey kabaragoyas flash prehistoric in slow water. The lotus seeds gathered on the bank could lie dormant for over a thousand years. A thunderstorm, a fallen tree, and overnight the boundaries of all this history could have shifted somewhere else.

The rain continues falling, spattering her arms. Renu feels as if she might be walking towards the embankment, just as she had walked there at about the time of her uncle's death, the two events now blurred so that his death and her discovery seemed to fill the same historical time. She had taken a skiff and rowed with one small oar, the oar drawing back over lilies and breaking open a bad smell. She had lifted the lip of a leaf to reveal a blackened form and can still feel it on her fingertips, the form congealing at her touch into the body of a man.

She withdraws her wet hand from the rain and wipes it on her clothes, uncertain of the order of these memories that refuse to die, not knowing whether the mourning or the horror came first.

Bradley too is awake, keeping watch in the car park of the hotel. It has been a loud, raucous night of festive music, dance and a poolside dinner that he heard from where he stood at the entrance to the drive. The last lights in the bar have been turned off. Bradley stands between a glistening wall and an ixora shrub, a black plastic jacket loose about his shoulders, lifted by the wind to reveal his wet arms and vest.

Bradley's long hair has been tamed by the rain close and shiny to his scalp. His wet face reflects the light of an overarching lamp and grows lighter as he approaches a car. This is one he has not seen before. He moves towards it, pressing his body against the bonnet of a van. He is used to moving between vehicles, aligning himself against half-seen things. There are only two lamps and an intermittent moon, but he can read the colour of objects despite the greyness of the hour.

The car is silver blue, a Mercedes from the previous year. It has a streak along its side that seems to attract light. Bradley had seen it enter a few moments earlier with three people inside. As the door opens, the streak of light is broken. Something in the footfalls, the alternate shift of rubber and plastic soles, catches his attention and he stops. A man's form lifts clear from the stillness of the car, stands as if ignorant of the rain. His face has softened with the years. There is a broad nose and brow, a pockmarked cheek and twist about the lips, but it is the cough that makes it certain he is a man that Bradley seeks. Something about this cough grows into a memory of a voice, a voice raised in anger that beats sharply down upon his father's hooded cry. Someone else steps out, then a third man straightens by them and Bradley sees them all before him in the brilliance of the moon. The men draw together in a murmur, one putting an arm about another, as they move on towards the steps and opening doors of Eden's Bay. Bradley follows behind, flitting between cars, the wind lifting up his jacket so it looks like he has wings.

IV

THE BLUFFING TREE

Romesh returned to the Fort after breakfast, stepping from the car into a morning clear of cloud. Despite being bearded and slightly potbellied, he walked up the steps of Dolmen in his heavy, formal shoes with a boylike spring and slapped Savitri-sister on the back, remarking how well she looked, how she'd caught the sun already. He pulled open a bottle of beer from the fridge and explained that he had come back two days earlier than planned to avoid the holiday traffic, what with Christmas and Poya all coming together this year. He would be a grumpy married man within just a few short days, he reminded them, as he tipped the bottle to his mouth, so they might as well delight in his youthful presence while they still had the chance. OK, said Savi pulling him from the chair and leading him by the arm to the lawn, let's see if you can still smash kaduru and hit a six at the same time.

Romesh's return made the family complete, just as it was about to be joined by a family from another part of the world. Fiona was spurred into action, counting out the doilies embroidered with sugar-bright flowers that she had been given by her mother-in-law, and matching the various shades of yellow and mauve with the tableware from photographs that her son brought. At intervals she would dash upstairs and stand opposite her full-length bedroom mirror, holding her shot-silk wedding sari against a range of sapphire and ruby jewellery sets, trying these under both natural and artificial light. She had already made several calls to check on the ingredients of the wedding cake when she realized she needed to remind the young woman who was making it that all the fruit stones had to be removed. At a previous wedding at Yala the bride had cracked a tooth while eating cake.

'Quite shocking!' Savi heard her exclaim. 'It's a disgrace for such a thing to happen at a superior hotel.'

The three cousins had gone to the beach and picked up small husked coconuts, taking turns to see how far they could throw them into the sea. They wandered to the rest house for drinks and scooped improbably tall ice creams with long-handled spoons and returned just before lunch to plant the small karapincha that Fiona had left out for them. Romesh prepared the soil while his sister lifted the plant from the pot. She asked Savi to hurry and fetch the sprats' heads from the kitchen.

Savi wanted to ask what this was for, but, seeing the soil dripping from Renu's hands, rushed to the kitchen where Josilin was slicing the small red onions whose tangy citrus-and-garlic smell always told her she was home.

'What's this for?' she asked, holding the dish of sparkling fish heads in her hands, but the cook only chuckled and said, 'Just see'. She went back to the garden and watched as her cousins sprinkled the heads about the roots of the plant, mixing them into the soil with their fingers.

'In celebration of your return,' said Romesh, dusting his hands, having smoothed the earth down with a trowel. 'Water this throughout your stay, Savi-sister, and you'll always have the tastiest, most flavoursome curries whenever you come home.'

They spent the few remaining days playing badminton, cards and carom until the Wednesday before Christmas when Eden took his son to Colombo to collect more provisions and call in on business associates. It was understood that Romesh would manage Tel after his father retired. 'Your destiny is set!' Renu had teased.

'Is he interested in hotel management?'

'No, but he doesn't mind. Why should he? He now has somewhere to take all the people he cannot invite home.'

The house returned to the quiet of the sea and calling birds. Savi and Renu were left together to help out. Renu had been given the task of finding something suitable for Savi to wear for the wedding, but was distracted by telephone calls from Mrs Fernando, the wedding manager, who wished to confirm details that would affect the conduct of the poruwa ceremony. Her mother was out at the market.

Yes, Savi heard Renu say, there were just two drummers, and as they had dispensed with flower girls this would surely not require too much time.

Timing, Savi discovered, was crucial. The auspicious moment for the bride and groom to ascend the poruwa and for the singing of the Jayamangala verses had to be carefully worked out. Mrs Fernando was a perfectionist and had measured the distance from the entrance doors to the poruwa and timed the verses so she had exactly the right number to fit the programme. She was a woman, Renu told her, who took time seriously.

'How is Linh taking to all this?'

'I have no idea. I have only met her once, when she stopped over on the way to Kataragama. She's a nice girl, Romesh's age – which is a relief. All his previous girlfriends were teenagers.'

Savi smiled, wondering if a younger woman might have suited her cousin better, then observed, 'I have only been to one wedding.'

She said this with a wistfulness that made Renu reflect how carefully her cousin avoided speaking of her own marriage. She could remember the wedding Savi referred to, remembered how the family discussed it afterwards. It was that of their second cousin, Crisanthi, when pandemonium had ensued.

'What a disaster!' Renu felt a twinge of anxiety that her cousin might think she was alluding to her marriage to Rob and hurried to explain, 'Crisanthi's wedding, I mean. Remember that little boy running into that huge oil lamp, twice his size, and banging his head.'

'Got oil all over his clothes, jacket and all,' Savi laughed. She had stored the incident in her mind in case her parents ever dared to call her clumsy.

'And the mother came rushing out and scolding at the top of her voice, *Who moved the lamp?* She was looking at Beryl Aunty with that hatchet face of hers and then tripped on her sari.'

'And Vernon Uncle went to help.'

'And Beryl Aunty said, *Damn fool, modaya. Why are you never there to help me!*'

'What's Crisanthi doing now?

'Three children and fat,' Renu drew her arms round her for emphasis.

'No! She was a stick.' Savi's jaw dropped.

'I tell you, fat as Josilin now.'

'I can't imagine.' Savi shook her head.

Renu laughed, less at the memory itself than at the way Savi was speaking just like one of them, the emotions pulling her features into exaggerated shapes, talking freely without a trace of the foreign accent that sometimes kept her apart.

'Yes, even Josilin said so, when Crisanthi came round with the kids.' Renu twisted her hair up into a knot and secured it so that it fell at the nape of her neck. 'But she looks happy. Filled into the role.' Her voice lifted, rounding 'role' with a full 'o' in the manner of her English mother, of Savi when she first arrived. Renu paused, unsure of the new voice.

'How is Josilin? She looks much the same. Happier if anything.'

'She got compensation so she makes ends meet. Not everyone was so lucky.' Renu stood up. She needed to fetch the saris from her room. The subject of Josilin's experience did not belong here.

'Her husband was an alcoholic.'

There was something about the way Savi said this that made Renu pause. It was made as a statement of fact, uncoloured by judgement. Renu was at the door with her hand upon the brass handle.

'Violent too,' she managed. 'Not much love lost there.'

They had never spoken about Josilin's marriage, had grown up with the knowledge that something was wrong that they did not have a name for. It was one of the large, unspoken events they had moved around, as if there was a danger that in touching it they might get hurt.

When they were children, the girls would hear their future being discussed by their parents. The girls would sit at the dining table with their talcumed feet dangling, listening to the ice clinking in glass tumblers as their parents argued on the adjoining verandah over the right age at which their education should end.

'Dom, you're asking for trouble. A-levels are just the thing. Enough to show they're capable but not enough to scare anyone off.' The girls were familiar with Eden's views.

'Look who's talking!'

'Yes, but Savitri is keen to study,' Savi's father continued, ignoring Fiona's dig at her husband. 'I don't think she will want to stop at that.'

'She's bright, granted. But, brother, I must say, she's quite a gloomy sort.' ('Gloomy, he says you're gloomy!' Renu had whispered as she leant over to hear more. Savi giggled and mouthed the word with exaggeratedly pursed lips.) 'If she keeps studying on and on it might make things worse. As for me, I'd be very happy to see Renu do A-levels or training of some sort…'

'What training? What are you training her for?' Savi's mother had a knack of confronting issues they would rather avoid. Renu, they all suspected, might be better off unmarried. Her parents did not know how to direct her.

Renu groaned. She hated the way these conversations always circled around her horoscope, as if the fact that some geriatric pedlar with nothing better to do than draw charts on predicted planetary changes, should have a bearing on her life.

'Training to get out of your silly plans!' she burst out.

The verandah fell into the silence of hissing ciçadas and belching toads as the adults paused and contemplated their drinks.

Renu had drifted into books on the wings of such conflicts. She never consciously decided to leave school. The constant closures and deferrals of exams meant she simply drifted free from formal study, carrying small leaves of knowledge back home as if they were objects that she'd stumbled upon in a walk along the beach. She grew up at a time when each day brought news so strange, so foreign to her understanding, that she would listen to it as if it was a subject she could alter with her views. Strikes and abductions by unidentified gunmen became the subject of discussion over meal times, Josilin bringing her own local knowledge to the table with each new dish of food.

One day her aunt Sunita, whom the children called Aunt Snooty, had appeared and recounted an event that related to one of her father's uncles.

'Have you heard the latest?' she said, seating herself down having embraced Renu and her mother gingerly with a peremptory sniff by the ear.

Renu's mother shook her head and drew up a chair.

'Lionel's estate was burned down.' Aunt Snooty drew her lips down into the deepest of frowns designed to convey her own dismay.

'What! Eldridge?'

'Yes. Over the weekend when Lionel was away. They came and ransacked the place, then set fire to it. The whole house is gone. All the rubber trees caught fire and all. There's nothing left.' Aunt Snooty clucked and consulted a manicured nail.

Fiona looked away towards the sea and Renu tried to read the significance of this news through her mother's slow, deep breaths. Lionel was her grandmother's brother. He was an old man whom they rarely saw on account of his ailing health but her father had always spoken of him with affection. Renu knew that all the old family photographs and the most valuable heirlooms were kept at Eldridge, a rubber plantation that had been in the family for generations. Her father had often said that some of these things would be passed on to Romesh one day.

'And the caretaker? Wasn't he there?' asked her mother.

'My dear, these are bad times.' Aunt Snooty sniffed and cast a glance in Renu's direction.

Renu was pretending to read the weekend fashion supplement that lay on the coffee table in front of her. She was still looking at the picture of Miss Sri Lanka in a cutaway swimming costume when her aunt leant towards her mother and hissed, 'Killed. They found his head on the gatepost, poor man. Can you believe it?'

Renu kept her head down. Her eyes were on Miss Sri Lanka's smile and her perfect pose with one leg raised and her arms holding on to the swimming pool rail. She was trying to imagine the rubber trees in flames, the man being pulled away and decapitated. It came to her as a scene in a film, distant and unreal. She could hear the crackling of the old house as it spat fire, could smell the burning of trees as they came crashing down, saw the photographs of her ancestors in Edwardian clothes curling into blackness, but none of it could make her feel anything other than a sadness that came from a distant place. She heard Aunt Snooty blow delicately into a handkerchief pinned onto her blouse, and went to her bedroom to read.

The news started becoming real to her when the military trucks appeared, disgorging army personnel who clustered about the Fort and in the town. They set up road blocks at junctions and the exit of the bridge, bringing authority and order with their smart uniforms and glossy guns. The family car would be stopped for security checks, an armed stranger peering at their identity cards, checking that their faces matched the photographs. She would look directly back, taking in the keen imperious eyes, the smooth jaws, the assurance that kept the soldiers aloof from them all. Despite herself, she was fascinated by these camouflaged men. They made her feel she was moving through historic times.

She could still remember her disappointment and frustration when her parents barred her from walking past the prison because it was not safe any more. Later she learnt that the prison held many hundreds of detainees from the government crackdown on the JVP. The prison was blockaded and the court rooms had grown busy, attracting people from miles around. Men gathered outside the paneless windows, chewing betel and smoking, while reporters checked their notes and waited patiently under the Bluffing Tree for an adjournment. As she was driven past them on the way to town, she would see on the one side the hot, quiet houses shuttered against the light, and on the other the open court rooms, hemmed in by vans and cars. She would peer through the car window, looking for the small island of shade under the Bluffing Tree where Punchisoma, the jailbird, would sit with his blanket and tin can, but even he had been cleared away with the litter of fallen leaves. A dozen policemen would be standing by, silent against the restless crowds, with their black belts and full holsters, doing little more than making themselves visible. Once their car had been stopped by a checkpoint near the entrance to the town, and their driver drawn aside and compelled to pay a fine. When she asked what the fine was for the driver shook his head and frowned.

'You don't argue with the police,' he said.

She then understood that all that was required of the police was to be visible by the courtrooms carrying their guns. It made little difference if people heard the proceedings or not.

As the breaks from school became longer, she found herself accompanying her father to Tel each day. It gave new order to her days and freed her from the cloying domesticity of her mother's chores. Tel was the family name for Eden's Bay, one that had stuck since she had first used it as a child. At Tel she could move from room to room chatting to Mrs Amaratunga, the hotel manager, and get to know the impossibly slim Vijitha Mendis, the main receptionist, who was not much older than herself. Vijitha, she was sure, had been hired for the purpose of making the guests feel fat. Renu would step into the lobby to see Vijitha rising and lengthening to reveal the full sweep of her green and gold sari, standing up and sashaying with her to the main office where Renu could ask the questions she wasn't able to ask at home. Mrs Amaratunga would complain of shop closures and their impact on the provision of hotel meals. Vijitha would speak quietly of the man she loved who had been taken away from the office for questioning the year before and had never returned. Renu had never known him but had heard that he had worked at the hotel. When she asked her father about the disappearance of this man he said the police denied ever taking him in. They have no record of him, her father said, in a way that suggested this man might never have existed at all.

Her father was delighted to see her take an interest in the business, and especially gratified when he saw her going through the accounts. He noticed, a few years later, that she even kept a notebook to hand and carried this in a canvas bag that matched her red sandals. The stars might have decreed that Renu was not marriageable, but visible evidence suggested the contrary, and he was glad that his friends and staff could see that this was so.

In just a few weeks Renu knew her way around every corridor at Tel. She could cover the walk from the lower kitchens to the laundry rooms and up to the pool bar within a minute. She could move, shadow run, quick and unheard, down the stone spiral steps from the fourth floor to the health spa where the therapy rooms were. These rooms looked onto a rockery of giant ferns, a cool dark space secluded from the wide arc of the main hotel. Staff would stand behind the plants, shaded from view, observing the swimming pool and beach where the tourists lay down to cook their skins. Like the staff, she had learned to follow her father's injunction to be on hand but keep a distance from the guests. She would speak to cooks, cleaners, dhobis and groundsmen, knew each one by name, the whole invisible workforce that helped keep the illusion of calm while the disappearances went on.

> *There are so many kinds of silence through which I feel I am moving like a shadow run… the black silence about the court houses and Vijitha's sadness which seems to drip from trees every-where as we sit down to dinner under a fan that scatters words away like flies.*
>
> *Ma's tight lips, Thatha's scowl, Romesh's glare, none of us talk…*

~

Renu could not remember the day she first heard of the rehabili-tation centre but could recall the conversation with her father that followed. It came back to her that she had walked out of the hotel to find a three-wheeler to take her home and had stopped to allow a car to pass. At the same time she noticed Wijepala, the handy-man, squatting on the grass verge beside the utility shed. She had taken him to hospital a few weeks earlier when he had fallen from a first floor balcony.

He was well, the handyman said when she approached him, but things were difficult as the boy who had replaced him was cheap, and with his injured leg he was unlikely to get another job.

He seemed to be trying to stand but she motioned him to stay down. Wijepala then lowered his head and looked away furtively as he explained that a new man from Colombo had told him he should get some compensation from the hotel, so he wondered if Miss might be able to put in a word for him about this when she next saw her father.

His lips turned awkwardly as he looked up to see how she received this.

'Who is this man from Colombo?' She was used to being approached for favours since working at Tel and knew how to deflect them while keeping the conversation alive.

'His name is Ranatunga. Arrived a few days ago. He's from some organization that is trying to help the families of the disappeared. He's set up an office in Kurundupola,' he rushed on, keen to make the most of the fact that she seemed amenable to his request. 'Will you ask your father, Miss?'

She said she'd speak to him when he got back from work and remembered the promise when she saw her father enter the living room that evening with a baila tune on his lips. He had changed into his home clothes and was ready to relax.

'You look pleased,' she said, getting up to mix him a whisky and soda, before sitting down beside him to explain Wijepala's case.

Her father looked more serious as he selected a newspaper from the rack beside him after listening to what she had to say.

'No problem,' he said, shaking the paper out, 'compensation isn't possible for casual workers, but I think we need a new pool attendant. Tell him to speak to Mrs A. in the morning.'

He stretched his legs before him and swallowed his drink, put the glass down on the table beside him and began to read. Renu was getting up to leave when he pulled down the paper and looked intently at her as if she might have strayed in some way.

'Renuka,' he cautioned. 'It's good to keep a little distance from the workers sometimes. They're not all the same.'

She paused to pacify him. She needed him to know she was grateful for his concern.

'Don't worry, Thatha. Wijepala is not a troublemaker. He can be trusted. He is a good sort.'

Her father raised his eyebrows so they carried his hairline back. 'You think so? You are sure? How do you know, huh?'

She had learned the importance of taking her time, of being wary of a sudden turn in conversation, and hesitated in the silence of this mistrust. She took a slow breath and relaxed into a smile as she exhaled, her lips skewed into a small, tight, lopsided twist that made her look embarrassed. Continuing to smile, she went forward and took the paper from his hands, and brought the footstool and lifted his feet on to it, still smiling as she refilled his drink, all the while remembering the long afternoon she spent with Wijepala and his wife at their home near the coastal road as they watched their niece play hopscotch. She had visited him after the accident and been given the sweetest cup of tea in a green enamel mug, the sugar turning bitter in her mouth. She had then removed her sandals and joined the child in her game, throwing a stone on the sand and jumping in the squares. The memory of the welcome from this family became a part of this long smiling silence, the memory of her childlike abandonment with them magnified by the restraint with her father at home, her early days of infidelity to him.

Her lips were drawn too tightly, he knew, the smile about to snap as she lifted his tired feet and slid off his slippers. Eden found this discomfiture most reassuring. It was to be expected in one who knew so little of current affairs. Renuka was really rather too sweet for this world, and he could see now that it was his good fortune that she would never marry after all. She would stay, tending him like this, till the end of his days.

'You are a dear good girl,' he had said, easing himself into the life of unsolicited care that was unfolding before him, as Renu left the room and went upstairs to sift through the cuttings in her file.

~

They had been rifling through the almirah in Savi's room and brought out the saris and matching blouses. Savi was sitting on a bed draped in yards of embroidered silk. Nothing seemed to fit. She stood up and held her arms out while Renu slipped on the last blouse. The problem with sari blouses was that it was pointless breathing in. They were designed to flatter the precise contours of a given a shape, the upper arms, shoulders, neckline, bust and upper waist of the woman they were made for, so they either fitted or didn't, with no compromise in between. At this rate Savi would have to unpick the seams and spend hours sewing every-thing back again. She could feel Renu's fingers brushing her neck, drawing the two sides close.

'I was sure this was your size.'

'I've grown fat on potatoes.'

'Is that all you eat in England?'

'No of course not. Look,' Savi took off the blouse and sat down. 'we'll have to try something else.'

'I have another one I wore a long time ago.' Renu lied to spare her cousin any sense of obligation. The sari she was thinking of was in fact an unused exchange with a schoolfriend, from the time when they were still trying out colours and styles.

'Were you fat at the time?'

'Stop it. You're exactly the shape of our filmstars. Now wait. I'll be right back.'

Savi stayed seated, wishing that she'd had the foresight to find something suitable in England to wear for the wedding, then remembered that all the shops had been full of dour winter clothes – all but the shops in the Lanes with their sequined skirts and delicate muslin kurtas. If she had worn something from there she would have looked like a gypsy.

'Here. Try this.' Renu handed her a roll of blue tissue. Savi pulled it back to release a sea of turquoise and silver.

'My! It looks new.'

'Stop fussing and try.'

Savi slipped on the blouse and felt it cool against her skin, reached behind to hook it close and found Renu's fingers under hers. She was unsure whose hand drew the blouse as the garment was found to be a perfect fit.

obliquely about the past

'Once we got four different versions,' he said as he drew down some files and laid them before her on the table. 'So you must be careful how you take the information down. Stick to the evidence and verifiable facts.'

Navin had been advising Renu on how best to tackle the role, describing an early experience when he had shadowed a case-worker reporting on disappearances in the northeast. The case-worker had been interviewing a Muslim child who had witnessed an atrocity on his family. Some men had come and abducted the boy's father in the morning, before returning at nightfall to gun down his mother and three sisters. The boy of five had hidden behind a water tank as his family had been taken outside and killed by a ditch behind their home.

'First the boy spoke of four men, lining up the family and shooting them one by one. He identified them as the same men who had taken his father and said they were from a neighbouring village allied to the LTTE. The second time, he said there were six men and he wasn't so sure who they were. By the fourth time, the story changed again and the identity of the men didn't bother him any more. Instead, he described his mother pleading with the man who was forcing the baby from her arms. He remembered his baby sister crying on until the final shot. He then said his father rushed in from nowhere and picked up this baby from the ditch and ran back with her to the forest. He said his father was still in the forest with his baby sister and that they would stay safe there till the fighting stopped. He insisted on this fact, even though we had found the bodies of them all.'

Since her first interview with Anoma, Renu has known that she needs to talk obliquely about the past. She would begin by sitting on the ground, drawing her feet under her, and casually remark on the new mat in the room, the taste of the tea, the pattern of a cloth. Ordinary, tangible things. It would have been like a game of blind man's bluff, reaching out to find new forms and textures in familiar objects, as if discovering them for the first time, had she not been reaching for something unknown that might never be found. She tried to make connections by drawing on personal details catalogued in her book. She would ask the vegetable vendor about the distance of travel, the old man about the tools required to mend an axle, the farmer's wife about the pre-monsoon harvest, and consult the herbalist about oil for sprains. She learned to steer the conversation so that her subject would relax and relinquish a crucial piece of evidence while imparting the story of an old sarong.

Savi later described a process that chimed with what Renu

sensed she was doing. She spoke of a writer who would never discuss his own books but would talk endlessly about jazz, of how his descriptions of the music that he loved did much to explain the extravagant digressions that erupted from his work.

'Was he aware of the connections between the music and his work?'

'I don't know. As I said, he never discussed his work.'

~

There was just one more day before the Christmas festivities began, and after that, Romesh's wedding on the twenty-seventh. For the Rodrigos, Christmas was largely a public affair. There was planning to do for the seasonal increase in European tourists and the rise in temporary staff, and there were charitable engagements that involved the buying and distribution of gifts, in particular gifts for children at the mission school that they supported in a bid to keep their reach non-partisan. There was little space for the kind of family bonding that took place in other homes. Fiona, who turned nostalgic at this time of year, would buy a token turkey and stuff it with a mix of spices and nuts, her own secret recipe to rival that of Colonel Sanders, she said. She stopped short of preparing a Christmas pudding that might require a communal effort around the baking bowl, because no one in the family cared for it but her.

This year the preparations at Tel had all gone well, buoyed up by the fact that the hotel was full. Bookings were the highest they had been in years and they had no rooms at all to offer the lower-paying local guests. Eden was relieved, not so much on account of the extra revenue but because, as he observed, Tel seemed to be attracting 'the wrong type of local' in recent years. Cocky youths with finger-snapping parents would drive down from Colombo in shiny new imported limousines, strip off their clothes without ceremony and move dripping and laughing from the pool to a raucous game of volleyball on the beach. They would test the patience of the staff while drumming songs and singing baila tunes on the terrace by the bar, then suddenly disappear into waiting cars with tote bags slung across their shoulders, leaving behind the harried pool attendants to right the tables, clear the bottles and trampled towels, without ever glancing back or giving a tip.

They came with little or no baggage, unlike the westerners with their large, hefty cases full of minimalist clothes, sun creams, insecticides, video cameras, technical toys, magazines, hats, batik shirts and sheer, glittering sarongs. Foreigners, the staff observed, brought so much luggage it looked as if they intended to stay for good, remain on the island in permanent fancy dress. Now in the lead-up to Christmas, the post-breakfast foyer would break into a chaos of stacked trolleys as the tourist coaches pulled in and emptied a frantic babble of French, German, Polish, Russian, English and Japanese straw hats and baseball caps. The staff made their way through the languages – the head porter had taken evening tuition in three languages, travelling by bus to get to classes in Galle; Vijitha was fluent in the cautiously slow Japanese she had learned from a correspondence course that came with a CD; the waiters could translate the menu into more palatable French terms, lifting the French back into English if it appeared that their efforts were producing an unidentifiable new language of its own.

In the midst of this globalized hubbub, the small homes at Kurundopola offered a soothing respite. Renu would keep checking her watch as her morning became an interminable round of receiving guests and ensuring that they all had their statutory welcome drink and iced face towel, checking names against room bookings, hurrying between kitchens and laundry rooms, ensuring that the temporary staff were settled in, before finally catching a steady moment when she would not be needed, when she might slip into her worn-out sandals, grab a couple of short-eats from the staff room for lunch, and head out on the dusty road.

On her last afternoon at the village she had stepped down from the three-wheeler to find the compound empty, the front doors of each home sealed into small coloured blocks of darkness. A garish billboard outside the Fort advertised a fair that had drawn the families away. Renu walked towards the office and saw the dark hole of the window frame where the glass had been smashed. The mobile unit had just one long fixed window along one side and one slatted pane above. An airless space. Navin kept the door open when he was at work. She could now see his desk clearly through the broken window. She stepped up into the office, feeling the floor beneath her tremble.

Navin was on his knees, wiping the floor with a cloth, brushing the glass into his hand.

'Careful.' She didn't want to startle him.

'It's nothing.' He didn't turn.

Renu looked towards the window and saw fragments sparkling on the sills. Someone must have smashed the window during the night, perhaps using a rock from the mine. Navin kept his back to her so she could not see his face. She felt he was brushing her away with the cloth.

She moved to his desk and picked up a file. It contained the latest report on the displaced in Batticaloa with his handwritten notes fringing the script.

'What's happened to your cousin?' It took her a moment to realise that he was re-entering an earlier conversation, as if withdrawing from the events that were scattered at his feet.

'I left her on the computer at Tel.'

'Isn't she interested in your work here?' He stood up and shook the cloth into a metal bin, then examined his palm for splinters.

'I think so. But I haven't encouraged it. She's been away a long time.'

Navin used the tips of his fingers to prise something from his palm and then looked up at her in a way that made her draw herself together. She brought her arms across her chest, not in resistance to him but because she was uncertain of the look in his eyes. His gaze seemed to have softened into a colour she had never seen before.

'I remember when you first came. You walked around as if you were apologising for being here, on the edge, looking in.'

Her lips turned in an involuntary smile that registered a discomfiture she did not wish to feel. A warm breeze was blowing in, bringing with it the smell of lime leaves and cinnamon. For the first time the office felt open to air.

'Then you carried away all the tapes and came back hidden behind the papers you had typed up. Somewhere behind this bundle of papers,' he motioned, 'you were. Hiding.'

His hair fell forward as he leaned across the desk towards her. She laughed and brushed her hand over his head, briefly.

'You hide too.'

'But not like you,' he said, moving round towards her. 'It is as if a part of you is always somewhere else, as if you cannot bear to be completely in one place.' He drew her to him, slipping his hand under her canvas bag, onto her hip, the tang of lime mingling with the smell of him. She was conscious of the lack of contact with skin and moved so that her arm pressed his.

'I am here now.'

His hand moved up, caught the edge of her scarf, her sleeve, making her aware of the contours of her body beneath her loose clothes, constraining her, pulling her down so she withdrew, gently, not wishing to unnerve him, took his hand from the darkness of her hair into hers and kissed his open palm, kept kissing all the small flecks of blood that lay scattered there.

The glare of the afternoon sun was lifting to reveal a clarity to distant objects as Renu and Savi walked along the beach later that day. They had just stepped off the low wall by the rest house and were making their way towards where palms stretched out to sea. Renu broke the silence with a question she had been waiting to ask. Would Savi like to visit the village again? Navin had suggested it, she said.

Savi kicked aside a young coconut that looked like a giant acorn and continued walking.

'Only if you tell me what you are writing in that book.'

Renu felt a mixture of annoyance and relief at the same time. For days they had been circling round the subject. She had noticed Savi glancing at the black book with its thick protective cover and gold stamp.

'I tell you what,' she said, pursing her lips, 'I promise that I will let you read it before you go. It's my notes really, but I am putting everything together into a file and I will give them both to you, as one does not make sense without the other. There are lots of details which may be difficult to follow, but there is a story somewhere there. In the middle of all the muddled facts. A story,' she turned to face Savi, 'that I am trying to pin down.'

Savi looked at the water swelling and withdrawing from her feet.

'And there's some personal stuff, too, which may get in the way of your reading. When you can't talk openly,' Renu brushed away a lock of hair from her mouth and clicked her tongue in exasperation, 'You end up writing, writing to talk to someone, to someone or something bigger than yourself. I often – and please don't laugh now, OK? – feel as if I am writing in the dark, reaching out for something, someone, but don't know who or where they are. A bit like Blind Man's Bluff – remember? – when everything is unknown except what you remember and what you carry inside.' She looked up at a roaring breaker as it frothed and broke open into a glistening spread of white, then shook her head with a smile. 'But you can skip those personal bits if you like. It's the story that matters in the end and a story only becomes a story once it has a listener, no?'

Savi, aware that they had entered new territory, found herself reaching for a foothold. Hard facts. 'You have just one story?'

'I think so.' Renu's words, sounding distant, swept back towards them as she spoke. 'All the stories are connected but I keep coming back to one. It seems to lie at the centre of things.'

Savi bent and picked up her sandals and felt the sand giving beneath her feet. 'Stories may be connected but that doesn't make them one.'

They both became conscious of a shift in tone.

'What about your manticore's tale. That's one story that gets repeated, again and again.'

'No. It is not one story.' Savi felt she was on familiar ground now. 'It changes each time it is retold. Each retelling is a revision in a different context. Each retelling makes a new story.'

She had moved apart, was almost sounding English with the haughty open 'o's. She paused and picked up a small shell from the beach, a turret shell, the spiral keeling into a perfect extension of the original curl, repeating itself in ridged whorls of speckled red, extending outward and curling back to a sharp point of intensity. As a child these were her favourite shells, the ones she kept for herself. She pocketed it and slipped her arm through Renu's to draw her closer.

'Tell me. When you interview the villagers, do their stories ever change?'

They were approaching a shelf of sand. Renu wanted to withdraw her arm but did not, felt in the contact with her cousin a memory of Navin return. She remembered his hands, the firmness of them on her as she pushed aside the notes on his desk, the notes that slid onto the floor so she had to pick them up later to carry them home. There, with the endless click and whirr of the tape recorder as she started and stopped it, she listened to short bursts of words, transcribing them, fragment by fragment, in anticipation of the all important verb that would fall at the end of the sentence. This would keep her guessing, as the murmur of voices filled her room, rising and falling in sadness, as she tried to pin words onto paper, fix each word so it could not run away.

'Not exactly.' Renu spoke from somewhere else, as if part of her was operating at a different level. 'Sometimes they remember an event and tell it again and again, using the same words each time. But it's hopeless, I think. What can you do when your own language cannot be trusted? *Kalabala, karadara.* Ordinary words, slithering like snakes, slipping out of your grasp and becoming something else, so even words turn and bite you. How can you speak when your language works against you? Sometimes they remember new things and you notice how it comes through in bits, and what they say doesn't fit in with what they said before. It's mainly a question of working through their silences, feeling your way in the dark. It's strange, come to think of it,' she said, pulling the scarf down so that it no longer swept across her face, 'to listen to the stories of women looking for the bodies of their men. It's like all we've got is a story without a body, while the authorities have bodies with no story. It sounds crude, I know, but it does not seem much to ask, to bring these two together. To make every life count.'

Renu was leaning on Savi's arm as their feet sank into a ridge of sand made by children earlier in the day, the beach pock-

171

marked with the laughter of small footprints, the memory of play.

'Come sit.'

Savi drew her down and they stretched their legs towards the sea. Renu bent forward and rolled her shalwar up so her calves were exposed next to Savi's. Their feet had the same square toes, the same signature swelling in the middle that marked their fallen arches.

The sea gained density from this angle, as if the momentum of the breakers was directed at them, gathering force and rolling into one long tumbling roll of spray that would enlarge and burst open before withdrawing in a sigh.

'When you finish your research, will you get it published?' Renu asked this in a way that suggested that she had been considering this question for some time.

Savi drew in the salt air as it blew into her face. She balked at the idea of someone watching, questions that made her feel guilty of some neglect.

'I need to finish it first.' Instantly they remembered that her father would speak like this with his need for circumspection, for uncertainty to breathe. They waited for this memory to fade, then Savi went on.

'Why do you ask?'

'I have often wondered what you hear of us in England. We listen to the BBC World Service, did so daily when things got very bad. There was more information there than in our own papers. Our journalists see much but are frightened. Yours are free and outside. We listen to foreigners to find out about what's happening here. It's crazy when you think about it.' Renu sighed. 'We get fragments of news and have to make sense of it in our own way, but where you are and how you deal with it makes a huge difference.'

Savi raised her knees from the dampness of the sand and sat forward. The sea was rising and exploding into ever larger disks of opalescence, the lowering sun streaking it with deeper and darker shades. She found herself falling into her old pattern of trying to catch the release of each wave with her breath.

'You cannot write about this place without being here.'

'You cannot write about this place without leaving.'

'Do you wish you hadn't left?'

'You speak as though I had a choice.'

Renu felt the cruelty of her words in her cousin's tart response. Savi had been expelled from the country before she was old enough to understand what was happening, caught in Uncle Dom's tussle between giving her a future and connecting her with her past. They had all been told that she was one of the lucky ones, for she had been spared the interruptions of those years, had the chance to gain the kind of education most of her friends could only dream about. They had all believed in her good fortune till her absence became a permanence and her father died.

Renu could have repeated the words back to her – she had no choice either as to whether she remained in the country or not – but she could feel her cousin withdrawing from her and rushed to make amends.

'Akki, why don't you stay. I mean stay here and not go back.' She slipped an arm about Savi's shoulders and felt them stiffen under her.

'How can I? What would I do?'

'Teach,' Renu said with authority, though the thought had just occurred to her. 'Teach English,' she added as the thought expanded. 'I've been reading some of those books you brought back, the ones with impossible polysyllables that make English a foreign language. I was even reading about testimony and 'heteronyms' – that's a way of finding another voice, right? You could stay and teach English as a foreign language. We need teachers like you!'

Savi laughed but her eyes remained sad. Everything Renu said made her realise how studying English had changed her, how the language seemed to have come between her and the world she wanted to reach. She touched Renu's hand and drew her fingers into hers, stroking the wrist with her thumb and began to ask about the missing years. About their lives when she had been growing up and away from them all.

Renu drew her arm back from Savi and rested it on the sand behind her, and told her of what she remembered of that time, reciting events as if she were handling old snapshots of the past. She told of disappearances and spectral violence, when people were forced to focus on tangible things. Her father, struggling to keep Tel going. Uncle Dom, busy in Colombo. The vehicles pulling in and out of the drive. Strangers banging on the door. Phonecalls from ghosts who breathed down the line but never spoke. Letters pasted to the door, written in spidery red ink. Hushed conversations. Sealed doors. A time when people would speak of things privately, name killers, but in public not at all.

'School closed suddenly, we were left to muddle through. I began to wonder what you were doing,' she continued, sifting the sand through her fingers and feeling small chips of broken shell. 'Ma said you should never have been sent away. I wanted to write but didn't know where to begin. What can you say when everything is changing so fast? I kept thinking of you sitting there in the dining room looking so young and so old, sitting and waiting by the coffin. All of us avoiding you because we did not know what to say and you did not seem to want us. We felt dreadful, as if we were responsible for what had happened. It was easier for us to leave you there, to wait for you to go, but I wish I had said something then. I want you to know that. We should never have left you alone like that and then let you go as if nothing had happened. You came for such a small time it made it easier somehow. Your father died at the worst time, when there were killings every day. You came and went so fast. It was only after you left that I realised that I hadn't spoken to you at all. I would sometimes sit in the same place and see the sun setting behind and think about you. Wonder if you might watch it too, later, on the other side, wonder if you ever thought of us.'

Savi drew breath with the roar of an expanding wave, closed her eyes just as it shattered before her, and listened, stilled, to the surge of a distant breaker. Behind her sealed lids she could see the darkness by the pier slowly extend itself like a terminal illness, gradual, sunless, without centre or definition, the sea at Brighthelm slow and sluggish. As she opened her eyes she saw a spray of light coming towards her, uncertain for a moment where water and sky met, and curled her toes into the sand, feeling the tiny sea creatures that lived on the strand line prickle beneath her feet. She felt small, vulnerable, discrete.

'I will always be a foreigner in England.'

Renu hesitated before the starkness of a statement, the words exposed as rocks.

She looked at the profile of Savi's face blending with the palm trees behind so her hair looked even wilder than usual. She could see the silver lines where the burnt skin was peeling off the tip of her cousin's nose.

'I am not exactly at home here either,' she said, barely audible, and then louder, to be heard, and with increasing urgency, began to speak of a moment that slipped into this time as if it belonged there, a moment that was as present as the waves that expanded as she spoke.

She told her cousin of the event she had never dared speak of till now, an event that took place shortly after the funeral, her words leading Savi by the hand, leading her down to that last afternoon of childhood when she had walked to the riverbank and stepped into the skiff, talking her through it so they stepped into this time together, their arms lifting the single oar and breaking the water of lily pads, pulling the boat on through the shifting leaves till it was stilled by what appeared to be an obstacle of wood. They reached down to release the unseen obstacle, their arms reaching through and breaking the small pieces of their own reflection that fell between the leaves, breaking through into another form. A girl's hand folding back a leaf. The disk of water on its surface beading up and rolling off, the leaf lifting clear to reveal a liquid space that became filled by the rolling, blackened face of a man.

Amongst all the debris swept down by the river, the oil cloths and jute sacks and plastic bottles and rusty tins, all the debris that would be cleared by the boatmen as they drew their nets along the water, all the debris that their gardeners dredged up and burnt in bonfires after the rains, all the stinking, putrid detritus of the town that they were repeatedly warned might find its way into their bodies if they dared enter the lagoon, not rubbish and sewage, not human faeces, but this human face gashed with anger and urgent appeal. Renu suddenly stopped.

'Who was he?'

'I don't know.'

'You told no one?'

'No.'

Renu exhaled slowly so that her lips tightened into a thin line. She stood up abruptly and began to shake the sand from her clothes, the wind lifting her scarf and blowing it about her arms and face so she was momentarily obscured as she turned and strode away.

Savi, trying to step in Renu's quick footprints, found that for some reason her steps were missing the mark.

~

Late that evening Renu hands Savi a package wrapped in brown paper, bound with wide elastic bands. A story, she says, that contains many others. It can be pieced together from the notes in the book and file. If she reads from one to the other she might find it, the story of a boy from the village who saw his father disappeared.

Savi takes the weight of it from her and holds it against her chest. She looks at the large, clear, amber eyes that stare back at her, as if challenging her to take on a responsibility she does not understand. She pulls back and carries the package to her desk, then turns round to tell her cousin she is not prepared to take this on, this other burden, this other grief, the killings that happened when she was away, that she does not think she could make head or tail of it if she were to try, that she has her own needs that she cannot shape into words, but she stays silent. To say such things would break her cousin's trust.

'It's unfinished,' Renu adds, twisting her lip, and leaves the room without closing the door.

Savi turns and watches the curtain lift and fall, lift and fall in the wake of her departure. The window is open with just two thin bars between her and a darkness that makes everything one. It is another moonless night, though somewhere, she knows, there must be a moon swelling into brightness as the tidal waves rise. *A moon*, she whispers to herself, *to draw the seaweed through*. She opens her diary, picks up a pen and draws a red line through the gridded number 24. There is just one day clear till December's full moon, and the next day, ringed 25, marks Christmas.

It was the Christmas Eve of her ninth year and Savi had packed her case for herself for the very first time. Her mother, too tired now and unable to keep shifting from wardrobe to suitcase, sorting out clothes and toys, had given her instructions from a chair in the room.

'Remember to put your books and heavy toys flat at the bottom of the case. Then fold the trousers and skirts over that. Then pack blouses at the very top. Squeeze underwear and socks down the sides of the case. Keep sharp objects, those pencils, folded inside.'

Savi had lifted her clothes in and made the case personal. This was the only useful lesson her mother had taught her, how to put away her things so that she might carry them with her, as if training her for a future of a portable life in which her world could be miniaturised and mobilised at a moment's notice.

Since arriving at Dolmen House she had watched her mother relax into a domesticity neither of them was responsible for, reading the papers in the garden where the guavas had been picked, the air thickening with the smell of tart sweetness exuding from the kitchen. Here she could move apart from her mother without guilt or accusation, answering her own needs while staying in touch. She went to join Renu in the kitchen where Josilin was stewing the unripe fruit.

Something about the process of softening and sugaring, of stewing and blending as the fruit morphed in the pan, made Savi reflective. She had just been learning about the differences between solids, liquids and gases, had just begun to see a physical order to the world. She was keen to test her knowledge.

'Is this solid or liquid?'

Renu looked at her. 'Both, stupid.'

'Can't be. It's got to be one or the other.'

'No look, these lumps are solid. This sticky stuff is liquid. So it must be both.'

Renu reached in and scooped up the hot mixture dropping the ladle back in the pot so that it splashed them both.

'Stop it!'

Josilin sniffed and took the pot off the cooker. 'Chup, chup, children, what's this. Solid-liquid, there's no difference to taste. Everything's changing, all time changing. So why argue about solid-liquid now. One moment solid, next liquid, next gas!' And she turned her round bottom up.

The girls laughed and sat down, inviting Josilin to join them on the back step that faced the sea. There was still time for a chat before they bathed. Savi picked up one of Josilin's soft hands and circled a small scar with her finger.

'It's Christmas tomorrow. Do you have a Christmas story for us?' she asked.

Renu groaned and stuck her fingers in her ears.

'A Christmas story is for Christians,' said Josilin emphatically, conscious of her role as cultural guardian.

'Exactly.'

'Another one then,' Savi persisted. 'What about a poya story? What happened on full moon in December?'

'What happened on full moon in December?' Renu repeated in an exaggeratedly high voice. 'An Indian princess brought the sacred sapling to Sri Lanka that's what.'

'There's much more to it than that.'

'That's it.'

'Savi child, come, I can tell you a story that you will both like. It is about the bravest and most devout princess from the island who later became the greatest lady this country has known. Queen Vihara Maha Devi.'

'I am fed up of princesses.'

'Shut up, Renu.'

'Quiet, girls.' Josilin hitched up her cloth to stretch a leg and ease the strain on her knee as the girls leaned towards the warm smell of stewed fruit and cinnamon she carried with her.

'You see the sea before you,' she said, as the girls glanced ahead, 'how beautiful and quiet it is, like a mother soothing a child to sleep. Well, it wasn't always like that. Once it rose up in anger like a giant and took this land and people.'

'Did everyone die?' Renu's interest was drawn.

Josilin sighed and drew the girls to her, and began to tell a tale that was both familiar and strange as they looked towards the waves.

178

So it was that the girls came to hear of the story of the misguided King Kelani Tissa, and the anger of the gods that caused the sea to rise and take the land. They heard of his devout daughter who consented to be sacrificed to the sea in a golden boat and who emerged from the calmed waves as the noblest of queens. And as they listened they were assured of the solidity of things, of the sureness of ripening, of the seasons of fruit and the certain pattern of the stars. For this was a story where evil was punished, of order and justice and heroines and gods. It was the oldest of stories where darkness came swiftly, drawing them close into one body, one story of the past, as the lights blinked on one by one in the darkening rooms of Dolmen House.

The girls had grown up in the shade of such stories. Savi would walk through the Fort cool and assured in her psychedelic T-shirt and white shorts, meandering through paths between the pale court houses. She was sometimes alone and sometimes with Renu, following her cousin to the wide open courtyard where she'd lean indolent beside her against the trunk of the Bluffing Tree, feeling its ridges press into her back. Here men of all ages would gather for a calming cigarette and discuss the on-going proceedings, along with rumour and local news. The random fragments of information and the multiple possibilities they contained kept the girls listening with their knees drawn up.

'Boss said 4.15. I should say I left at 3.'

'Why. Does it matter when he wasn't even there?'

'No better say 3 in case. Someone might have seen.'

'They say that goonda is back in town. The Justice is in his pocket.'

'Yes, true. It might not make much difference what I say.'

'Times have changed. It would be different if Justice Dom was still in charge.'

'He's in Colombo. Too important for this sort of thing.'

Renu prodded Savi and smiled. 'See. Your father is a big man now.'

Savi looked at the man who had just spoken to see if he might notice her. She wanted him to know that Justice Dom's daughter was right there listening. Her father had worked in the city as long as she could remember and this recognition of his work at the Fort strengthened her sense of connection to the place. To think that these people knew him too. She was no mere interloper, she belonged under this tree with them, and could see him just as they did, a figure of authority in their lives.

In later years she reflected that she had found out most about his work through such snatched conversations and only remembered him talking directly about it once. It must have been on one such occasion, after eavesdropping under the Bluffing Tree, that she found herself at his side, as he sat in an easy chair in his brother's home. She was looking at him through the eyes of one of these men whose life might depend on his judgement.

Have you ever, she asked him, sent someone to jail but felt it was wrong to do so?

He had just put his drink down and looked at her in a way that made her feel much older, as if he was looking beyond her at the person she might become, his hand still raised above the glass.

The question – good question, he said – seemed to make him pause at some gap inside himself. Then, as if he found what he was looking for in the emptiness of his raised hand, said to her, 'The law as it stands is in good shape, though enforcing it is not always easy. But when official law and natural law are in conflict, we need to find a path that runs between them.'

She wanted to ask what he meant, how such a path was to be found, but was stayed by the grownup nature of his words and that small moment of uncertainty when he fell silent. They made her feel privy to a part of him she had not seen before.

'There is a famous Greek myth,' he continued, 'that deals with the conflict between official and natural law. I know you like myths so listen well.' He leant towards her. 'There are these two brothers, Eteocles and Polynices, who kill each other in single combat over a dispute over who should rule the kingdom of Thebes. Creon, their uncle, who was now the undisputed king, decrees that Polynices was a traitor as he had challenged both his rule and that of Eteocles. He commands that Polynices' body should be left to rot where it fell, that he should not be accorded the normal burial rites. Imagine that! Leaving his own nephew's body to rot! Polynices has a sister, Antigone, who is of course horrified by this and goes to bury her brother, thereby breaking the law. She is caught and sentenced by her uncle to be buried alive. A prophet, Tiresias, then proves that the gods are on her side. Creon rushes to make amends… but is too late. The girl has hanged herself and her mother, too, has taken her own life.' Her father sat back and cracked his knuckles by clasping his hands over one another. 'The girl was following natural law in insisting that her brother must be buried. Her uncle was following official law as he was the king.'

Savi got up from her chair and went across to make herself comfortable on his lap. She relished these moments when her father took the time to explain things.

'Is natural law then whatever people believe to be right?' she rested her head against his chest and breathed in the smell of his aftershave balm.

'Not always. I think it's better described as what makes us human, or the part of us that connects us with the gods.' He looked down at her furrowed brow and smiled. 'Or to put it another way,' he drew his arms about her and whispered, 'I love you, so will do anything for you. *That's* natural law.'

It was hard to believe he'd said that. She laughed and looked away from him, turning her back to him, looking towards the open window to try and hide the delight in her eyes.

Renu, too, would listen closely to fragments of stories under the Bluffing Tree and find herself quickening to the conflicts she found there. These sudden glimpses into the experiences of those about her took her into homes beyond the Fort and made her feel she was connected to people who led invisible lives. It was under this tree that she first heard the voices that would one day fall silent while her parents and their friends lapsed into the verbal shorthand that became the common language during the years of open violence. Under this tree she came to see how seemingly small domestic details that gave the world pulse could be part of a larger story of mutable justice, and how the unreliability of such justice was at odds with the easy logic of Josilin's tales.

Josilin, who had been part of Renu's home ever since she could remember, was more closely connected to the men who gathered under the tree than she could ever be. A bad night for Josilin would be written on her body with bruises that swelled into unnamed shades of damage. She never spoke of her husband in front of the children, but they had heard him mentioned by their parents, who seemed even more resigned than Josilin was to the fact that there was nothing to be done.

'I have told her to try and talk to him, but she says he's always drunk when he gets home. I can't get involved or else I'll have him at my door too,' her mother would say.

'What to do. It must be her karma,' Savi's mother observed. 'We all need to put up with things beyond our control.'

In such broken conversations Renu came to find a common thread between narratives that reordered her understanding of events. When she cut through Josilin's tales, removed the false elaboration and hyperbole, she found in them a core, a moral spine that held them together, and realised that they were all connected to a single idea, an idea she had grown up with from her earliest years. Karma, she reflected, all the stories came down to this. The ancient logic of cause and effect. It was King Kelani Tissa's bad karma that led to the loss of his land and untimely death. It was the princess's good karma that protected her. It was the Leper King's good karma that led to his recovery. Similarly, she found in karma the reasoning that explained the responses of those around her to the instability of the times. It was Josilin's bad karma that led to the beatings, her aunt's karma that led to her illness, her own karma to remain unmarried, and the karma of those who gathered outside the court would doubtless determine their fate too. Things were as they were meant to be, events were preordained, and evil would always be punished in this life or a life that had yet to come.

So when the curfews started and silence entered the Fort, it seemed to Renu that Karma was the only law that was respected. Nobody seemed to speak out, to question, to open events up to scrutiny. She saw a connection between her mother's silence in the face of Josilin's bruised body and her parents' refusal to get involved when Josilin's husband was abducted. Karma, it seemed, could rationalise almost anything. He was killed because of his karma, the unprovable truth, the unprovable lie. Even those who appeared to live a blameless life could be caught in the loop of a previous birth and be abducted, tortured and killed for a misdemeanour they were not conscious of having committed. No one was exempt. As for the killers, bad actions lingered, would exact revenge some day. They might go home to their families, continue with their daily tasks and live under the bowers of honour, but they would surely stumble in another life if not this one. Justice would be meted out in a future beyond the grave.

This was the lie they seemed to tell themselves, those who crept into bed and sank into the darkness of willed amnesia. This was the lie they all lived by, a lie that linked rich and poor, killer and victim – for was not every killer intimately connected with those he has killed? – the lie that there was no point in trying to enforce earthly mechanisms of justice. It explained everything to the growing girl who did not know of the fugitive resistance of those who did fight back. It explained why Josilin had called not for justice but compensation. It explained why Navin, whom she'd admired even before she met him, never called the police. Even Anoma, whose broken voice Renu could still hear despite not having spoken to her in years, seemed to be divided between the need to bring peace to her husband's soul and bringing him back to her.

It was natural, therefore, that Renu's search for coherence in the stories she recovered came to centre on the man who stood apart from it all, isolate and alert, asking nothing of her but the right to be alone. Bradley – the youth whose body was no longer quite his own – seemed to be searching for more than what was taken away, more than bringing his father back, more than the mere restoration of his former life. She would enter the driveway to Tel and watch him withdraw into his cabin, knowing that he had tested out all the possibilities of the night, and feel she was entering a world that was diminished by his sleep.

It was a clear afternoon in April, about a week before the New Year, the Sinhala and Tamil New Year that marked the Sun God's crossing, a time when families gathered, when communities were drawn together by a faith in renewal. The sun was moving from Pisces to Aries, the house needed a fresh coat of paint and there were rites to be followed at auspicious times. There was a time for drawing the first water from the well. There was a time for boiling the first milk. There was even a time for touching the jak fruit tree.

Before all this there was a period when the sun was in the process of moving out from the old year to the new, a period of transition known as *nonagatha*, a time of no auspicious moment. This was a time when precautions were necessary, when music ceased and the hearth remained cold. In years to come Renu would reflect on how her later childhood could be described in relation to such a transitional time. This was a period of her life, she would tell Savi, without an auspicious moment.

She had not been to school for several weeks and could not remember now whether this was due to the normal school holidays or to enforced closures by the government or the JVP. Holidays cropped up without warning, sapping energy from days and wiping out weeks of study and collective play at a stroke. The home tutors her parents had found for her cancelled classes when bus strikes gave way to election violence in the town. She dreaded being released into this empty time. It made her conscious of a lack of direction to her life.

Romesh had been drifting apart from her, aware of a destiny she did not share. He did not need to justify his indolence, his daily disappearances when he went off to meet his friends; he knew that no matter what he did he would end up taking on the role prescribed for him. Renu had been left to muddle her way through, left to grow into womanhood without recourse to maps.

Her mother would put books on the table for her and she would take one with her on her walk, tucked under her arm like a statement of intent. She felt secure with this solid block against her body. It gave her identity, purpose. She would take the grassy path behind low houses and move directly to the sea, then turn left along a short stretch of sand that led to the esplanade. This was the only way she could escape the Fort now that she was barred from going through it. If she dared to venture near the courts she would be seen and reported by neighbours and her father would almost certainly end up grounding her at Dolmen. She had taken the beachward path so often it had almost become invisible to her, so she would sometimes find herself walking along the paved sea walk with a crowd of near strangers, walking ever further from her home, completely unaware of having taken the hidden path to the sea.

She would listen as she walked to kitchen conversations, market news, election speculation and tales of workers' unrest. It did much to explain the clipped conversations at home. Words had become suspect, people were having to learn a new language, anything 'Indian' carrying with it the wrath of insurgent gunfire. On one of her walks she heard how a chemist had been killed the previous day for selling an Indian acne cream, breaking the JVP ban on the sale of Indian goods. On another walk she found out that a wedding announcement in a national paper had been read as a coded message about a bomb attack, resulting in the police detention of the couple who were due to get married. She had read in the papers how the army had taken over television and radio stations and fetched journalists and technicians from their homes, forcing them to work and break the strikes that had been forced upon them by the JVP. If they went to work the journalists risked being killed by the JVP, if they did not they risked arrest by the army.

News from overseas was now more limited than before. Foreign television reports on the political violence were subject to the static buzz of censorship, the evening news broken by an effervescence of grey dots that wiped out stories of conflict and human loss. Renu would make her way through the scattered pieces of information, step over the rubble of the former post-office, and climb up the fifty-four steps to St Bridget's convent to sit with her back against the gate, a book open on her lap until the cooling sun told her that the army trucks would move in to enforce the curfew soon. That Rodrigo girl, people said, she really needs to be at school.

On that afternoon in April she had not taken her customary walk as she'd sprained her ankle climbing the convent steps the previous day. Instead she was in the garden at home, moving through grasses that grew taller as she approached the water's edge. The wooden skiff hidden in the reeds had once belonged to a neighbour who had used it for recreation. It was not much larger than a child's cot and had a plank for sitting on and just one good oar, the other having broken on an unseen rock. She had sometimes stepped into it and pushed herself clear using the unbroken oar to slowly circle through water plants. She had never gone far from her home. She would watch the cool columns of Dolmen flash through grasses and trees.

That afternoon, heavy with the frustration of a morning spent at home, she rowed in ever widening circles, moving the oar slowly from one palm to the other, enjoying the luxury of giving direction to the boat. It seemed to carve its own sure path through the lily leaves as she moved closer to the stakes that stood midriver to keep crocodiles away. Perhaps one day, she might be able to row with enough sureness to go up river and on to the very edge of the prison walls. She had always wondered what the prison looked like from behind, wondered if there was any possibility of escape from its high windows.

She was approaching the stake barrier when the boat hit an obstacle and she lifted the oar clear to see what it was. There was something the size of refuse sack moving under the lilies, something dark and crumpled that was up against her boat. She saw the rough shape of it as a disturbance in the leaves. She looked over the side of the boat and saw a part of it lifting to reveal something that had the texture, the colour of rubber, though too porous here, too soft, with feathers perhaps. For a moment she thought these might be kitchen scraps, but as she put her hand in the water, turning back a dark leaf, she saw a round form turn its face towards her, the eyes rolling round so she was caught in the full sweep of the white gaze as the body rose into definition and an arm came towards her, the arm moving up as if reaching for the boat. Her gaze entered the gash on his temple, the underwater shirt and sarong.

The oar slipped from her hand, beyond the blackened body,

out of her reach. She struck out and pushed away from the dead man, pushed against the mangled darkness of him, his body the only object that offered enough resistance to push herself free. Her hands were wet against his coldness, her hand reaching out and catching the detail of his face that rippled into definition at her touch, the flailing arm trailing after as she tried to get away, the boat rolling and erratic with broken lilies till it suddenly rose and tipped to one side lifting into grass. She turned and clambered into wetness, her skirt instantly heavy against her throbbing foot, felt a burning up her arms and noticed the lacerations made by leaves.

Later that evening, after scrubbing herself with Lifebuoy soap and a brush, scrubbing all the small red wounds as if in doing so she might cover the old pain with a new one, she sank into the hollow of a wicker chair, cradling a tumbler of ginger beer. Her skin was burning, the glass in her hands too cold. She began to feel the glass release the roughness of a hard, wet head into her hand, in her palm the tissue of a loosening jaw, the pressure of a nose and individual teeth. Her fingers fell into the hole of an open mouth, caught a small lip of flesh under her nails as she pulled away and the glass fell in a shriek of splinters on the cement floor.

She refused to speak or leave her room the next day.

'Is she ill? She's shaking like she's got dengue fever.'

'No, it comes and goes. Her temperature was up but it's back to normal now. I think she's just exhausted. She's grazed herself, probably doing something she shouldn't.'

Her mother had sat by the bed embroidering flowers on linen, while Renu lay still under the shroud of a mosquito net, her hands held tight between her knees.

A clear night in December, about a week before the New Year, and Savi was descending the stairs. She had gone to bed leaving Renu's package untouched and the curtains wide open in case the moon travelled by. But she'd been unable to sleep. The waves had been breaking to reveal an image that Renu made real. As her cousin had been speaking, earlier that afternoon by the sea, telling her of a man's face turning in the water, she had seen the face too well, all the details drawn into definition by her cousin's anguish:

187

the face turning towards her, turning and slowly congealing into that of her father as she'd last seen him, darkened by drowning with a bruise at his throat. She had blinked it away and let her eyes settle on the silver line of the horizon, focusing on the experience of the young cousin lost to her during her years abroad. In the solitude of her room the image kept coming back, the boat lurching on broken water, the oar drifting, and her father lunging towards her with outstretched arms. She was reaching for him, for the embrace that might save them both, but her arms had opened onto nothing but Renu's words.

Downstairs, she felt her way along the length of a wooden settee. She could see pale squares of cushions, the furniture of the room two dimensional in the dark. She went past the tall chairs at the dining table to stand before Renu's door. It had been left slightly open and as she pushed it she stepped into moonlight.

Renu was lying down with the sheet drawn to her chin and the grey parachute of a mosquito net knotted above her, unused. Her breathing was restrained, and though her eyes were closed, Savi thought she might be awake and tested the possibility with a whisper.

'I couldn't sleep.'

'I know.' Renu shifted and slid herself up against the head-board. 'Did you start reading the story I gave you?'

'I will start tomorrow.'

Renu switched on the light over her bed, placing herself in its pale circle and revealing the greenness of the net above. Her dishevelled state in the green light made her look sour. It occurred to Savi that she was offended that her gift had been left untouched.

'I'm looking forward to reading it.'

She sat down in the wicker chair by the window in half-shadow, curling her feet under her, taking in the old furniture of the room, the red chairs they used to cover with a bedsheet to make a den to hide in, the family of carved ebony elephants they used to play with on the floor, looking at these and taking in the memories they evoked, when there was a splatter of gunfire, a volley of sharp cracks, and they both sat up, instantly alert. It took a few moments to register that these were crackers, to the fact that they could relax. Renu checked her watch.

'It's Christmas of course,' she said.

'I hate that noise.'

'You get used to it.'

'Why set off crackers? Doesn't it scare them, the noise.'

'Not when you're the one setting them off.'

Renu got up to open the wardrobe door. She brought out a tall bottle to the bedside table, pulled two plastic cups from a polythene tube, and passed one to Savi.

'With the compliments of the management.'

Savi raised her cup to Renu and it darkened with the liquor; she smelled it, gulped and winced.

'I haven't had this for a long long time. It tastes just as bad as it did then.'

'You've been away too long,' Renu said flatly, and then settled into the bed, lying so that Savi could see her face clearly in the reflected light, her skin thick, shiny as wax against the tousled hair, the eyes glass chips.

'Did you take it from Tel?'

'There's always a surplus. Thatha brings it home and I help myself.'

There was something about the way she said this that made Savi uneasy, a coolness and sharpness that seemed new.

'Happy Christmas!'

Savi just lifted the cup. Renu drained hers and poured herself another drink.

'Does your father bring much back from Tel?' Too late she recognised the unintended haughtiness, the tone of accusation in her voice.

Renu looked coolly at her, this England-returned cousin who would never understand the corruption of time. She had exposed her memory to her, revealed it, raw, glistening, this memory that she had kept deep inside for years, deep enough to avoid touching the culpability that now stuck to her hands, the man's silent appeal which she could never wash away. Savi would always be able to sit there with those wide eyes and open hands, like an incorruptible witness to her fall.

'You really have been away too long.' She measured out the words, drawing out the distance between them.

'Perhaps.' Savi put the cup down and slipped her feet back into her slippers. Perhaps, it had been a bad idea to come downstairs, to try to talk during a time of unbidden dreams. But she could not leave with Renu looking askance at her like this, needed to explain why she hadn't started to read the story, explain that she never meant to pass judgement on Eden, explain, above all, the anguish in her father's turning face that had drawn her to Renu's door. The questions about his death could only be answered if they spoke freely, with compassion, without blame. She was about to speak, to explain, when Renu began to talk into another crackle of fireworks.

As for *your* father, Savi heard, and then was unsure of the words that followed, unsure whether she had heard correctly, for what came through began to make her feel cold from the inside, ice trickling through her veins to the thin membrane of her skin.

She wondered, for a moment, if the crackers were breaking the words into a new order, but there was meaning in what she heard between the bursts of noise, a meaning punctured into sense, as if in the short spaces of understanding she was catching everything Renu meant to say, stripped of the softening 'maybe' 'perhaps' 'might', the conditionals intended to cushion her as she learnt that all the years spent in England, spent away from home, might have been paid for by money secreted abroad, money that might, perhaps, and never to be known for sure, have come from sources that were illegal and unsafe, that her father had done this for her, to keep her from the violence at home, that he had tried to leave too, leave them all behind, but had died first, and that his death was indeed, perhaps, maybe, never to be known for sure, swallowed up in the forgiving darkness of the times.

Renu drained her cup and squeezed it so it split.

'He got death threats,' she said with finality, as if this proved his guilt.

Savi was alone, with just the tainted possibilities of her father's love, his death. She reached for the door and walked into rooms where the furniture grew large and solid against her, found herself reaching with unseeing arms, trying to find a way to the open release of the stairs.

~

Christmas Day broke into Dolmen House with the sound of the horn of Eden's white Mitsubishi Outlander. Eden came out of the car, cheerily announcing that Father Christmas had come bearing gifts with one of the not-so-wise Men, and opened the boot to reveal several boxes and multicoloured bags containing wedding paraphernalia. Romesh climbed heavily up the front steps, calling for someone to carry things in. No traffic in Colombo, he remarked. He couldn't remember when he had last seen the city that quiet.

Fiona and Renu were in the living room packing red and yellow packages of toys into large carrier bags. They were going to take them to the community centre before preparing lunch. Eden greeted them with a peck on the cheek and went up to his office.

'Where's Savi?' Romesh went over to the table to pick up the morning paper, ignoring the parcels that lay scattered by his feet. 'Is the jet lag getting to her again?'

Fiona looked up. 'She's normally up by now.'

Romesh sat on the settee, spreading his legs wide, and opened the paper before him so that he looked nearly all legs.

'Ma,' he said in a voice his mother recognized as placatory, 'I've invited some friends for lunch.'

Fiona did not respond. She was counting the packages on the tips of her fingers. Romesh looked over the paper and waited till she'd finished.

'OK?'

Fiona drew herself up with a hand on her hip. She would have understood better if Romesh had invited Linh and her family to stay, despite the inconvenience such a visit would have caused them. This, however, she did not understand. It was difficult enough gathering her family together for Christmas lunch without having to suddenly cater for unknown guests as well.

'Who are these friends?'

'Kit and Tilak – maybe one more.'

Kitsiri was to be his best man, his school friend who had gone in for military service and whom she had not seen for several years since his posting in the East. Tilak was someone Fiona did not know. Romesh could be exasperatingly selfish when it came to domestic arrangements.

'This is typical of you Romesh – so absorbed in your wedding that you've forgotten everything else. You know I can't arrange a meal at the last minute. If you'd told me earlier we might have managed, but with Josilin away there's no help and I've cooked just enough for the five of us. Why don't you take your friends to Tel?'

'Can't do. It's fully booked,' said Eden as he came downstairs. 'Bring them round for drinks this evening. Sixish would be good.'

Eden was used to making swift decisions, had spent a lifetime adapting to unexpected changes – a cancellation, a wrong delivery, an accident, the death or disappearance of staff. He could have swung it for his son even with a full hotel, but he was quick to resist his son's suggestion, was able to counter Romesh's impulsiveness with his own. The truth was he didn't want to risk seeing Romesh and his friends having a drunken send-off in front of his staff. It would be bad for business and give a poor impression of the future proprietor of Eden's Bay.

Romesh stood up, folding the paper. 'They're already staying at Tel. I just thought you'd like to see them and give them a chance to have home food. I'll call and tell them it's drinks at six instead.'

He left the room abruptly without looking at his parents, making them feel they had let him down in some way.

V

TEL

the coolness of red cement

Savi lay on the floor, taking the coolness of red cement into her skin. She used to do this as a child on the hottest nights of the year in March and April, or when she was ill and had a fever that burned through her, as it did now. She would lie first on her back till the hardness hurt her head and then on her stomach with the cold stone pressing her cheek and thighs. If the floor hadn't been polished properly she would wake to find red wax smeared across her body like fresh blood.

She didn't know how long she lay there imagining the different ways in which her father might have died, hearing once more the ruptured words that revealed his hidden life. He had not spoken to her much when she was a child, the communication between them reduced to those long, blue letters that avoided recognition of the fact that they were apart. Over time, he had stopped becoming a physical presence to her, contained as he was in words, memories and aphorisms from the past, portable things she carried with her wherever she went. When she came back for his funeral and saw the embalmed face, the body so small and finite in the coffin, she realized at once that he was a thing that could be touched.

Now Renu's words were bringing him back more vital than before, reaching the living heart of him and fleshing him into fallibility. Our work, her father would say, defines us, gives us dignity, calls us up as human beings in the wider world, but our loved ones are there to restrain our vanity. She had dreamed him reaching out for her through water, till this knowledge of the night came to fill her understanding. He was no longer just her father but a man who knew fear, someone whose love for her had carried him into conflict with everything he believed of the law. He'd been planning to leave the country and join her at the time that he'd died. She felt herself growing older with this new knowledge of him.

They called him traitor, Renu said, *because he challenged the abductions.* Her words exposed his demons, made the connection with him complete.

She turned over and became conscious of her arm brushing the stippled surface of a wall. Her eye was pressed against the floor so she could feel herself blink. She could see the legs of the desk that stood near the open window and the clean outline of a package resting on the top. It lay like a monument on the smooth line of the desk. She watched as it gained definition in the dark. It must have been about three or four o'clock in the morning. Josilin used to call this the hour of a thousand buddhas in anticipation of a thousand bodhisattvas gaining enlightenment before dawn.

Savi righted herself against the wall and reached for the package, slipping off the bands that held it together. It felt satisfyingly solid in her hands. She tapped the switch next to her and the desk light came on. Her head began to clear as objects settled into focus. It was Christmas day. This was the only gift she would get this year. In Brighthelm, Hannah would have spent the night arranging presents under the tree for Natalie. She remembered the young girl curled up on her lap and her words, 'Go back'.

She spread the brown paper on her lap and lifted out Renu's black notebook. It lay on a manila folder with two sheaves of paper pinned together with a giant paper clip. The gold stamp on the cover indicated that it was the notebook of a military man. She opened the book. There were jottings in Renu's small precise hand, but they were too disjointed for her to make out, and, at the back, on gridded pages, there were some genealogical maps in different coloured inks. She flicked back to the first page and saw a note made out in an unfamiliar scrawl, 'For Renu, Love, and only love, Kit.'

Kit. Kitsiri. Of course, the plump boy with the loud laugh. She remembered Romesh's spotty friend, could see him leaving Dolmen after an afternoon of play, his pockets sticky with kiri aluwa, singing raucous songs. Kit must have kept in touch with her cousin and joined the army at some stage.

She turned to the first sheaf of paper. This contained more names, dates and charts, with the names Bradley and Sirisena sometimes circled, sometimes underlined several times. She put these on the floor beside her and opened the second manuscript. The original title, 'A fragment', had been crossed out and above it a new title, 'A Postscript to the Years of Terror', followed by a small script that was even and tightly packed. She flicked through the pages and stopped at a point where the lines broke off into a series of disjointed sentences and floated free. The broken paragraphs reminded her of the letters from her father, the script interrupted by personal reflections. The words she read came in Renu's voice.

except as an absence, a space I write around
I do not believe I will ever know him ^ . He has been silent
all this time. The secret of his grief taunts me.
I know everything and nothing.
His identity is clear though no one seems to know exactly
when he was born. Their history is marked out in private ways
I cannot reach.

His grandparents run through the beads of their past, again
and again, like some mantra. They know their history in a way
I never can know mine. They live it again and again.
And Anoma nods and talks in many voices rubbing her
hands over one another as if washing them clean. She does not
speak of her son.

Who am I to try and write this man's story? I who live cut
off from everything and spend too much time in a fancy hotel.
And yet I must write. I know that despite the distance between
our worlds there are connections to be found that explain things,
that because of the distance between our worlds I am bound to
write.
The past is no longer past when it is remembered. It becomes
something else. And when it is remembered and unvoiced it lies
in wait to burn us all.

I'm still searching for the words to fill the silences I meet. These silences are ~~like~~ inky pools. The only way forward is to write with looseness, which will mean rewriting everything that has gone before.

And there is <u>so</u> much talk from the other side. 'He escaped from police custody', 'he took his own life', 'he was killed by vigilantes', and you know justice has jumped ship. Some people really believe these things. Even Ma, who can be maddeningly obtuse sometimes. And Romesh, who just smiles and says that there's no smoke without fire.

And the present is too full. The violence builds up, though it is not constant as the foreign press keep making out. Sometimes I feel the weight of the present is squeezing out what came before. Perhaps we need to push the past from us in order to cope with everything that's happening now. To unpick one thread would require us to unravel the whole.

I remember Uncle Dom saying how it had become lawful to bury a body without a public inquiry. And the last legal defence against murder was a writ of some sort, the demand for simple evidence of a life being lived. How I wish he were here now. Perhaps he could explain how we ended up like this. The silences have invaded every family, even ours. There is no place to belong to any more.

And the rehabilitation centre is useless. I can't speak of this to Navin though I'm sure he knows. We can only carry on with our work if we stick by the rules and remain deaf, silent to calls for accountability. This knowledge lies between us but also holds us together.

The next six lines had been crossed out.

We ignore the past at our peril. It sounds bookish – even trite – but it's true.

I believe that the way is clear for it to all happen again, just as it continues to happen, to repeat, in that parallel world of memory, in that parallel time.

The sky was slashed crimson, like a bird's wing on fire. Savi pressed her face into it and felt feathers of wind that came from the sea. She remained by the window, feeling the force-ripe richness of crimson break into orange and molten gold on her skin. Somewhere, in the distance, a gate was drawn open and a car came up the drive, hooting three times. Men's voices, laughing and calling for assistance. Her uncle and Romesh were back. She leaned forward so that she might see them, leaned so far forward that she felt she might lose balance, swinging into the space where guava leaves had caught her hair.

Romesh climbed the stairs and entered Eden's office. His mother had left with Renu for the community centre and his father had gone to Tel leaving him to himself. His parents might have blocked his chance to see his friends for lunch but everything else appeared just as he wished. The boxes of wine had been stacked by the office door. On the back of the door was his wedding suit in its transparent protective covering. He had everything ready for his early trip to Yala the next day. The rest of the family would follow him in the Outlander after lunch. Romesh poured himself a drink and sat down. He had looked forward to spending his last day of bachelordom at home with his closest friends, but they were staying at the hotel. His father's peremptory dismissal of his small request played upon his mind.

He picked up the phone and dialled. He could talk freely now that he was alone. The receptionist answered. Romesh asked for Kit and waited, picking his teeth with a paper clip.

'I'm sorry Sir, there's no response.'

He clicked his tongue and asked for Tilak, waiting another full minute, only to be told that there was no answer there either. He bent the clip in two between his fingers and tried to stay calm.

'Who is this? How long have you worked at reception?' he said, breaking the clip and running the pieces between his fingers, 'Well this is... Yes, that's right. I would've thought you could manage the exchange now. Put me on to Mrs Amaratunga. Not in? What sort of outfit are you running. It's...' Romesh checked his watch, 'eight fifteen in the morning and you're telling me that the guests are out and the manager isn't there. I've a good mind to come round and see for myself.'

He slammed down the receiver and considered phoning Linh to tell her he'd be round in time for lunch the next day, when he heard a door open. He became aware of someone walking down the steps, a hand sliding on the banister. He had almost forgotten that his cousin was there.

'Savitri!' he called after her. 'So how, Savi. Come and tell me what you've been doing all this time.'

Savi was at the dining table with the newspaper spread out in her hands. It was bulky with the weekend and Christmas supplements. She looked up at Romesh and noticed how much he looked like his father when he smiled, with the same clear brow and smile full of teeth, though his hair was thinner and softer than Eden's, combed into submission. Under the full sunlight of the window he appeared even paler than his sister, his face thrown into colourlessness by the darkness of his beard.

'I'm sorry I'm late. I meant to go to the community centre with them.'

'No problem. Will you join me for an omelette? I should be able to find some simple, honest eggs amongst all this clutter.'

He went to the kitchen and started shifting things around. Savi began to talk of the changes she'd noticed at the Fort and of the many guests at Tel and how busy it was. It was easier to talk to him when he was busy, not facing her.

'So you still call it Tel?' he called out, above the sizzle of the pan.

'Of course.'

'Renu calls it Tel too. It's Eden's Bay to me. A business, family business, and right now it seems to be run by prize idiots. I couldn't even get a call through this morning. I sometimes think Thatha employs the wrong types.'

Savi didn't respond. She was reflecting on the similarities between Romesh and his father – the way their good humour could be expunged by problems at the hotel – and on the name of the resort, its aptness, linking as it did Eden's ownership of the place with the edenic dreams of tourists. Ever since a Tuscan friar had spread the rumour that Eden's fountains could be heard in the island, travellers had been charting their own private journeys to paradise. Little did they know that the resort owed its name to a dashing English parliamentarian with whom Eden's mother had a lasting but imaginary affair. Savi's grandmother, Lavinia Samaraweera, then seventeen, large-eyed and dimpled, had fallen for Henry Rodrigo when he walked out of the smoking room and into the foyer at the Nuwera Eliya Hill Club. Henry, chisel-boned and elegant in waistcoat and cravat, had leant across the counter and placed upon his tousled head the brimmed and banded hat known as an Anthony Eden. In that instant the gentleman and the hat became the young woman's combined object of desire, a relationship made more complex when Lavinia, newly returned to Colombo and still flush with the encounter, opened the morning papers and fell in love with a picture of the said Conservative MP – the suave progenitor of the hat – wearing it askance as he talked to Winston Churchill. The three-way affair between Lavinia, Henry and Anthony Eden was to last a lifetime, and became a subject of some amusement to her sons. They would tell friends over drinks that their mother's weakness for the cut of an English hat meant that anyone who wanted to win her favour had to come 'hat in hand'. The story had been embellished many times since her grandparents had died, one soon after the other, of pneumonia over ten years ago.

Savi turned to Romesh as he came in with plates steaming with delicious smells.

'For me,' she said, as he put them down before her, 'it will always be Tel.'

towards the coastal road

The last of the presents had been distributed when Renu closed the door of the community centre and started walking back towards the coastal road. Her mother had taken the car and left half an hour earlier to finish preparing lunch.

Renu walked outside and looked down the road for a three-wheeler. A kingfisher darted from a telegraph wire. The path was quiet and clear. As she began to walk down it, she realised that if she tried to walk back home she would be late for lunch. She turned around and looked back, squinting in the sun.

The community centre stood between a church and the village school. She would have a better chance of finding a three-wheeler if she went back towards the centre where the children were being collected by their parents. She could still hear the children's screams as they tussled over gifts. She began to walk back, drawing a scarf over her head to shade her face.

She went past the school wall where bicycles were stacked and crossed the courtyard, stepping aside to let two girls with candy-floss dresses giggle past. There was no sign of a three-wheeler here. A mother nodded to her and smiled. Renu pulled her scarf aside and smiled back. She turned the corner of the community centre and carried on walking. If she was lucky she might find Jazeel in a lay-by between the centre and the church.

The door of the community centre was closed, just as she had left it, but as she went behind the building she noticed that a storeroom window was slightly open. This was where books, sundry tools and play equipment for the mission school were kept. She had entered the storeroom earlier that morning to fetch some scissors, but knew she had locked the door before leaving and pressed against it to make sure it held.

She looked at the window. The gap was small, but there was enough room for a hand to squeeze through. She hesitated, wondering whether she should go back inside. Soon everybody would disperse for the holiday and the buildings would be unattended and vulnerable to theft. She was still deciding what to do when she heard someone say something from inside the store. She moved into the shade of the eaves. It was a man's voice, one she knew. She turned and stretched up to look into the room.

In a thin slant of light she saw a man's chest exposed, the dark hair of it rising and falling as he breathed, the small rise of the clavicle near his outstretched neck. She saw the familiar blue jeans, the worn leather strap of his watch, the long fingers that lay upon a loosened waistband. Navin was seated on a chair with his head tilted back, some three feet away from her with his eyes closed. His lips were lifted in pleasure as someone's supple fingers rubbed his temples in slow, smooth circles.

'That feels good,' he said. 'That feels very good.'

Renu could just see a woman's arms, thin and darkly glossy with scented oil, moving across the line of his jaw. She had seen those arms before, working themselves up into a frenzy, when Anoma spoke. Those hands were on Navin now, sleek with sandalwood oil, moving into the darkness behind his ears. There was nothing she could do to reason them away.

She turned and ran down the path, out of the shadow into the glare, hurrying past the church where people were gathering for service, her scarf unravelling behind her, till she came up short against Jazeel who had just pulled up in his three-wheeler.

'Miss Rodrigo.'

'Take me home.' She entered the vehicle with the image of those moist fingers still cradling Navin's neck.

A few minutes later the three-wheeler slewed across the road and righted itself. She was thrown from side to side, hitting her head on a metal bar.

'Bloody fool!' Jazeel shouted after the retreating man. 'OK, Miss?'

Renu was dazed. She turned to look behind her and saw a man walking down the road in the opposite direction, his body lithe and fluid, as though his limbs were on springs. He was wearing brown trousers and a white shirt and carried a holdall on his shoulder that seemed weightless from the way he sauntered on. She did not recognize him at first, but there was something familiar, as if he'd once been a shadow that had now gained physical form. Later that evening, after she had hurried back from Tel, she realized she had seen Bradley, vigorous and whole, walking as if floating down the coastal road.

She could still feel his face against her palm.

'You are not as I thought you were,' he had said, as she lay against the dampness of him, her face against his cheek.

'That's good.' Renu had smiled and run a finger across his brow, feeling him without seeing him, tracing the indentation behind his ear and drawing her hand across the line of his jaw.

'Renuka,' he said, turning so she felt her name blown back

towards her face. 'Did you know that in India, Renuka is a goddess, a protectress of the dispossessed.'

'Apo, what nonsense!' She pushed his head with her palm and smacked him lightly on the cheek.

'They say it means other things too,' she said, nuzzling down and tucking her head under his chin, 'like "born of dust". Renu is an ancient name for dust, the smallest particle of matter. I think that's me.'

He cupped her breast. 'Not so small.' He smiled and brushed her forehead with his lips.

They fell quiet, breathing in a cool breeze that came from the broken window.

'How long will you be away?' She had often asked him this. It was the last thing she would say before leaving his office. He could be away for days or weeks depending on commitments in Colombo and the demands of other rehabilitation centres. The question was weighted now and she felt him tighten against her.

'My parents expect me for Poya. But I'll get back as soon as I can.'

He was shifting from her so she had to lift her head. She wished to reassure him, to make it clear she made no claim on him.

'That's OK, we don't have to meet till the New Year. My brother's wedding is next Monday. I'll be away in Yala for a while after that, so it will be difficult anyway.'

She had left him in the cabin with the wind cutting through the jagged shards, left him with his head propped up against a book. Left him now without looking back.

~

I do not believe I will ever know him except as an absence, a space I write around.

He has been silent all this time. The secret of his grief taunts me.

I know everything and nothing.

~

A hotel cleaner found the bodies in their beds that afternoon. Three male guests, asphyxiated with pillows. Two of them had pillowcases tied over their heads, one of them with such force that his neck had been broken. Another had his underpants stuffed in his mouth. All of them had been beaten and lashed by their own belts, the welts standing out in purple weals. The ferocity of the attack shocked even the police. They were frequent witnesses to brutality, but this brutality was neither casual nor premeditated. It was driven by something they did not recognize, something that gave them cause to fear.

The staff were to be interrogated. Special importance was placed on interviewing the security guards and night watchman. But Bradley, the night watchman, could not be found. It was most unlike him to have disappeared, the others told the police. He was the most attentive watchman they'd ever had. He was not a suspect, of course. It would've been impossible for him to commit the crime because his arms didn't work, but they needed to talk to him as a matter of urgency. An officer went to find Anoma in case she knew where he was.

Events moved quickly in the next few hours. All Renu could remember of this time was a blur of indecision and response. She remembered arranging a staff roster at some point and talking to several police officers, drawing waiters one by one, with a touch on the arm, away from the live music of the banquet room. She was making calls all night and moving up and down the corridors among people who were unrecognizable in their semi-dazed state. The day staff were roused from their beds at home, the night staff were still in uniform. The subterranean corridors of the staff quarters were lit by emergency lamps to ensure that guests were not disturbed. Staff who were barely awake looked especially vulnerable, as if they could have been persuaded of anything, to say almost anything, at such a time.

Renu could not recollect seeing her father for more than a few minutes that evening. He might have stayed near the rooms where the bodies had been found, perhaps in some misplaced desire to make amends for a wrong he couldn't comprehend. Romesh, she knew, had gone to Dolmen to contact the families of his dead friends. She could see that he needed to get away from the frenetic activity at Tel; the news he had to convey required a quiet, unlit room. Later she heard that he'd spent hours at the morgue, cajoling the disbelieving locum to fast-track the autopsy results.

It was almost three in the morning before they were back at Dolmen. Renu stepped inside to see Savi and her mother folding clothes into suitcases that lay across the arms of living room chairs. By them was an ironing board laden with wedding clothes, her brother's elaborate marriage reduced to an inconvenient domestic task.

When they finally went to bed they were all too exhausted to find relief in sleep or dreams, their minds restless as ciçadas on a windless night. The striking of a match would make them all look up, though each had retreated to their own room, drawing a thin sheet of doubt about themselves.

'Are you awake?'

'Yes.'

'I can't sleep.'

This was the longest and slowest night of their lives. They had been thrown into a new landscape, found themselves sifting through the details of secret character, searching for a pattern to the personal past into which the killings might fit. They were trying to find a space for the murders and arrange events into line, as if a belief in cause and consequence was all that might be necessary to bring order into being. But this long, slow night would be forgotten, lost in the events of historical time, just as all private memory can be washed away in the instant generation of a collective past. In just a few hours, tragedy became local, tragedy became global, tragedy became the distance between hands that failed to touch.

Shortly before 9 am, a tsunami struck the south coast of the island, having swept down from the eastern shore. It came in three waves that swept over the bay and swimming pool of Tel, sweeping into the lobby and reaching onto the coastal road. The first wave was over six feet high and flooded low-lying areas of the hotel grounds. The second was the largest and rose taller than the palms. By the time the last wave came it was too late to make a difference.

'And the gods were so angry that they caused the sea to rise and take the land, carrying people and homes in its wake. Wave after wave came, taking more and more people, so the King understood he had done a serious wrong...'

'Reports are coming in that a sizeable tsunami generated by an underwater earthquake off the west coast of Sumatra has resulted in a significant loss of life...'

People climbed trees, people ran for the stairs, people climbed through windows and onto tiled roofs. All the hotel staff and guests scrambled and survived. Renu took quick steps up the spiral staircase that was breaking as she climbed. In Peraliya, the southbound train to Matara was torn from its tracks and tossed inland. Over twelve hundred passengers and crew died in what was to become the largest rail tragedy in history. The waves wiped out almost three-quarters of the island's coastline and left an estimated thirty-five thousand people dead. Reefs and bays dissipated the energy of the tsunami, the safest point in water being the crest of the wave. Your survival depended largely on where you were at the time, your destiny marked by chance, accident, a random combination of unpredictable elements. Thousands of people were carried off, hundreds surfaced into new identities. There was plenty of scope for multiple rebirths, for speculation about who had lived and died. It took just ten minutes for the waves to destroy a locality. It would take several hours of aerial TV footage to show the extent of the devastation to a people too shocked to speak.

The number of dead and displaced was estimated in figures that rose by thousands with a speed that matched that of the tsunami. The waves were to reach twelve countries across two continents in six hours. While local communities, the military, guerrilla forces and aid agencies united on the island to attend to the disaster, the parallel need that emerged in the coming weeks was to understand things historically, causally, to find an origin, order and logic to events. Local newspapers made appeals to members of the public for medical supplies, scissors, surgical gloves, bandages, antiseptic cream. People rushed to find loved ones, heedless of destroyed roads. It was a time of untold compassion and untold greed, when many gave their lives to save others, when people hacked rings off the fingers of corpses that lay bloated in the sun. Some looked to karma, others spoke of Fate, a woman in the hills spoke of God's retribution against the ungodly, everyone everywhere searched for reasons to explain and understand the event. The global scramble for the comfort of material facts became almost as urgent as the scramble for medical aid and food supplies.

The epicentre of the quake was identified (250 km south-south-east of Banda Aceh), the size of the faultline between tectonic plates (600 miles), its magnitude (9.3), its speed (as fast as a commercial plane), its height (up to 30 feet), its reach (three miles inland), the number and scale of aftershocks (121 with 21 above a magnitude of 6), and its force which speeded up the earth's rotation by a few microseconds and increased its tilt. The energy released by this tsunami was equivalent to twenty-three thousand atomic bombs.

Such exponential devastation can make classicists, calibrators and determinists of us all, but none of the explanations provided answers that helped people give meaning to their loss. In the open hands of strangers, of doctors, priests, of soldiers and fisherfolk unprepared for such suffering, in the small consolation of touch, observance, a meal, a dry floor, new nets and tools to start again, in the connections made across communities unknown to one another, or at war with one another, there was potential here for a new landscape to emerge, but no language as yet tough enough to bear the magnitude of such change, no language strong enough to bear the weight of suffering.

The swell, we are told, is produced by an abrupt and violent shift between the earth's tectonic plates that generates a massive displacement of a column of water at the boundaries where different histories meet. It feels a gravitational pull and attempts to restore equilibrium, its height increasing as its speed drops, drawing disparate elements together as it increases momentum. It is a fluid narrative whose displaced components gain an unpredictable force as it reaches the end, just as everything transient carries the measure of its own time and energy within itself, just as lines of influence remain indirect and uncertain. On reaching shallow water it is slowed down, the energy of its speed transferred to gaining height and power in a penultimate chapter. A coastal road is wiped out like a gap in the plot. Small disturbances capable of generating such disasters take place unnoticed every day. They are molecular, subatomic, unmeasured, unseen and unheard, like trees that fall in a forest of quiet, undiscovered birds.

On the coastal road, Romesh was driving through sleep. He was exhausted, having spent the night in the rank air of a shuttered office where the smell of the morgue seemed to collect. His body ached and his mind kept going over details that resisted order or sense. He rubbed his eyes to keep them open, steering only with the sight afforded by his fingertips. The news of Kit's death remained unreal to him. He'd only been able to read it through its impact on the staff, catching in the expression of their faces a shock he could not yet feel. He'd caught a glimpse of a man's naked body lying limp on the bed, darkened by asphyxiation and swollen with weals, and left the room as he was not ready to see more. It bore no relationship to Kit who had, just months before, told him how much he was looking forward to getting leave from the army, before swallowing his anticipation in a gulp of arrack. The war had changed his friend, spiking his gregariousness with thorns of irritability. Kit would sometimes pause between the spluttered safety of sexual jokes to lambast politicians and journalists who, he claimed, spoke from the sidelines while his comrades took the flak. Tilak and Sujith, more cautious with their words, would interject from time to time and support Kit's outbursts with an occasional hint of blundered operations in the East. In the past their dedication would not have been in doubt.

The last time they'd met they'd been in a Colombo casino, all three ganging up to remind the future groom of his rough seduction skills. They had parted as brothers, asking Romesh to pass on their condolences to his bride. During this time they'd reflected on their personal lives. Romesh could not remember details, he was not one to remember such things, but it had taken him back to the days of their youth when they were vital and free, when they could walk roughshod over the present and leave the imprint of their boots behind. Those days seemed like a world away now.

Romesh continued to drive on through his thoughts, along a

road clear of traffic, easing past a stray bullock cart driven by an unseen man with a switch. He had been down this road many times. He knew its depth and its shallows, its potholes and sudden arches, the places where it tipped into gullies, the places where it broke into lost, forgotten towns. There was no need for him then to attend to a distant rumble, the sudden hooting of a horn, there was no need for him to attend to the calls running down the road, as he turned inland, and the thunder came, with water that rose from nowhere, lifted him and smashed the windscreen into a spray of silver stars. The car was swept along with him lurching and rolling over, pulled out in the tumbling car for about a mile, rolling over with broken trees and boats, people thudding against the vehicle, legs scrambling on top as the water came in and kept rising, rising in him and above him, rose so high that in just six frantic minutes it grew crimson, dark and heavy, pressing around him and in him, crushing all memory and desire.

It took them three days to find his body, to find the torso crushed against the open car window where an arm had been torn off.

Less was known of what happened at Dolmen as Fiona could not remember much. She had been putting away some personal belongings in her room at the time. Eden and Renu had got up early and left for Tel where armed officers, many of whom had kept vigil during the night, were spreading assurance and alarm, alarm in their assurance, among the early breakfast guests. Fiona had remained at home to pack her husband's clothes and hers. She was folding something into a bag when she thought she heard Savi singing. She had not heard her go downstairs but someone seemed to be outside. She thought she heard someone call out in wild loops of sound, calling, as if singing, as Savi used to sing as a child when the swing carried her up and down, up and down, her voice rising as she lifted into the air and the sound was released and suspended, then rising again when she was carried up again, as if catching the earlier cry before it could fall and touch the ground.

Fiona had paused in this release of rising words when she heard a rumble like a thousand express trains and the house juddered and broke, heard the sudden smash of glass and split furniture, the roar of a wall shifted, being swept away. From the open French windows she saw the vast surge of water thrash below, spraying her room, the tops of trees marking the place where the garden had been. She stepped outside onto the balcony, over the heaving blackness of it, and instinctively lifted herself onto the roof, her angular feet finding a foothold on the filigreed eaves. She leant against the tiles and dug her fingers into the grooves feeling the bump, bump, bump of individual tiles moving against her bones as she inched past. She could see the smooth flatness of the porch roof covered in moving water, water that kept rising and moving on, carrying people and screams, limbs appearing and disappearing in a rush of broken wood. There were two children, swirling, their arms ringing one another, holding each other in one long wail of distress, and in the distance a woman, someone who might have been Savi, being drawn down the swell as it moved across Land's End, moved down into the heart of the Fort where it joined another swell that swept over the rest house and esplanade. She called out Savi's name, but her voice was lost in water. Then something fell upon her and the lights went out.

The night before, Savi had been unable to sleep. She had never seen her uncle in such a state of agitation. He was shouting at Fiona who was wringing a tea towel, then wiping his brow on the towel he'd snatched from her hands, shouting, shaking and crying out his anger, before ripping the towel and flinging the shreds to the floor.

'All these years,' he kept saying, 'after all these years of keeping the devils from my door, paying them off, wining and dining them, turning a blind eye, why after all these years of being yes-man to every pompous yakko in town, why this bloody murder – not one, not two, but three bloody murders! – who are these perethayo? – Why now, why this, why this bleeding shame before the wedding?' He was crying out and resisting Renu as she tried to lead him to a chair.

The phone kept ringing, the family whispering, calling,

remonstrating with one another, moving from one room to the other and back again, each following the other like magnetic beads.

Savi sat on the stairs watching them, with her night shirt pulled over her knees. She did not move till someone came to her, was relieved when Renu finally approached.

'Renu,' she stopped her cousin, 'is there anything I can do?'

Her cousin looked at her as if she almost didn't recognize who she was, then gave a small smile.

'I'm sorry,' she whispered, 'about what I said about your father last night.'

'It's OK. You told me what I needed to know.' Savi wanted to talk, but not about this. She touched the step beside her but Renu leaned back against the banister, one arm running along its length. She was standing two steps further down.

'I started reading your notes,' she said, trying to lift her cousin's spirits. 'I saw the connections you were trying to make. And I liked those personal bits. They said a lot. They took me into your world.'

Renu looked directly at her and beyond her as if her focus was elsewhere. She was silent as she thought of the package she'd given Savi, the black book that had been a casual gift from Kit and the files that contained her efforts to put together Bradley's story. Both men had gone suddenly in the space of a couple of days.

'Kit gave me that notebook.'

'I know.'

'He said it was weatherproof and perfect for recording time and place. He didn't know what I'd use it for, of course, but he was right,' she sighed. 'It was perfect. I began Bradley's story there. And now Bradley's gone missing. We've been looking for him all night.'

Renu thought of the man she'd seen from the three-wheeler that afternoon and her hesitation in recognising him. Bradley had been walking with a bag slung lightly over his shoulder, along the crest of the road past the empty fish stalls and beached catamarans, walking with assurance, as if he'd claimed ownership of himself, walking without impediment as a free man. It was a backward glance at a retreating form, but something about his straight and steady step made her feel she was seeing him for the first time.

She saw the events of the last hours rearranging themselves. Three of Romesh's military friends had been killed in their hotel beds. Bradley, the night watchman who'd seen his father's three abductors, now disappeared without warning. All her years of observance, of collecting the statements of witnesses, of trying to make connections between disparate facts, had taught her that the truth often lay in a deep hollow between seemingly discrete pieces of evidence. She had been coming up against this again and again over the years, though held in check by her fear of jumping to conclusions – she'd always liked the expression 'jumping', how appropriate, she felt, given the possibility of a fall – by the awareness that there was a need for caution too, for facts to be verified and checked before any dangerously incriminating claims were made. Too many people had been killed during the troubles on the basis of a sudden rumour. She was now hesitating before a possibility that might call her to account, call her into Bradley's story in a way that might make it complete.

The phone rang again. Renu looked down and saw her mother seated on the sofa with her head resting on her open hand. Fiona's eyes were closed but she was not asleep.

'I'll get it,' she said, moving swiftly on from Savi into the shaded darkness of the stairs.

Savi was left alone, free to pick a path through the broken pieces of the family's distress. She went up to her room and stood by the almirah, looking at the closed suitcase that lay on the floor. She had barely unpacked it before she had to repack it again for the wedding in Yala. It now lay ready for her departure the following afternoon. The papers Renu had given her to read still lay on the desk. She leant back and curved her fingertips about the ebony lion's paws at the base of the top wardrobe. She had not opened the almirah since her return. She turned a key and opened the drawer beneath. Some of her mother's silk scarves were folded at the back, and in front were three round parcels wrapped in faded white tissue. She took the parcels to her bed and unwrapped them

213

one by one, leaving the paper around them so that they opened into pale petals of crepe. She knew the objects at once. They were the jade incense burners her mother had used, each with just one small eye to hold a joss-stick in place.

She went back to the almirah and brought out a packet of incense, withdrawing three sticks from the sheaf. She placed the holders on her bedside table and put the joss-sticks inside, struck a match and watched each stick light, feeling her mother's thin hand upon her own, steadying her to ensure they were properly lit. Each small flame melted into a thick lash of glowing orange as wisps of smoke ascended and disappeared. She watched them burn down, slowly curling into long tendrils of ash, bending and breaking, leaving a patter of dust on the table. She knew that her mother was thinking of her now, in this place they had shared, thinking of her as the hours folded in on one another, in the wholeness and stillness of this time.

The sky was lightening, the mauve streaked with bold seams of gold, when Savi entered the garden and walked through the leaves. She could hear a car start up behind the house as Renu and her parents called after Romesh who was pulling out from the damp gravel of the drive. After he left she heard them walk back, knew they would have their arms about each other as they climbed up the steps. She was released, forgotten, superfluous to events. She could go where she wished without being seen.

She moved on through the garden and into the new day, watching a squirrel scamper up the prop roots of a wetakeiya palm, its tail flicking in time to an urgent pipping cry. The first birds had started to call, slashing the sky into more colour, the competing cries of male and female koels, birds of the April New Year, the rising kew-yoo of the males broken by the hard kik-kiks of their partners. Some ioras joined in, whistling and rattling when a leafbird threaded its own whistle, then mimicked the koels' calls.

She walked through the open gate and down the road, without shadow, walking past the small temple with its wall of white-washed lotus flowers. Her gaze was drawn to the preaching hall which had been built in memory of her grandparents. She saw a monk making his way to the shrine room. He paused on the step, passed a palm over his bald head, yawned, then slipped a key in the door and went inside. She had once attended Sunday school here. She remembered going with Renu and hearing a story about one of the Buddha's previous lives. In one such life the future Buddha had been a rabbit and had thrown his body onto a fire that he had lit himself, sacrificing himself to feed a starving ascetic. It had been the holy day of alms and all the animals had offered something. The jackal gave meat and milk, the monkey ripe mangos and the otter offered fish, but the rabbit had nothing to give but bitter blades of grass, so he'd given up his body to save the life of the old man. The ascetic who was none other than Shakra, the lord of gods, was moved by the compassion and courage of the creature. Shakra drew the rabbit from the fire and carried him to the heavens where his image was to be found every full moon day.

Savi could still remember the monk who told the tale. He'd had a formidable forehead and his head seemed to grow longer when he asked them to contemplate the meaning of the rabbit's sacrifice. Savi had been left subdued at the thought.

'I can't imagine doing that,' she had said, as they kicked the dirt from the temple steps and picked up their sandals.

'It's just a story, silly,' Renu laughed, 'to make you good.'

But they were both to carry this story with them for as long as they lived.

As she passed the temple she saw children walking in, neatly groomed in white. She watched them as they stepped onto the sandy floor of the temple grounds and stopped chattering, slipping off their footwear by the preaching hall. She watched them enter the room of blue walls that carried her great-grandfather's name on a brass plaque by the door, watched them and knew the hardness of the stone floor upon their knees, the sudden hush as the priest entered and took his place on the lofty preaching chair. She felt she knew these things as if she was still a part of them.

She continued walking down the waking road, on past the gabled house where Aunt Snooty's sister and brother-in-law lived. They'd had a white dog with a ruff of fur about a mouth of snapping teeth. In the past she had been scared of this dog and had given the house a wide berth. Now there was nothing to stop her from going up to it, nothing to stop her from calling; the aunt and uncle, who had been no more than a peripheral presence then, seemed all too solid now that she was standing before their home. She stepped aside and watched a motorbike speed by in a spray of dust, then turned down a path that was shaded by a tree of yellow frangipani flowers. It screened a house she had lived in when she was too young to remember, a house they had occupied when her father worked in the Fort, before she had memory and need for this place.

She passed it unawares and went on towards the De Saram's former home, this family of lawyers as established as her own. Her father used to come here for a chat with Maxwell De Saram in the days when their evenings had been reduced to her mother sleeping in a garden chair. He would leave her rocking gently on the lawn with a book upon her lap, kissing her cheek before he left, as if she were a tired child. Sometimes he took Savi along to play in the De Saram's garden as it had a tree-house she could climb on if she was suitably dressed.

As she approached the house she saw a woman glance up at her as she opened the gate, swinging it wide so that the driveway was clear. She was smiling as Savi came up, her face creased into a spidersweb of lines about the eyes.

'Eden Rodrigo's niece, no?'

Savi brightened, the recognition felt natural somehow. The De Sarams had left during the troubles, but this generous smile made her feel she was home again.

'Yes. And you?'

'Susitha Vaas.'

The name was familiar but she could not place it. She scanned the almond trees to see if the tree-house was still there, and then glanced down at the finely veined hand that lay on the open gate.

'Are you expecting visitors?'

'I teach English. Some pupils are coming soon.'

She looked up, nodded and smiled uncertainly. Susitha Vaas was appraising her with a mixture of curiosity and affection.

'Good morning, Miss,' someone called.

They both turned to let the girl pass. Savi looked on as she swung her bag up the steps and entered the arched room where her father used to spread his papers on a table, talking with Max into the afternoon. Savi continued watching, holding on to the open gate, feeling the reassuring firmness of the iron bar beneath the flakes of rust, standing still by this garden she had known. The girl had drawn up a chair and emptied her bag, was opening books upon the table in a way that made Savi want to go and read what was inside.

'Perhaps one day I may return and teach English here too,' she said. And in that instant it became real, not a whim or a languid dream, but as real as the solid bar under her hand, as real as Susitha who was looking back at her, warmly and smiling her assent. She had the urge to leap up and swing over the gate as she had done as a child.

'I'm sorry, Savitri child,' Susitha said, responding to some expression in Savi's eyes, 'I would invite you in if I didn't have this class, but please come, see us soon. Freddie said you're here a short time for the wedding, so without fail you must come.' She squeezed her arm, 'Dom's daughter, no? You are family to us!'

Savi laughed and said she'd love to drop by, lifted her hand as Susitha went inside, smiling all the while to herself, and carried on without any aim, because there was no need for certainty when she could walk lightly like this. She turned away from the road and took a hidden path between two derelict outhouses that led directly to the beach. Some instinct, perhaps the sound of buried water, told her it was there. It was the same path Renu had taken when she was forbidden to walk through the courts. Savi felt the ground soften beneath her, walking through the patch of scrubland that marked where the boundary walls had been. She was now outside the residential area of the Fort, an area that had been out of bounds when she was young. It was thick with vegetation until it broke open into a rivulet that spewed onto the beach. She heard the splash of water, the swing of a bucket. Someone was doing their washing beyond the trees. She felt her feet sinking into the sand, the grains brushing against her toes, then stepped onto purple-flowered beach vines that flowed along the shore. Pale ghost crabs scurried off, dissolving in ripples of sand at her approach.

She came to the sea wall by the rest house where she sat down and kicked off her sandals. Once there had been elephant stables here in the days of coastal trade, but for her this place was just a rest house where her parents sometimes stopped off for a light meal. It marked the place where the history of the Fort gave way to the chaos of an expanding town. She looked up along the length of the esplanade towards the edge of the town and saw a group of holidaymakers step down from a white van. They were assembling their bags on the pavement. A woman in the group was looking out towards the sea. She followed the woman's gaze, making it her own.

The sky was now bleached into glare, the sea lifted into a crush of silver sequins, the horizon a long luminous line, clear of trawlers and fishing boats. It was as if all the properties of light were contained in the sea and it was this light that was thrown up to illuminate the sky. The stretch of ocean here lay uninterrupted by land till it reached the South Pole. A bus hooted as it passed the clock tower; the bells of St Bridget's began to peal. It was Sunday, of course. The fishermen were Catholics so were not at sea today.

She could hear someone sweeping the ground with an ekel broom and turned as a car pulled out of the rest house drive. Romesh must be well on the way to Yala by now. She would be joining him there later that day, and she really should get back to Dolmen before the others noticed she was gone. She had to remain invisible, to slip seamlessly into the family's needs at this time.

On her way back to the house she became conscious of curtains drawn open, the whirr of ceiling fans, of radios being tuned across a slur of songs and languages, of spices crushed and rolled on grinding stones, of the somnambulant drone of a meditation class taking place on a shaded verandah. These were the sounds of homes she had moved through as a child.

At the farthest reach of Land's End, she turned into the road that led to her uncle's home. As she went down towards the house she noticed that the gates had been drawn open and Eden's car had gone. Something about the absence of the car, Renu's probable departure for Tel, made her suddenly feel as exposed as the ground she stood upon. She went past the house and into the garden, going round the lidded well to climb onto the wooden swing. There was refuge to be found here in the broken light of leaves. She would spend a few minutes in the garden before going back inside.

The swing hung low on coir ropes from a high branch of a jakfruit tree. It had been put up one April New Year and been renewed with fresh coir every new year since, although the children it had been made for were not children any more. It overlooked shrubbery that fell away to the beach, and gave an unobstructed sea view when the swinger was at its utmost height. For fleeting instances it was possible to see the whole coastline break into sky.

Savi began to swing slowly, in gentle, steady strokes that gave her momentary glimpses of the lifted sea. In torn moments she saw that the water had thickened, the horizon now marked by a thin pencil line. She carried on swinging, breathing into the lifting wind till the bird cries stopped and she was left in the rhythmic hush and rumble of the waves. In the distance a tatter of crows littered new clouds. She began to sing a song, a song from the past, a few climbing notes matching her movement on the swing. It was a melody that arched and fell back, a melody that belonged in the sky, a melody that slewed and filled the absence of birds. She lifted herself higher to reach the song that now seemed to come from outside, moving deeply into air, so that she nearly reached leaves, nearly caught her own words. She was now swinging with the abandon of a child, kicking harder and harder to catch the moving words, her body pushing on in an ever steeper arc.

She could see the spread of sea now unbroken by leaves, the waves rolling, pulling back, rolling forward and pulling back, in a rhythm that challenged her movement on the swing. She had gained a momentum beyond her control, her body overcome by the ebb and flow, zooming close into a sky that expanded as she approached, when in a fleeting, high instant she saw the waves withdrawn, folded back, extending the beach into a shimmering sheet of sand.

There was a low whistle as she began to sweep forward again, a whistle that broke into excited shrieks as, swooping, she saw the dark tips of exposed rocks and small sticks of children rushing forward for the stranded, flipping fish. Then another blank instant as her breath drew back after her and someone was calling, shouting, cries leaping down the road, calling so clear that it took a lost moment for her to make sense of what she heard, *Run! Run! The sea is flooding!* Her body propelled on now, carried forward by the thrust, carried on towards a black roar that obliterated the small stones of words.

The swell came churning towards her, growing and darkening, rising so high that it reduced the sky to a broken pane of light. There were cries, *Ma-maa*, overlapping one another, children's screams like sea birds, as a surge so dark and dense it might have come from Brighthelm, grew larger, came towards her in an ever rising wall. She was carried by her momentum, a creature of lashed air, swinging loose in the scattered words of a childhood song. The swing carried her upwards to the near safety of the tree, carried her to a vital split second when she might have reached the high branch of a different destiny, but she was torn from the moment, carried in the opposite direction, her body tossed, shattered wet and tumbled in the roll of a wave. She went far and fast, swept in a surge of broken wood, and found herself reaching for something that came towards her as a dining-room chair. It swept past her and on towards someone else, another woman struggling to keep afloat as low roofs spat their tiles into the swell. The trees were gathering clothes about them as people struggled to hold on, all of them drawn into this surge of single time. She saw the woman's head bob up and down, her arms flailing for the chair, when suddenly she felt something flip and struggle in her arms. A child was naked against her, pulling her into heaviness at her neck. She put her arm about the child, held her high against her, the water thrashing them against one another and then tugging them apart, her own grasp binding their nakedness as one. She held the child fast, found herself in this strength of holding, and felt the child become weightless as she redoubled her grasp, the girl's body emptying out and filling her own. Somewhere on this body she felt a tiny grip tighten and turned to see her face, turned to find the child was too close for definition, a blur of wet skin and hair. *Go back*, she heard her say, *Go back*, words that came from another place and time.

They were being swept on towards the roofs of the court offices, swirled past prison walls heaving with the writhing bodies and cries of those who'd scrambled on. *Here quick*, someone shouted, and she saw his arm reach towards them, but there was nothing she could do, unprepared for such release, her arms full and heavy with the child. She saw the man looking after her, a man in rough prison clothes, looking after her, sunk into the emptiness of his hands, as she was carried away with the child and spun into a new course.

They were being drawn back, back towards the court house roofs, past the creamy cupola of the Dutch Reformed Church when she slowed momentarily and heard a litany of cries, slowed and found relief in the leafy steadiness of a branch. They had been pushed to the farthest reaches of the Bluffing Tree, its exposed branches a scramble of limbs and climbing forms. She gripped the child more firmly, checking the push and pull of water against her, and released the full strength of her free arm.

She tried once, twice, then managed to get a grip on a stump of a splintered branch, the sudden jerk of this hold compelling a new equilibrium. She held on, trying to lift the child clear, but the girl now clung on to her, refusing to let go, clung on to her in an embrace that hurt her with its weight. She kept pushing her up while the swell drew them both back, feeling her growing heavier against her, adjusting to this new strength of the child's resistance. Then, without warning, the child let go and released her from her body. She saw her quick limbs climb air and disappear in leaves.

It was too quick, this sudden shift in balance, the shift to weightlessness that caught her unprepared. The loss of the girl's grasp came as a loss of her own hold. She was pulled into her own exhaustion, set loose into the giddiness of it, the swell claiming her indecision and dragging her clear into its rage, away from the broad reaches of the tree.

She was pulled with such force that she lost all sense of definition, all sense of boundary, pulled hard and fast over a horizon that left her body somewhere in the small girl's grasp. All she could hear now was the hollowness of her breath coming back to her, coming in ever shrinking circles, her breath hollowing in underwater echo, hollowing and pulsing louder and more slowly, as she breathed in and out in a deepening tunnel of sound, in and in and in one long last heavy breath, breathing in the booming, slowing permanence of the sea.

fifteen months after

The light lifts slowly in March. The sky thins into a milk white haze of heat so it is possible to see small particles of dust suspended in air. It is a dry time of parched wind, unbroken by rain, the heat entering everything like an unseen snake. Along the coast, fifteen months after the wave train came and destroyed everything in its path, sand and soil that had long lain saturated with silt and saltwater, has evened and lifted into dryness. There is a heady sense of space and lightness in this open ground that could persuade someone living here into reckless abandonment or despair. The drained wind finds little to play with now. The earth has been cleared of shards and iron fragments, picked clean of fallen tiles, broken bricks, awnings, cooking pots and sarongs, children's shoes dimpled with toe prints where skin pressed warm against the soles. The leaves breathe easier now the stiff flags of clothes have been removed.

There are instances of high activity on the road where this quiet is interrupted, but beyond the noise of mechanical diggers, the calls of construction workers and the shriek of billboards proclaiming redevelopment schemes, beyond the still angry boats that had been lifted from the road, between the rush of palm trees punctuating even ground, there are many, many half-houses to be found. They are not the same homes that Savi moved through on her return, not those half-finished homes of raw brick with their windows of high shrubs and stairs that scrambled into open weather. Those statements of hope were a future broken by the waves.

These half-houses stand open as a scream on the cleared land. They are all that is left of the time of tall water. All that is left, stumps of footworn steps, broken archways of wind, a frieze of green tracing a freestanding wall. All that is left, the clay hollow of a blackened hearth and endless, interminable squares of smooth cement that break the ground like oversized mosaic tiles and mark the space of forgotten floors. This is the geography of a specific time. It marks the moment history broke into two inaccessible halves.

On the ground by the temple lies a loose pyramid of votive coconut shells. The coconuts have been split, dashed open by those trying to make peace with the gods. For over a year Renu has been walking through this landscape with her hands thrust deep in suffering. A touch from a stranger would send her falling into a communal well of pain.

This was a time of much talk, few words. Politicians and village headmen haggling over the distribution of funds came to speak a language so universal that it entered the western press. It all came to her as a communication of need. She now knows how much rice is required to feed a family of six for two weeks, she knows the registrar and place where identities are reclaimed, the room where deaths can be registered with speed, the cost of a plywood coffin, the blue nylon used to mend fishermen's nets. She tries to order this knowledge into the biography of the time and finds herself shifting fragments of sand.

A year ago, in the city, streamers of white hung across the roads that led down to the coast. The view of the sea in Colombo became one vast ocean of mourning flags. There was no sea any more, only these pale waves of grief tumbling down towards the shore. She had walked along the promenade at Galle Face, her hand sunk deep in the fold of her father's thinning arm. Loudspeakers on the lampposts were broadcasting the *Ratana Sutta*, a sonorous chant to heal the land. No one spoke. A few black birds lifted and were carried into a line of verse. All the walkers looked from time to time towards the sea. Renu had walked and said nothing, just held her palm above the warmth at her father's elbow, pressing it occasionally so that he would know she was there.

She has spent little time at the Fort. The beach has been cleared of property and trees. It is now clean and pitted as a lunar landscape. On the esplanade near the rest house stands a wind-blown memorial, a cascade of white steel crescents. They might be waves, they might be sails, they might be pieces of the moon.

The sculptor who designed it has kept all these possibilities alive.

All the houses at Land's End have been washed and rearranged. They have been claimed into a past of which few are aware. Each house has been documented, its genealogy attached like a gift tag, the value of each almirah, each lost lamp, has been added up. Each detailed calculation results in a new interpretation of dwelling, each an acknowledgement of the fragility of ownership. All the waterside houses bear a shiny plaque carrying the name identifying the foreign aid agency that sponsors them. The plaques are attached to mildewed walls. The dolmen stone rests in silt between earth-washed colonnades. The house has been earmarked for rescue by the Swiss Red Cross.

Renu has been staying at Tel in a room of her own. Her parents occupy a suite on the floor above. For eight months the family moved through the washed hotel in the blind grief of separate rooms, her mother's stifled cry carried down to her in a rock pigeon's beak.

Renu looks out on the sea from two balconies near her desk. They are positioned on different sides of the room so that the South and West are held apart as she writes. While the words form she can feel Savi as a touch on her wrist, the bangle her cousin gave her pressing against the thin sheet of paper. She can imagine the sun's slow fall into water as she tilts warm liquor down her throat. *They will not call you idle for dying with the sun.* Her parents have discovered her destiny. She is to learn her father's craft. She is to enter the space where her brother had been. The slim badge on her blouse identifies her as the Entertainments Manager for Eden's Bay. She is to book dance troupes, magic shows, the events that give colour to a two-dimensional tropical night. She spends her time reading stage magazines and watching cultural shows in search of new acts. Each time she searches for these things she wonders whose eyes she is looking through. Her father's plans for the hotel have been pared down to this.

In the middle of the day she will find release in a walk on the beach, away from Tel, away from the Fort, away from those places on the map where damage has been named. She will sometimes take the car inland and sit in a grove of parakeet calls. She will sometimes walk towards the moonstone mine and enter a disused cabin of dust. She will sometimes park within the arm of a quiet bay. She needs these walks that take her back into herself, where she can feel her feet grow wet with coldness in this river where Romesh washed his canvas shoes; she needs these times when she can step upon the rough rocks of notes that called Savi into song. The unhistorical landscape remains unchanged. The private gardens continue to grow.

One afternoon she finds herself walking on the railway track that runs by the coastal road and enters the place where over a thousand people died. She had not intended to come here, has taken the track only because it offered a steady path for her thoughts. As she walks down she is conscious of entering a different order of time. A train was thrown by the waves here, at this shoulder of track, at this point in Peraliya. It takes her four minutes to step over 162 wooden sleepers. She has been taking care to step in the grassy space between them. Something in the counting of these sleepers has made her believe that they might move and come alive. She feels a small vibration of earth, the rattle of an engine the colour of blood, and steps aside as eight carriages slew past. The train is an explosion of humanity, people squeezed on footrests, billowing at open doors, bubbles of children at the windows, a sudden froth of cotton sleeves, white, blue, yellow rushing past. It must have been this crowded when the surge threw it into air.

She looks after the retreating train as it draws towards the place where the broken carriages had been carried, looks after it as it enters the ghost of its former self. She is left alone in a shrinking funnel of sound.

On the open ground before her lie the floors of blank cement where village homes have been. She crosses them one after the other, moving through walls of lost rooms towards the temporary shelters that line the coastal road. These shelters are arranged symmetrically in a rough, open grid. They all have the same tin roofs and green water butts. All but one have been deserted. Only someone without a family would choose to remain here.

Beyond the road, before the reach of waves, there is a wide, metallic memorial depicting the chaos of a train that tumbled into trees. The memorial is a rising black crescent resting on the ground that curves about a stone plinth. Underneath lie the bodies of hundreds of unnamed victims that were disposed of quickly to avoid the spread of disease. A foreign tourist stands before the plinth with his back towards her. He has hair the colour of straw and a shirt that clings with wetness on his back. He moves aside as she walks forward to read the inscription on the stone. She reads and then steps back to observe the human forms on the memorial. They have been carved in light relief, caught in the moment of struggle with steel, against the weight of a twisted railway carriage, caught and half-rising from the surface, limbs lifting from metallic water into the hot light of the day. The artist has tried to personalize each individual, to mark the quick flame of a moment before a life shaded into doubt. There is something in the contrast between the visual wave of suffering and the words on the inscription that gives her pause. Later she will find the language to express her unease about this.

There are inscriptions meant for foreigners that stand proud in English letters. This one offends me with its vanity. It commemorates the pride of a president, the ostentation of a minister, and relegates the victims of our tragedy to a blur of anonymity. Anyone reading this would think the president had the power to command the waves to stop.

She stands before the memorial as a lorry laden with coconuts rumbles past. She turns into the shadow of its movement and sees the tourist moving within the crosshatched path of shelters. He holds a bulky, large-lensed camera in his hands, and walks with precision towards the lone man sitting at the earth entrance of one of the shacks. She watches, not certain at first of what she sees, as he bends down within spitting distance of the refugee and lifts his camera up. The man does not move. He rests in the thin shadow of a tin roof, as if he has not moved for some time. Even from this distance she can tell that he is old. He might be ill, he might be lying in the hollow of some hunger, he might be asleep, unaware that this stranger is catching a quick moment of a waking dream. She walks across the road with feet of fire and goes straight into the path of entrapment.

Are you alright? I asked the old man, going close enough to smell the trace of woodsmoke on his hair. Do you mind this foreigner taking a photograph of you?

I deliberately ignored the tourist who pulled at my elbow and kept my focus on this man who seemed indifferent to us both. He was small and wiry, naked but for a sarong. His body reduced to the dark essentials. Behind him I could see the contents of his home. A plank for sitting on, a cup, a bucket, a cloth and some other pale material strung on a loose line. A small wooden platform on the ground the only evidence that there might be a place to cook a meal.

He had the calloused fingers of a fisherman used to drawing nets. I believe he had ownership of his solitude before it was broken, had drawn silence to himself like a net of silver fish. He had remained motionless as I came up but then looked up slowly, taking a distance of time to look at me. When finally his eyes met mine, I felt myself being drawn onto a level where there was no measure of time or place.

What matter? he said breathing faintly. What matter now. Everything is gone.

Two miles away, in a railway siding overgrown with grass, stand the buckled carriages of the Samudra Devi, the train that made headlines as The Queen of the Sea. *The carriages have been righted and put into order. They stand patient as if waiting to be repaired. They have been cleared of clothes and shoes, bags and human bodies. There is nothing to suggest what happened here. The door of a carriage bears an election poster of a political leader's beaming smile, as if the train might be useful for bearing other news.*

Five months after the tragedy, after the media had left, tourists from all over the world, continued to come to photograph the train. They wandered up and down the siding taking pictures from different angles and then climbed inside and continued their work there. See the broken seat, a smashed door, the luggage rack that saved a child. They would walk through the train ignoring the growing shouts of protest that came from outside. Get out! It is dangerous in there! It is not safe! These were the cries of those who knew it was a grave. Who knew what spirits walked through the carriages at night.

Renu remembers as she writes and wonders if her thoughts lack moral logic, a curve of uncertainty warping her rational mind. As she looks from one window to the next she sees the solid block of wall that divides her view of the sea. The sun is sliding somewhere behind this wall, between the South and the West; it is hidden from her view as she continues to write. She turns a page and relaxes in this space, writing in loose, disjointed lines that fall obliquely on the paper, writing her uncertainty, Savi's songs, her brother's left-handed bowling, the history of a man who held his memory in his arms. She continues to write, writing the new page in the light of an unseen sun.

ACKNOWLEDGEMENTS

My thanks to enablers: Sharmilla Beezmohun, Vicky Blunden, Denise deCaires Narain, Neloufer De Mel, Abdulrazak Gurnah, Susheila Nasta and Sarah Williams, who read and commented on the manuscript. To Michael Meyler, lexicographer. And to Jehan Perera of the National Peace Council of Sri Lanka. To Hannah Bannister and Adam Lowe. And to my editors, Jeremy Poynting and Jacob Ross. To Jo Chevlin. To Gail Bolland and Fiona Goh of the SI Leeds Literary Prize. And to Elise Dillsworth.

Thank you to Darshini Gunasekera, for voices salvaged. To Trilby Perera, for the loan of a tree. To my parents, Indira Salgado and – long ago and much remembered – Kenneth Salgado, for dwelling places. To Roshan and Dilhan, and to Shaun D'Arcy.

★

The following were drawn upon in the writing of the book: the reference on p. 40 is to Ediriweera Sarachchandra's play *Sinhabahu*, English version and a pre-production image by Namel Weeramuni (Sarasavi Publishers, 1999); the italicised lines on pp. 48 and 176 are from Leonard Cohen's, 'Song To Make Me Still' in *Stranger Music: selected poems and songs* (Random House, 1993); information on the dolmen in Sri Lanka can be found in D.T. Devendra's *This Other Lanka* (Visidunu, 2004); the title of the novel is a loose transcription of words attributed to the Buddha, cited in Pankaj Mishra, *An End to Suffering* (Picador, 2004); Pablo Neruda's words cited on p. 68 are from 'Lamento Lento' (or 'Slow Lament') in *Residence on* Earth, trans. Donald D. Walsh (Souvenir Press, 2003); the italicized lines on p. 82 are from 'Goodbye to Love' by

Richard Carpenter and John Bettis; the italicized phrase on childhood on p. 84 is from James Goonewardene's, *Dream Time River* (1984); words describing Ceylon, found on p. 74 draw from K.M. De Silva's *A History of Sri Lanka* (University of California Press, 1981); the fictional Fort of the novel bears some correspondences to the Dutch Fort at Matara; lines cited on pp. 84-85 are from Dylan Thomas's 'The Visitor' in *A Prospect of the Sea and other stories and prose writings* ed. D. Jones (Everyman, 1986); Jona Oberski's *A Childhood* trans. Ralph Manheim (Hodder and Stoughton, 1983) is cited on p. 98; the reference to a poet's quest for his father alludes to Michael Ondaatje's *Running in the Family* (Picador, 1984) and the phrase 'the distance of a shout' on p. 93 is the title of a poem by him in *Handwriting* (Bloomsbury, 1998); the allusion to heteronyms is clarified in the translator's note to Fernando Pessoa's *The Book of Disquiet* (Serpent's Tail, 1991; trans. Margaret Jull Costa) in which they are described as 'imaginary authors to whom he gave complete biographies and who wrote in styles and expressed philosophies and attitudes different from his own'; the newspaper citation on p. 97 is from *The Island*, 1 February 1990, also in *Extrajudicial Executions, 'Disappearances' and Torture, 1987-1990* (Amnesty International, 1990); the last sentence in Renu's journal on p. 77 draws upon a line in Shoshana Felman and Dori Laub's *Testimony: Crises of Witnessing in Literature, Psychoanalysis and History* (Routledge, 1992).

I am indebted to Patricia Lawrence for the notion of the safe witness, found in her article 'Violence, Suffering, Amman: The Work of Oracles in Sri Lanka's Eastern War Zone' in *Violence and Subjectivity* ed. Veena Das et al (University of California Press, 2000); to Alex Argenti-Pillen's *Masking Terror: How Women Contain Violence in Southern Sri Lanka* (University of Pennsylvania, 2003) for drawing attention to the language used by southern women in Sri Lanka to describe political violence, referenced on pp. 145-146, and to Sasanka Perera's *Stories of Survivors* (Women's Education and Research Centre, 2006).

The parents' words cited on p. 97 are those of the mother of the late Dr Rajani Thiranagama who was killed in Jaffna in September 1989, cited in John Merritt, 'The Battle for No Man's Land', *Observer Magazine*, 29 March 1990. The italicised words on p. 126, found in Nimal Mendis' interview, draw upon the words of Dr Manorani Saravanamuttu whose son, the poet Richard de Zoysa, was abducted, tortured and killed in February 1990.

ABOUT THE AUTHOR

Minoli Salgado was born in Kuala Lumpur and grew up in Sri Lanka, South East Asia and England. She has written extensively on postcolonial literature and is the author of the critically acclaimed book, *Writing Sri Lanka*. In 2012 she was selected to represent Sri Lanka in London's Poetry Parnassus, part of the Cultural Olympiad, and was the winner of the SI Leeds Literary Prize for unpublished fiction.

An extraordinary novel of a country trying to come to its senses, to see and hear the thousands 'disappeared' by political conflict and environmental catastrophe. Minoli Salgado's delicate, determined lyricism compels us to think of Sri Lanka's missing and the silenced, always conscious of the formidable challenges of reading and writing about those displaced from us by time and tide. The result is a literary latticework of remarkable craft and subtlety that brings into focus Sri Lanka's troubled past while shaping a necessary ethical response upon which the future might depend.

— PROFESSOR JOHN MCLEOD, University of Leeds

Bold and delicate. I loved it.

— DENISE DECAIRES NARAIN, University of Sussex

It is a great book – a wonderful elegy to a childhood and country lost.

— SUSHEILA NASTA MBE, Editor, *Wasafiri*